BRUTAL

BRUTAL

Mandasue Heller

MACMILLAN

First published in 2019 by Macmillan
an imprint of Pan Macmillan
20 New Wharf Road, London N1 9RR
Associated companies throughout the world
www.panmacmillan.com

ISBN 978-1-4472-8840-4

1 3 5 7 9 8 6 4 2

A CIP catalogue record for this book is available from the British Library.

Typeset in Arno Pro by Palimpsest Book Production Ltd, Falkirk, Stirlingshire

Printed and bound by CPI Group (UK) Ltd, Croydon, CR0 4YY

Visit **www.panmacmillan.com** to read more about all our books
and to buy them. You will also find features, author interviews and
news of any author events, and you can sign up for e-newsletters
so that you're always first to hear about our new releases.

For my beautiful mum, Jean Heller.
Always in my heart xxx

Acknowledgements

All my love, as ever, to Win, Michael, Andrew, Azzura, Marissa, Lariah, Antonio, Ava, Amber, Martin, Jade, Reece, Kyro, Diaz, Auntie Doreen, Pete, Lorna, Cliff, Chris, Glen, Nats, Amari, Aziah, Dan, Toni, Rayne, Joseph, Mavis, Val, Jas, Donna, Julie, Brian, Ian – and the rest of mine and Win's families, past and present. Love also to Liz, Norman, Paul, Betty, Ronnie, Kimberley, Katy, John, Jayne, Laney, Shirley Levi, Jonathan L, Colin, Amanda, Jac, Brian, Rick, Chris, Judith, Dr Sue and all my old friends from Hulme – too many to mention by name, but you know who you are. Thanks, as always, to Sheila, Wayne, Alex, Jez and all at Pan Macmillan. Also Carolyn C, Anne O'Brien, Nick and Cat. And, lastly, eternal gratitude to my loyal readers and supportive FB friends. You guys rock!

Prologue

'What are you going to do?' the man asked, staring in horror at the wispy hair sticking out of the top of the rolled-up quilt the two men had carried into the room.

'Shut it!' the smaller of the pair hissed, dropping his end of the bundle and shoving him forcefully down onto a chair. Then, turning to his mate, who was carefully setting down his end, he said, 'Quit fucking about and go fetch the chainsaw. The pigs are waiting to be fed.'

The seated man's face drained of blood when he realized what was about to happen, and his heart was pounding so hard he thought he might faint.

'Please don't do this,' he croaked. 'It's barbaric.'

'I thought I told you to shut it,' the smaller one roared, kicking him and the chair over.

'Pack it in!' the other man snapped. 'We haven't got time for this. If you're gonna do it, get on with it!'

Flashing him a dirty look, the small one pushed past him and made his way outside.

'Please don't let him do it,' the man begged as he hauled himself up off the floor. 'You're not like him, and I know you don't agree with any of this. But it's not too late to start over. I've got money; I can help you. You just need to—'

'Oi, dickhead, don't be telling him what he needs to do,' the smaller one sneered, walking back in at that exact moment and kicking the door shut behind him. 'He'll do as he's told – same as you. Now, quit snivelling like a little bitch, and start this fucker up.'

He shoved the rusted chainsaw he was carrying into the man's hands.

'You'll be doing the honours,' he said, grinning nastily. 'And no funny business, or the grunts'll be getting double rations tonight.'

PART ONE

1

Jo Cooper waved the last of the guests off from the porch of her parents' farmhouse. Once the car's tail-lights had faded into the distance, she gazed at the bleak landscape on the other side of the lane. A low-lying mist lent a sinister atmosphere to the moorlands, and she shivered as she remembered the terror she had always felt whenever she'd had to walk home after dusk when she was younger; convinced that the twisted trees with their leafless, claw-like branches were going to come to life and drag her off the path.

The front door creaked open behind her, and Jo smiled as her father came out to join her. At sixty, Frank Peters was still a handsome man, but the dim bulb above their heads high-lighted the silver strands in his once jet-black hair and deepened the shadows framing his kind grey eyes.

'You look tired,' she said, slipping her arm through his.

'I am,' he admitted. 'It's been a long day.'

'Nice, though.'

'Aye, it was,' Frank agreed, gazing out into the gloom. 'Looks like summer's coming to an early end.'

'You're not kidding, it's absolutely freezing,' said Jo. 'Let's go back in and have a brew, eh?'

As her dad went back into the living room, where her brother, Evan, was lounging on the sofa in front of the open fire, Jo headed into the kitchen to make the drinks. Every surface of the usually orderly room was littered with used paper plates and plastic glasses, and the old oak table was covered with disposable silver trays bearing the remnants of curling sandwiches, half-eaten sausage rolls, and wilted salad from the buffet. Her mum's apron, still dusty with flour from the last pie she'd baked, was hanging on the back of the door, and a wave of sadness washed over Jo when she realized she would never again taste her mother's cooking, or share a pot of tea and a gossip with her over this table.

Determined not to start crying again, because it felt as if that was all she'd been doing for the last few weeks, Jo glanced at the clock hanging above the window. It was almost 9 p.m., and she bit her lip when she realized that she'd forgotten to ring her husband, Sam, to check that he and their five-year-old daughter had got home all right. This was the first night she had ever spent away from Emily and, even though she knew that Sam was more than capable of looking after her, she still felt guilty that she hadn't been there to tuck her in.

Teas made, Jo carried them through to the living room. Evan smiled as he took his cup from her.

'I was just saying, I reckon Mum would have been proud of the way Dad handled himself today. He did a belting job, didn't he?'

'Brilliant,' Jo said, taking a seat on her mum's chair and covering a yawn with her hand. Apart from the hour she'd spent perched on the uncomfortable pew in the village church that morning, listening as the boring vicar droned on and on for what had felt like an eternity, this was the first time she'd sat down all day.

'Your mum arranged everything in advance, so I can't take any credit,' said Frank. 'If I'd had my way, she'd have had nothing but the best, but she made me promise I wouldn't change anything, so my hands were tied.'

As he spoke, his gaze drifted to a framed photograph on the mantelpiece. It had been taken on his and Maureen's wedding day, and she'd looked like a beauty queen with her long blond hair in curls, and her sapphire eyes sparkling with the joy of being a new bride. Her physical appearance had changed after moving out here; her smooth skin coarsened by the unforgiving weather of the countryside, her waistline expanded from the hearty meals she'd cooked. That extra weight had dropped off her at an alarming rate in the months following her cancer diagnosis, but her fighting spirit had stayed to the bitter end, and they'd had some blazing rows over her refusal to take the course of chemo she'd been offered. *'What's the point?'* she'd argued when Frank had begged her to go for it. *'We're all going to die eventually, and I don't want to waste whatever time I've got left being pumped full of poison that'll make me even sicker than I already am.'*

'Are you all right, Dad?' Jo's voice pierced Frank's thoughts.

'Just thinking what a stubborn woman your mother was,' he sighed.

'She certainly knew how to keep *you* in your place,' said Evan. '*And* me, come to that. As tiny as she was, I didn't dare answer back when she told me off. That's why I was always out in the fields with you.'

'Pity you didn't keep it up,' Jo sniped. 'If he'd had more help since his heart attack, he might not have had to retire so early.'

Evan's grin evaporated and he fixed his sister with an accusing glare. 'I didn't see *you* offering to give him a hand.'

'I've got Emily to look after,' she reminded him. 'And you're their son, so it was your job. Anyway, you live closer.'

'I've already got a job, *and* a disabled wife.'

'Marie manages just fine while you're at work, so you could easily have switched to working here instead. And her so-called disability doesn't stop her from going to bingo, so I don't see why you have to run round at her beck and call all the time. I'm sure she puts it on to keep you away from your family.'

'Why do you always have to be such a bitch?' Evan glared at her. 'It's all right for you, with your Pilates, and your yoga, and all that other hippie me-me-me shit you're into. But you don't see Marie when she's struggling to breathe, and . . .'

Frank closed his eyes and rubbed his throbbing temples with his thumbs. His kids had got along OK when they were small, but they'd started fighting like cat and dog as soon as they hit their teens: Evan using crude humour to get a rise out of his sister; Jo lashing out with the razor-sharp tongue she'd inherited from their mother. But they were both nearing their thirties, so they really ought to have grown out of it by now.

Unable to bear any more of it when their voices rose in volume, Frank slapped his hand down on the arm of his chair.

'Right, pack it in, the pair of you! If you must know, we didn't want *either* of you helping out on the farm, because you were both useless at it.'

Jo guiltily dipped her gaze. She'd been ten and Evan twelve when their father had lost his engineering job and invested his redundancy money in this place. It was only thirty or so miles from their old terraced house in Manchester, but it may as well have been a different planet for how isolated they'd felt. Out of sheer boredom, Evan had half-heartedly helped their dad on the land, but Jo had defiantly resisted their mother's attempts to teach her how to cook, grow vegetables, or tend to the stinking chickens. As soon as they had been old enough to leave home, they had both hot-footed it back to the land of the living, and only visited for special occasions now, like Christmas, and their parents' birthdays.

The fire crackled loudly as the wind howled down the chimney, and the three lapsed into silence and drank their tea. On the verge of falling asleep by the time he'd finished, Evan leaned forward and slammed his empty cup down on the table.

'Oi, spud face.' He kicked Jo in the ankle. 'Fancy a fight?'

'Don't even think about it,' she warned. 'I used to want to kill you when you roughed me up. And I *mean* kill,' she added ominously. 'If you'd known how many times I plotted to murder you and bury you under the cowshed, you'd have steered well clear of me.'

'Oh, I knew,' he chuckled. 'You wrote about it in your diary – in very gory detail, might I add.'

Jo's mouth fell open. 'You read my diary?'

'Course I did,' Evan said, without a trace of remorse. 'It used to give me and my mates a right laugh. I can't believe you didn't know.'

'You little shit!' she squawked, her cheeks flaming at the thought of him and his spotty school friends reading her private thoughts.

'Yep, that's pretty much what you called me back then, as well,' said Evan. 'Little shit, little mong, little dickhead, little cu—' He paused and gave her a curious look. 'How come it was always *little* something, when I was so much bigger than you?'

'How am I supposed to know? I was a child.'

'But you just did it again . . . called me a little shit.'

'Yeah, well, I guess old habits die hard, don't they?' Jo sat forward and put her cup down. 'Right, that's me done. I'm going to head up to my room and give Sam a quick ring.'

'Why don't you go home, love?' Frank suggested when she stood up. 'There's no need for you to stay over.'

'I'm not leaving you on your own tonight,' she insisted. 'You need company at a time like this.'

'No one needs company when they're asleep,' he reasoned. 'And you can go, as well, Son,' he added to Evan. 'You shouldn't leave Marie by herself overnight; it's not safe round your way.'

'She's got the dog to protect her,' Evan argued. 'And I've already told her I'm staying.'

'Well, now I'm telling you you're not,' said Frank, rising stiffly to his feet. 'Go on . . . get yourselves back to your families.'

'You're our family, too,' Jo reminded him, ashamed of herself for already mentally packing the little bag she'd brought over that morning, containing her pyjamas, toothbrush, and make-up bag.

'I know.' Frank patted her shoulder. 'But you've a long drive ahead of you, and the sooner you get going, the sooner you'll get home.'

'Only if you're absolutely sure you'll be OK?'

'I'm positive.'

Aware that there was no use arguing once their father had made up his mind, Jo and Evan headed up to their old rooms to collect their things.

Frank was standing at the foot of the stairs with their coats in his hand when they came back down. Jo took hers and was slipping it on when her mobile started ringing.

'It's Sam,' she said, glancing at the screen. 'Won't be a sec.'

She rushed into the kitchen to speak to her husband in private, but she didn't close the door properly, and Frank and Evan exchanged an awkward glance when her voice carried clearly out to them.

'Hi, I was just leaving. No, I haven't had a chance yet. I was going to do it in the morning, but he's told me to go home so it'll have to wait.'

There was a pause while she listened to whatever her husband was saying. Then, sighing, she said, 'OK, I'll do it now. But he's not going to like it.'

'Everything all right?' Frank asked when she came back out into the hall.

Unable to look him in the eye, Jo shook her head.

'Not really. There's, um, something I need to tell you.'

'Uh-oh, this sounds personal. Think that's my cue to leave,' Evan said, reaching out to open the front door.

'No, stay.' Jo touched his arm. 'You both need to hear this.'

Curious to know what was going on, the men followed her into the living room and sat down. Nervous, because she had no idea how they would react when they heard what she had to say, Jo licked her lips and clasped her hands together in her lap before starting.

'Right, this isn't going to be easy. And I know it's a terrible time to tell you, but Sam says I can't keep putting it off.'

'You two are OK, aren't you?' Frank asked. 'You're not thinking of splitting up, or anything?'

'God, no!' she spluttered. 'It's got nothing to do with Sam. Well, not in that way, anyway. It's just . . .'

'Come on, our kid, spit it out,' Evan said impatiently when she tailed off. 'You've got us thinking all sorts here.'

Breathing in deeply, Jo said, 'We're going to Australia.'

'That's nice,' Frank said, wondering why she'd been so worried about telling them. 'It'll do you both good to take a break, and Emily will love it.'

12

'I don't mean for a holiday,' Jo said quietly. 'I mean we're emigrating.'

'What?' A deep crease formed between Frank's eyebrows. 'When?'

'Two weeks.'

'Bloody hell!' Evan drew his head back and stared at her in disbelief. 'And you're only telling us *now*?'

'I'm really sorry, Dad,' Jo addressed her father guiltily. 'I wanted to tell you ages ago, but every time I tried, Mum got worse, so I couldn't.'

'So you thought you'd wait till the day of her funeral instead?' Evan sneered. 'Classy, that, Sis. *Real* classy.'

'I'm sorry,' Jo said again, struggling to keep her tears in check. 'If there'd been any way to tell you sooner, I'd have done it. But there wasn't.'

Frank stared at her for several long moments as if he didn't know what to say. Then, leaning forward when a tear trickled down her cheek, he tugged a tissue out of the box Maureen kept on the hearth and passed it to her.

'Don't cry, love. You've no reason to be upset.'

'Evan's right, though,' she sniffled. 'It's totally the wrong time to be telling you something like this. But it's coming up so fast, and I might not have had another chance.'

Frank sat back and drummed his fingertips on the arm of his chair.

'So . . . Australia, eh? Can't say I was expecting that.'

'It's not that long since *I* found out, so it was a shock for me, as well,' Jo said, dabbing at her eyes with the tissue. 'But Sam's been asked to manage his company's new branch on the Gold Coast, and it's twice the salary he's getting now, so we'd be stupid to turn it down. They've leased a house for us, with a really good school close by, and a beach at the end of the road.'

'Whoopty-do,' Evan said scornfully, staring at her in disgust. 'He buried Mum today, in case you've forgotten, and now you're going to abandon him?'

'I'm not abandoning him,' Jo protested, even though she felt she was doing exactly that – and hated herself for it. 'It's only for two years, and we can call and email each other all the time. We can even Skype – if you can get your head around it, Dad.'

'I'm sure I'll manage,' said Frank.

'Never mind Skype,' Evan interjected bitterly. 'It'll be winter soon, and who's going to look after him if he gets snowed in or has a fall? Or – God forbid – another heart attack?'

'That's not going to happen,' Frank said before Jo could respond. 'This is a great opportunity for them, and I'd never forgive myself if they missed out because of me.'

'But your heart—' Jo said lamely.

'Is stronger than it's ever been,' said Frank. 'I haven't had any problems since the doc put me on that new medication, and there's no reason why that should change.'

'She still shouldn't be going at a time like this,' Evan argued. 'She's being selfish.'

'And *you're* not?' Jo rounded on him. 'Expecting *me* to stay in case Dad needs looking after, when you're only an hour's drive away?'

'You're his daughter.'

'And you're his son – when it suits you.'

'What's that supposed to mean?'

'Oh, come off it!' Jo snorted. 'You only ever visit when you want something, and he doesn't see you for dust the rest of the year.'

'You're no better,' Evan retorted angrily. 'When was the last time you—'

'*Enough!*' Frank barked, shocking them both into silence for the second time that night. 'Have you any idea how much it used to upset your mother when you squabbled like this? She hardly saw either of you from one year to the next, and she'd lay on a lovely spread whenever she knew you were coming. And how did you thank her? You'd wreck it all with this ridiculous, childish bickering – *that's* how! It's no wonder Sam and Marie can never get out of here fast enough when you fetch them over, because they can't bear the flaming atmosphere you two create. *None* of us can.'

Frank's face was puce by the time he finished, and Jo stared at him open-mouthed.

'I'm so sorry, Dad. I had no idea you felt like that.'

'Well, now you do,' Frank replied bluntly. 'I'm only glad your mum doesn't have to suffer any more of it, because she deserved better.'

'Yes, she did,' Evan agreed. 'But all this with me and Jo, it's just banter. We don't mean anything by it.'

'Maybe not, but it's time you both grew up and started treating each other with respect,' Frank said gruffly. 'If these last few months haven't taught you the value of family, nothing ever will.'

When they both apologized again, Frank released his irritation on a long-drawn-out breath. Then, pushing himself up to his feet, he said, 'We're all tired, so let's draw a line under this and call it a night, eh?'

After kissing her dad goodbye and telling him she would call round to help him clean up in the morning, Jo gave her brother a rare hug before heading outside. Evan followed seconds later, and Frank watched from the porch as they reversed their respective cars out onto the lane.

A blissful silence settled over the house when he closed the door, and he felt the tension lifting from his shoulders as he went back into the living room. It was years since the kids had left home, and he'd grown used to the peace and quiet. Today, with the house bursting at the seams with mourners, the noise had been deafening, and all he'd wanted to do was hide in the barn until every last one of them had gone – Evan and Jo included.

Especially them, by the end.

Frank lifted the larger coals out of the fire and made sure the embers were safely contained. Then, stuffing his hands into his trouser pockets, he gazed at the photograph of Maureen again.

She had loved the peace and quiet as much as he had, and they had both enjoyed sitting in here of an evening: Maureen knitting and doing crosswords, while Frank scoured the internet for spares to renovate the old cars that now occupied the barn where his cows had once been housed. Now it would just be him, and his heart ached at the thought.

Sighing, Frank switched off the lights and went out into the hall. The doorbell rang as he was about to head up the stairs and, thinking one of the kids must have forgotten something, he opened the door without checking, only to find Yvonne Caldwell, from the cottage at the other end of the lane, standing in the porch with a foil-covered dish in her hands.

'Evening, love.' She smiled out at him from the circle of fur edging the hood of her coat. 'I saw your Jo and Evan driving past and thought I'd pop round to check how you're doing? And to give you this . . .' She thrust the dish into his hands. 'It's nothing special; only a spot of stew I had left over from tea last night. I noticed you didn't really eat much earlier, so I thought you'd probably be hungry by now.'

Frank wasn't hungry, but he didn't want to appear ungrateful, so he said, 'Thanks, love. Much appreciated.'

'You're welcome,' Yvonne said, pulling the collar of her coat around her chin to shield it from the wind. 'It was a lovely send-off, wasn't it? Great to see so many people paying their respects. Mo would have been pleased by the turnout.'

'She would,' Frank agreed. 'Anyway, I'd bes—'

'I don't think she'd have been too impressed with that vicar waffling on like that, though,' Yvonne continued. 'No offence, because I know your Mo took her religion seriously, but I reckon she'd have been as bored as everyone else was.'

'Probably,' Frank said, pretending to stifle a yawn in the hope that Yvonne would take the hint and go home.

'Your Evan's speech was very moving, though, wasn't it?' she went on, as if she hadn't noticed. 'He had me in tears a couple of times. Oh, and didn't your Jo's girl look a picture, all dressed up like a little doll?'

'She's bonny, all right,' said Frank. 'Anyway, I'd best get this inside.' He held up the dish. 'Thanks again.'

'My pleasure,' said Yvonne. Then, tipping her head to one side, she peered at him thoughtfully. 'I could always come in and warm it up for you, if you like? Give you a chance to put your feet up.'

'To be honest, I'm pretty tired,' Frank said politely. 'I was on my way to bed when you knocked, so I'll probably save this for breakfast.'

Yvonne's smile faltered, but she quickly recovered.

'Oh, right. Well, you know where I am if you need me. I'll pop round in the morning for the bowl.'

Frank thought about transferring the stew into one of his own bowls so she could take hers with her. But he had a feeling it would be hard to shift her if she got her foot through the door, so he nodded, and murmured, 'Night, then,' before closing the door.

A frown creased his brow as he carried the bowl into the

kitchen. He was pretty sure Yvonne had been wearing make-up, and that was odd, because he didn't think he'd ever seen her made-up before. Then again, he'd never paid much mind to her appearance whenever she'd popped round to have a brew and a gossip with Maureen in the past, so she could have been plastered in it each time for all he knew.

He scraped the stew into the bin and washed the bowl, then placed it on the hall table, ready to hand straight out to Yvonne when she called round in the morning, and then headed up to bed. He hadn't slept properly in months for worrying about Maureen taking bad in the night, but now it was all over, he hoped he would manage a few straight hours.

After undressing in the dark, he climbed into bed and pulled the quilt up around his shoulders. Almost immediately, the house came alive with noises he'd never noticed before. The creak of floorboards settling . . . the rhythmic ticking of the clock on Maureen's bedside table . . . the drip of water leaking from the bathroom tap . . .

Only one sound was missing: that of Maureen breathing softly on her side of the bed. In all the years they had been married, apart from the times when she had been confined to hospital after giving birth, and the two weeks Frank had been kept in ICU following his heart attack, they hadn't spent one single night apart, and the realization that he was never again going to hear her breathe, or feel the warmth of her body as they lay back to back in this bed, caused the tears Frank had been holding inside all day to spill over.

2

Woken by the sound of a car pulling onto the driveway the next morning, Frank peeled an eye open and squinted at the clock on Maureen's bedside table. Shocked to see that it was 10 a.m., he shoved the quilt aside and dropped his feet to the floor. As a farmer, he'd grown accustomed to waking before dawn. And, even now, some two years since he'd sold his livestock and rented out most of his crop-bearing fields to neighbouring farmers, he tended to wake before the sun had fully risen.

Wincing at the sound of the doorbell echoing through the hallway below, he stood up and quickly got dressed before clattering down the stairs and peering through the spyhole. It was Yvonne, so he snatched the bowl up off the table before opening the door.

'Morning,' Yvonne said cheerily, taking in his tousled hair and the stubble on his chin. 'Didn't wake you, did I?'

'No, I've been up for ages,' he lied. 'I was, um, getting ready to go out, actually. I've got an appointment, so I hope you won't think I'm being rude if I don't invite you in. Oh, and thanks for the stew. It was delicious.' He thrust the bowl into her hand before reaching behind the door for his coat.

'You liked it?' Her face lit up.

'Very much,' he said, looking around for his car keys. Spotting them on the table, he leaned back to get them, giving Yvonne a clear view of the hallway and the kitchen beyond.

'Oh, my,' she exclaimed when she saw the mess. 'You're going to need a hand clearing that lot up, so why don't I—'

'It's OK, I'll do it when I get home,' Frank cut her off.

Yvonne drew her head back and gave him a stern look.

'Not on your own, you won't. I've got nothing important on today, and four hands are better than two, as my old mum used to say, so I'll stop here and make a start while you go to your appointment.'

'There's really no need,' Frank said, shivering when he stepped outside and pulled the door firmly shut behind him. It was bitterly cold, and he really didn't fancy getting into the car with its frost-coated windscreen. But now he'd lied about having an appointment to go to, he had no choice.

'It's no trouble,' Yvonne persisted, linking an arm through his and walking with him to the car. 'This is what friends do for each other at times like this. Your Maureen looked after me when I lost my Don, so now I'm going to look after you. And don't bother arguing, 'cos I won't take no for an answer.'

Frank gave her an uneasy smile as he clicked to key-fob to unlock the car doors. Last night, he'd wondered if Yvonne might always have worn make-up. But, now, seeing her in the cold light of day, with her kohl eyeliner and scarlet lipstick, he was pretty sure he'd have noticed if she'd ever looked like this in the past.

'What time will you be back?' Yvonne asked, letting go of his arm when he pulled the car door open. 'Will it be more lunchtime, or teatime, do you think? Only, if I'm coming over to help you clear up, I might as well pop something in the oven, so I need to know whether to do a light lunch, or a proper meal?'

'I'm not sure how long I'll be, so it's probably best if you see to yourself,' Frank replied evasively. 'I'll pick something up in the village.'

'Oh, I didn't realize you were going to the village,' Yvonne pounced. 'I was going to pop down there myself, so why don't I leave my car here and come with you? I can do my shopping then wait for you in the café.'

'I'm not actually going that way,' Frank backtracked. 'I was thinking of stopping off at the bakery on my way back, that's all.'

'Well, there must be shops where you *are* going, so I could still—'

'No!'

Yvonne drew her head back as if he'd slapped her, and Frank immediately felt guilty.

'Sorry, I didn't mean to bite your head off. But I really need to get going, or I'll be late for my appointment.'

Yvonne nodded and patted his arm.

'Don't worry, love, I understand. You've had a rough time these last few months, so you're bound to be feeling a bit fraught. But please stop thinking you've got to cope with it on your own, because I'm here to help. OK?'

'OK,' Frank conceded, sighing as he climbed into the driver's seat.

Before he had a chance to close the door, Yvonne leaned in and planted a kiss on his cheek. Then, leaving a trail of cloying perfume in her wake, she waggled her fingers at him before heading to her own car.

Shoulders slumping when she'd driven away, Frank started the engine and reversed the car to the back of the house, before jumping out and opening the barn doors. Yvonne meant well, but he'd never been the best at making small-talk, and the thought of being trapped in the house with her filled him with dread, so he would park the car out of sight in the barn, he decided; make her think he was still out if she came back round.

Letting himself in through the back door after hiding the car, Frank had a wash and brushed his teeth, and then drank a cup of coffee and ate a slice of toast before getting stuck into the cleaning.

Afraid that Yvonne might be checking to see if he was back yet when the phone started ringing an hour later, he left it to go to answer-machine, but quickly snatched it up when he heard his daughter's voice.

'Morning, love. Did you get home all right?'

'Obviously, or I'd be lying in a ditch somewhere instead of

calling you,' Jo replied bluntly. Then, sighing, she said, 'Sorry, Dad; didn't mean to snap. Sam's arranged for a letting agent to call round this morning, and I'm stressing out because the house is an absolute mess. But never mind me . . . how are *you*? Did you manage to get any sleep?'

'Like a log,' Frank lied, deciding not to mention the tears he'd cried, because that would only make her worry. 'I actually had a lie-in,' he went on. 'Didn't wake up till Yvonne called round at ten.'

'Wow.' Jo sounded surprised. 'It's not like you to sleep so late, so you must have needed it. What did Yvonne want?'

'She came for her bowl.'

'Bowl?' Jo repeated, suspicion in her voice now. 'What bowl? Everything in that kitchen belonged to Mum, so she'd better not be trying to lay claim to anything, or I'll—'

'It was hers,' Frank interrupted. 'She'd noticed I didn't eat much yesterday, so she called round with some stew when you and Evan had gone home.'

'You didn't eat it, did you?' Jo asked. 'She gave me a piece of cake once, and it had half a dead cockroach in it.'

'Don't worry, it went straight in the bin,' Frank assured her. 'And I know she's only being neighbourly, so I shouldn't complain, but like I told you and Evan last night, I don't need looking after, so I'm hoping she's not going to start calling round all the time to help out.'

'Good luck with that,' Jo snorted. 'Anyway, subject of helping you out, that why I'm calling: to let you know I won't be able to get over to yours till later this afternoon. Can you bear with the mess till then?'

'I've already taken care of it,' Frank told her. 'And I was actually thinking I could pop over to help you. There must be loads to do if you're leaving in two weeks.'

'I'd rather you didn't,' Jo said sheepishly. 'No offence, Dad, but I've got a routine, and you'll only get under my feet.'

'Like mother like daughter,' Frank chuckled, remembering the way Maureen had always shooed him out of the kitchen whenever he'd tried to help.

'Oh, no,' Jo groaned as her doorbell chimed in the background. 'The letting agent's early, and I'm nowhere near ready for him.'

'You can't pack up ten years' worth of belongings without making a mess, love,' Frank said. 'I'm sure he'll have seen worse.'

'I don't want him seeing it like this and thinking it'll be OK to shove any old scruff-bag tenants in,' Jo replied edgily. 'We've worked really hard on making the house nice, and we want people who'll treat it with respect.'

'Stop flapping,' Frank said calmly. 'Everything will work out fine.'

Jerking the phone away from his ear when Jo yelled, 'All right, I'm coming!' at the sound of her bell ringing again, Frank said, 'Love, go and let him in. I'll speak to you later.'

He replaced the receiver in its cradle and shook his head as he picked up the bags of rubbish and carried them out to the bin. Jo had two weeks to sort the house out, but, as usual, she was trying to do everything at once, and her stress levels would be through the roof by the end of it. Still, there was nothing he could do if she didn't want his help, so he'd just have to leave her to it.

3

The two weeks' notice Jo had given Frank flew by, and before he knew it, she'd jetted off with her little family to start their new life in the sun. She rang the following afternoon to tell him they had arrived safely, that the weather was fantastic, and the house was amazing, with its own swimming pool and three enormous en-suite bedrooms. As happy as Frank was for her, the realization that he wasn't going to see her again for two years settled over him like a lead weight, and the future began to look like a bleak and lonely place.

Still grieving for Maureen, and now missing Jo and Emily as well, Frank only left the house if he absolutely had to during the next three months. Evan hadn't called round since the funeral – mainly because Frank had asked him not to; and the few conversations they'd had on the phone had been brief. Jo, who had always been better at keeping in touch than her brother, had phoned every Sunday for the first few weeks, but that had gradually petered out, and Frank felt truly alone for the first time in his life. He had no desire to 'join some groups and meet new people' – as Jo had ordered him to do before she'd left. And he had neither the energy nor the motivation to resume renovating the cars in his barn, which had once been his passion. Most days, he couldn't even be bothered to get dressed, and he was sitting in his stained pyjamas with a glass of whisky in his hand when he got a rare phone call from his son early in November.

'All right, Pops,' Evan said cheerily, as if it hadn't been weeks since they had last spoken. 'What you up to?'

Ashamed to admit that he was wasting another day away watching mind-numbingly boring daytime TV, Frank said, 'Just cracking on with some jobs around the house.'

'Great stuff,' Evan said – sounding relieved, Frank thought, that he wasn't wallowing in grief. 'I won't keep you if you're busy,' he went on. 'I only wanted to let you know we're having Christmas dinner at ours this year.'

Frank couldn't think of anything worse. Not only would this be his first Christmas in some forty-plus years without Maureen, he would now be subjected to a day of being growled at and eyeballed by the mangy dog his daughter-in-law treated like the child she'd never had.

'I'm not sure what I'll be doing yet,' he said evasively. 'I'll have to let you know nearer the time.'

'Marie's already started organizing it, and she needs to know how many she's cooking for,' said Evan. 'Anyway, what you on about – you don't know what you'll be doing? We're the only family you've got left, so you'll be spending it with us – end of.'

'I'll let you know,' Frank repeated. 'Now, is that all? Only I'm in the middle of something here.'

'Cut me off, why don't you?' Evan snorted.

'Sorry,' Frank sighed. 'But you know what it's like when you stop halfway through a job – it's really hard to get started again.'

'All right, I'll get off and leave you in peace,' Evan conceded. 'But can I ask you a favour first?'

'What kind of favour?' Frank asked warily, taking a swig of whisky.

'I don't suppose you could pop round to Jo's and check on the boiler, could you?' Evan asked. 'The letting agent called me this morning and said the tenants have been bugging him about it. I know I said I'd handle the maintenance, but I'm snowed under at work, so I'm not sure when I'll get the chance.'

'It's fine,' Frank said, relieved that Evan hadn't asked for another loan, as he'd been expecting. It wasn't that he minded lending him money, but Evan had a habit of forgetting that he'd borrowed it, so Frank rarely if ever got it back.

'Cheers, Pops, you're the best,' Evan said. 'And I'll tell Marie to count you in for Christmas, 'cos there's no way I'm suffering her folks on my own.'

Frank shook his head when the call was finished, and raised his glass to take another swig. Instantly changing his mind, he placed the glass on the table and headed upstairs to get washed and dressed. He didn't really fancy the hour-long drive to Jo's house, but now he'd promised, he didn't have much choice.

Surprised to find that it was snowing when he left the house,

Frank pulled his gloves on to clear the car's windscreen. It was early for snow, and he hoped it didn't augur another terrible winter like the one they'd suffered a couple of years earlier, during which the central heating had broken down and he and Maureen had almost frozen to death before the engineer had finally managed to get to them.

Making a mental note to stop off at the village garden-centre on the way back, and stock up on extra coal for the fire, Frank set off down the lane – putting his foot down as he passed Yvonne's place, in case she spotted him and tried to flag him down. For the first couple of weeks after the funeral she had called round almost daily, bringing food he never ate, and offering help he neither needed nor wanted. Unable to bear it, he'd politely asked her to give him a bit of space, and to her credit she hadn't called round since. But it wouldn't be long before she was back at his door if she saw him out and about, and he wasn't sure he was ready for that.

Jo's house was situated at the end of a quiet cul-de-sac, and her neighbours were mostly retired couples – who clearly had a lot of time on their hands, judging by their well-tended front gardens. Both too busy – and neither particularly green-fingered – Jo and Sam had employed a gardener to tend their front and back gardens, but the tenants who'd moved in a few weeks after their move to Australia had obviously decided not to bother with his services, and Frank eyed the overgrown lawn and weed-infested borders with disapproval as he parked up on the driveway and climbed out of his car.

No one answered when he rang the bell, so he let himself in using the spare key Jo had given him. The furniture belonged to Jo and Sam, as did the white goods in the kitchen, but the personal effects belonged to the tenants, and Frank felt like an intruder under the gaze of the strangers in the photographs hanging on the hallway walls. The house smelled completely different, and the absolute silence in there, which was totally at odds with the chatter and laughter he was used to when he visited, only served to remind him of what he'd lost.

Desperate to get out of there as quickly as possible, Frank hurried through to the kitchen and checked the boiler. Pleased to discover that all it needed was a refill and for the pilot to be relit, he dealt with it and then rushed back to his car.

Worn out by the long drive after months of inactivity, Frank dumped the bags of coal he'd bought on the way home in the shed, and then made his way inside. After heating a tin of soup and buttering a couple of slices of bread, he settled in his chair to watch TV while he ate. When he'd finished, he reached for the glass he'd left behind earlier, and topped it up with fresh whisky.

Relaxed, he gazed around the room, looking at it properly for the first time in months. The bowl and saucer he'd just placed on the coffee table was surrounded by yet more dirty crockery and microwave-food containers, and every piece of furniture was coated in a thick layer of dust. He didn't need to imagine how disgusted Maureen would be if she could see the state of the place – or the state of him, with the dark bags under his eyes, the messy, unwashed hair, and the peppery half-beard he'd grown out of laziness rather than desire. He felt as if he'd aged twenty years since the funeral, and if Maureen were here she'd be telling him to pull himself together. And she'd be right to, because he had fallen into a pit of self-pity that was sapping the life out of him.

It was time to start living again, and he would begin by getting an early night. Then, in the morning, he would open the curtains and windows to air the place out, before tackling the dusting and the vacuuming. And then – *maybe* – he would make a start on clearing Maureen's clothes and shoes out of the wardrobe.

That last thought had been hanging over Frank for ages, but he'd resisted putting it into action because he hadn't wanted to admit that Maureen was never coming back. But that was the truth of it, and he knew that she'd have packed his stuff off to the charity shop a long time ago if the shoe had been on her foot instead of his, so that was exactly what he was going to do, he decided.

Sure that Maureen would approve of his plans, Frank carried his glass and the whisky bottle upstairs and placed them on the bedside table while he got ready for bed. He knew he'd been drinking too much lately, and that was another thing he planned to address. But not tonight.

4

Despite his intention to get an early night, Frank couldn't sleep, and he was re-reading an old book about serial killers, third whisky in hand, when he heard a loud bang coming from the back of the house at 2 a.m. Conscious that it might be burglars – like the gang who'd broken into a neighbouring farm not long before Maureen had passed away, and beaten the farmer and his wife so badly they'd been hospitalized – he shoved the quilt off his legs and groped under the bed for his cricket bat.

Clutching the bat, he crept down the stairs, avoiding the ones that creaked, and quickly checked the front and back rooms before heading into the kitchen. The moon was full and high, floodlighting the snow-covered yard. Able to see the garden and the outbuildings clearly through the window, he did a scan of the land, his gaze sweeping from left to right and back again. Seeing nothing suspicious, he decided a fox must have knocked one of the bins over. But as he was about to head back up to bed, a movement between the old chicken coop and the barn caught his eye, and when he squinted to get a better look, he was sure he could see someone crouching in the shadows.

Aware there could be more than one of them, Frank stood the bat in the corner and quickly unlocked the cupboard where his shotgun was housed. In all the years he'd lived on the farm, he had never used the gun – and he hoped that wasn't about to change as he loaded it now before unlocking the back door and stepping outside.

'I can see you, and I'm armed,' he warned loudly as he aimed the gun in the direction of the figure. 'You've got five seconds to get the hell out of here before I start shooting . . . Five . . . four . . .'

'Please, no shoot!' the figure cried, lurching up from its hiding place, hands in the air.

Shocked to hear that it was a woman, Frank narrowed his eyes and peered at her. Most of the people who lived in the area were Yorkshire born and bred, but this woman sounded foreign. And she definitely wasn't dressed like a local, because no one who'd experienced a winter out here would go out at this time of night in the short skirt and thin blouse she appeared to be wearing.

'Are you alone?' he called.

'Yes, is only me,' she replied shakily.

'It's OK, you can put your hands down,' he said, lowering the gun.

Visibly shivering, the woman lowered her arms.

'I am sorry for disturb you,' she said. 'I mean no trouble. I was only look for warm place to sleep.'

'Are you hurt?' Frank asked when he noticed a dark shadow on her cheek.

'No.' She shook her head and covered her cheek with her hand. 'I fall. Is nothing.'

Guessing that must have been the bang he'd heard, Frank said, 'Is there someone you can call to come and pick you up?'

'There is no one,' she replied. 'But is OK. I will find another place to sleep.'

Concerned when he saw her sway, Frank glanced around again to check that nobody else was hiding, and then jerked his head at her.

'Come inside and sit down for a minute, love. I'll make you a warm drink, and then I'll give you a lift home.'

'No!' Her eyes widened and she took a step back. 'I cannot go back there.'

'Well, you can't stay outside in this weather dressed like that,' Frank said bluntly. 'You'll be frozen solid by morning – if you make it that far.'

The woman bit her lip and gazed around. Then, turning back to Frank, she said, 'Is safe to come inside?'

'Absolutely,' he said, stepping away from the door and waving for her to enter ahead of him.

She hesitated for a moment, as if weighing up her options, and then limped across the yard and stumbled over the threshold into the kitchen. Frank followed her in and locked the door.

'Whoa, steady,' he said, catching her by the elbow when her legs started to buckle. 'Sit there and catch your breath.' He guided her to a chair. 'I'll put the kettle on.'

When she was seated, Frank switched the light on and frowned when he saw that the bruise on her cheek was worse than he'd initially thought. Her clothes were filthy, and her torn blouse appeared to be spattered with dried blood. There were more bruises on her arms, some more recent than others judging by their varying shades, and yet more on her legs.

Strongly suspecting that this was the result of an assault and not a fall, he said, 'Who did this to you, love?'

'No one,' she replied quietly, dipping her gaze. 'Was my fault for be clumsy.'

Frank didn't believe her, but he couldn't force her to talk about it if she didn't want to, so he locked the gun away and then filled the kettle.

'I think I may be sick,' the woman mumbled, covering her mouth with her hand. 'Where is bathroom, please?'

'Top of the stairs.' Frank pointed the way. 'First door on the right.'

She rushed out of the room, and Frank took two cups out of the cupboard. About to put teabags into them, he dropped the canister when he heard a heavy thump on the floor above, and ran up the stairs.

'Hello . . . ?' He knocked on the bathroom door. 'Are you OK in there?'

When no answer came, he tried the door. It wasn't locked, but something was obstructing it, so he had to use his shoulder to force his way in. The woman was sprawled on the floor behind it, her face as white as a sheet, the bruises even more livid under the bright light. Squatting down beside her, Frank gently shook her.

Her eyes fluttered open, and she swallowed loudly before asking, 'What happen?'

'You blacked out,' he told her, slipping his arm under her back. 'Let's get you sat up, eh?'

'I do not feel good,' she croaked, leaning against his shoulder when he eased her into a sitting position.

Concerned that she might have some kind of internal injury, Frank said, 'OK, stay there while I get my phone. I'm going to call for an ambulance.'

'No!' Panic flaring in her eyes, the woman clutched at his hand when he made to stand up. 'You cannot tell anyone I am here. If he find me, he will kill me.'

'You're safe here,' Frank assured her. 'And you'll be safe in the hospital, too. Tell the police who did this to you, and they'll—'

'You do not understand,' she cried. 'I cannot talk to police because I am not meant to be here. I will rest for minute, and then I will go.'

'If you try to go back out there in this condition, you won't last ten minutes,' Frank warned.

'I do not care,' she murmured, tears glittering in her eyes. 'Death is better than . . .'

She didn't finish the sentence, but Frank got the gist, and he shook his head sadly.

'Love, no one's worth dying for,' he said. 'I don't know where you came from, or what you've been through, but you obviously need help, so let me—'

'*No!*' She swiped away a tear that was trickling down her cheek. 'Thank you for be kind, but no one can help me, so I will go now.'

She tried to stand up, but immediately fell back down. Catching her, Frank made a snap decision.

'Look, you're in no fit state to go anywhere tonight, so why don't you stay here?' he offered. 'You can sleep in my daughter's room.'

'You have children?' She gazed up at him. 'I am sorry, I did not think. I hope I have not disturb them?'

'Don't worry, they left home a long time ago,' Frank said, helping her to her feet.

'You do not look old enough to have grown children,' she said, leaning against him.

'Believe me, I am,' he said, guiding her into Jo's room.

'Will your wife mind me be here?' she asked, clinging to him as they walked.

'She passed away a few months back,' Frank said, lowering her onto the edge of the bed. 'But, no, she wouldn't have minded. Now make yourself comfortable. I'll finish that tea and fetch it up for you.'

'Thank you. You are very kind, Mr . . . ?'

'It's Frank,' he said, backing toward the door.

'I am Irena,' she murmured, sinking back against the pillows.

Nodding, Frank left her and went back downstairs. He switched the kettle on, and while he waited for the water to reboil, he stood peering out through the window looking for signs that she'd been followed. He didn't know where she'd come from, but he doubted she'd have been capable of walking far in her condition, so he figured it had to be fairly local – in which case, the man who had hurt her might not be too far behind.

Aware that the man might track her to his door, Frank took the shotgun back out of the cupboard and carried it upstairs with the tea. Irena was fast asleep when he entered Jo's room, so he left the cup on the bedside table and quietly closed the door before going to his own room.

He switched the lamp off and, taking a seat on the chair by the window, gazed out at the moonlit lane. This was the only route to and from the village four miles away, and it ended in a dead-end some three hundred yards past his gate. Very few people ever ventured this far unless they were visiting him, and, from here, he could see them coming from a mile off, so there was no chance of anyone catching him unawares tonight.

5

Frank didn't realize he'd nodded off until he opened his eyes the following morning. It had snowed again during the night, and everything was covered in a blinding sheet of white as far as his eye could see. Stiff and cold, he started to rise from the chair, but quickly dropped back down and cried out in pain when the shotgun slid off his lap and landed on his foot.

The door flew open, and Irena appeared with a panicked look on her bruised face.

'What happen?'

'It's OK, I dropped the gun. Nothing to worry about,' Frank said, grimacing as he leaned down to rub his injured foot.

'He is not here?' She looked nervously around, as if expecting the man to be hiding somewhere.

'No one's been near all night,' Frank assured her, averting his gaze when he noticed that she was naked beneath the sheet she was clutching around herself. 'If you give me a minute to get dressed, I'll root something out for you to wear. Leave your clothes on the landing outside your room. I'll stick them in the washer then make you some breakfast.'

Irena nodded and backed out of the room, pulling the door shut behind her. Ignoring the pain in his foot, Frank quickly got dressed before rifling through Maureen's wardrobe. Most of her clothes were old and far too big for his slim young visitor, but she'd lost a lot of weight in the final months, and he was pretty sure the jumper and leggings Jo had bought for her last birthday would fit Irena. Maureen had been too tired by then to even try them on, so they were brand new, and a wave of sadness washed over him when he took them out and saw that the tags were still attached. Shaking it off, he gathered up his own dirty clothes before reaching for the shotgun.

As he'd asked her to, Irena had left her skirt and blouse on the floor outside her door. Exchanging them for the new ones, Frank made his way downstairs and locked the gun away before loading the washing machine. That done, he turned the heating on to take the chill off the house, and then looked in the fridge and the cupboards in search of something for breakfast.

There wasn't a lot to choose from, because he hadn't bothered stopping in at the supermarket after picking up the coal the previous day, but he found a couple of eggs that passed the stand-in-water test despite being out of date, and a dig through the ice in the freezer uncovered a bag containing a few slices of bread.

Irena joined him in the kitchen as he was serving up, and she thanked him when he placed a plate in front of her.

'Hope it's OK,' he said, sitting across from her with his own plate. 'Maureen reckoned I could burn water, but you can't go far wrong with scrambled eggs, can you?'

'Is good,' Irena said, taking a tiny bite of toast and delicately wiping the crumbs off her lips.

'How are you feeling this morning?' Frank asked, trying not to stare at the bruises circling her wrists.

'A little better,' she said. 'Thank you for let me sleep in daughter's bed, is very comfortable. And thank you for clothes.'

'You're welcome,' Frank said, leaning back in his chair to reach for the two cups of tea he'd left on the ledge. 'That colour really suits you.'

Irena gave him a shy smile, and then gazed around the room.

'This is very nice house. Have you live here long?'

'Coming up for twenty years,' Frank said, covering his mouth with his hand to prevent himself from spitting toast crumbs at her. 'It was a functioning farm for the first eighteen, but I had to retire a couple of years back, so I sold off my livestock, and now it's just a house.'

'Is nice,' Irena said again. 'It remind me of farm houses in Prague when I was child.'

'Ah, so that's where the accent's from,' said Frank. 'I did wonder. But, tell me . . . where did you come from last night? Somewhere local, I'm guessing?'

Irena dipped her gaze, and Frank frowned when he noticed that her chin was wobbling.

'Sorry if it looks like I'm prying,' he apologized. 'I was only curious, but it's fine if you don't want to tell me.'

'Is not you.' Irena sniffed. 'I just don't know what I am to do.'

Frank put his fork down and rested his elbows on the table.

'Look, love, I totally get why you're scared of that man after what he did to you,' he said softly. 'And I know you're terrified of involving the police, but there are people who can help you without involving them. I don't know if you have the same thing in your country, but we have refuges for women in your position. They keep you safe while you're there, and they can help to get you rehoused where the people who've hurt you can't find you.'

'You do not understand,' Irena replied quietly. 'Nowhere is safe, because I am not meant to be in country. He – he take my passport so I cannot leave, and he say police will put me in prison if they catch me.'

'Is he your boyfriend?' Frank asked, noticing that there was no ring on her finger.

'No, he is *monster.*'

'Then why were you with him?'

Irena looked down at her hands, and Frank could tell she was struggling to keep her emotions in check when she bit her lip and breathed in deeply.

'I was not *with* him,' she said after a moment. 'My father meet him and tell me he is good man who will bring me to England and help me find me job and place to live. But it was lie, because Nikolai take me to house and lock me in room when I arrive. He say I owe him money for flight, and I must sleep with men to repay.'

Frank was shocked. He'd seen documentaries about these types of things, but he had never imagined they could be happening so close to home.

'When I tell him I will not do it, he beat me,' Irena went on. 'And he say he will kill me *and* my family if I try to run away.'

'Does your father know any of this?' Frank asked, trying to imagine how *he* would react if anything like this were ever to happen to Jo.

'My father does not care,' she replied bitterly. 'He is only interest in money.'

'What about your mum, then?'

'She die, like your wife. But my father is not strong, like you. He is angry, and he drink too much. Then he lose job, and there is no more money to pay for my brother to see doctor.'

'Your brother's ill?'

'In here.' Irena touched a fingertip to her temple. 'He is . . . *difficult*,' she went on. 'Our father blame him for make our mother unhappy and take her own life, and he beat him with stick and call him devil. But is *him* who make our mother unhappy, not Karel.'

'I'm so sorry,' Frank murmured. 'It must have been a terrible time for you.'

'My mother is free now, and this make me happy,' said Irena. Then, sighing, she said, 'I promise Karel I will send for him when I have earn enough, but I did not know this was never going to happen – that Nikolai would not allow me to keep money.'

'Where's the house he took you to?' Frank asked, wondering if he could pass the address on to the authorities without telling them about her.

'I do not know.' Irena shrugged. 'He say is Manchester, but this mean nothing to me.'

'*Manchester?*' Frank's eyebrows shot up. 'That's an hour's drive away. How on earth did you get here?'

'I walk. Was very far, and I fear I will not make it. But I was more afraid that he will find me if I stop, so I keep walk until I think I am safe. And this is when *you* find me.'

'Christ, no wonder you didn't want to go back when I offered you a lift,' Frank said, struggling to get his head around what he'd heard. 'But how did you escape?'

'Last man hurt me, and when I cry he say I am not please him and he will not pay. Nikolai beat me, and then he say he will kill me when he come back from deal with man. But he forget to lock door, so I run.'

'Good for you,' Frank said.

'No, is not good,' Irena countered. 'I was afraid to be there when he come back, but now I am afraid what will happen when he catch me, so I think maybe I should have stay.'

'Definitely not,' Frank argued, reaching across the table and placing his hand over hers. 'You did absolutely the right thing getting out of there while you could, and I wish you'd let me call the police, because he needs to be taken off the streets before he does this to anyone else.'

'He has done many times already,' Irena said, staring at their joined hands. 'And I know you are right, but I cannot risk go to prison.'

'You're the victim, so I very much doubt they'd arrest you,' Frank said reassuringly. 'They might even be able to arrange for you to go home – if that's what you want?'

'My father will not accept me with empty purse, so I have no home,' Irena said bitterly. 'And if Nikolai hear that I am there, he will come for me, so I cannot go back.'

Before Frank could reply to that, the doorbell rang, and Irena snapped her head up.

'Is him!' she cried, panic in her eyes. 'He has find me.'

'I doubt it,' Frank said, scraping his chair back. 'But stay here while I take a look.'

'Please do not open door,' Irena said fearfully. 'If he see me with you, he will kill us both.'

'Don't worry, I won't let anyone in,' Frank promised, patting her shoulder before walking out into the hall.

It was Yvonne, and she waggled her fingers at him when he peeped through the spyhole. Too polite to ignore her when it was obvious she knew he was there, Frank cracked the door open and peered out at her.

'Hello, stranger,' she beamed. 'I saw you drive past yesterday, so I thought I'd pop round to see how you've been getting on?'

'It's not really a good time,' Frank croaked. 'I've, um, come down with some kind of bug, and it might be contagious.'

'Oh, you poor thing,' Yvonne sympathized. 'But I've had my annual flu shot, so I should be immune to most things. Now let's get you inside and I'll warm this up for you.' She held up a bag containing a large Tupperware bowl. 'Chicken soup – how's that for a coincidence? You're ill, and I turn up with nature's perfect remedy.'

Frank pulled a face, as if the very thought of eating nauseated him, and clapped a hand over his mouth, mumbling, 'Sorry . . . got to go.'

Yvonne opened her mouth to speak, but he closed the door before she had the chance, and he felt guilty when he peeped out at her and saw the expression of concern on her face. Relieved when she turned and headed over to her car, he went back to the kitchen.

'It was only a neighbour,' he told Irena. 'I said I wasn't feeling well, so she's gone now.'

Almost as soon as the words had left his mouth, the letterbox rattled, and Irena cried out in alarm when she looked round and saw a pair of eyes peering at her.

Annoyed, Frank marched back out into the hall and yanked the door open.

'What the bloody hell are you playing at, Yvonne?'

Visibly flustered, the old lady took a step back.

'I wasn't being nosy, pet, I was worried about you. But I didn't realize you had company.'

'It's my niece. She's come to stay for a few days.'

'Oh . . . I didn't know you had a niece. I don't remember seeing her at Mo's funeral.'

'She couldn't make it,' Frank said, tempering his tone, because he knew he'd overreacted. 'Anyway, sorry for shouting, but you gave me a shock.'

'Oh, goodness, what was I thinking?' Yvonne clapped her hand over her mouth. 'I completely forgot about your heart. I hope I haven't done any damage? Do you want me to call the doctor out to check you over?'

'No, there's no need for that,' Frank insisted. 'But do me a favour, and stick to ringing the bell in future, eh?'

'Absolutely,' Yvonne agreed. Then, lowering her voice, she said, 'That's a nasty bruise on your niece's face. Has she had an accident?'

Struggling to keep from snapping at her again, because this was none of her business and he didn't appreciate being forced to explain himself, Frank said, 'Yes, and that's why she's here. For some peace and quiet,' he added pointedly.

'Oh, that's good,' Yvonne said, missing the sarcasm. 'There's nothing like a bit of fresh country air to heal wounds and soothe the soul. But if you're both not well, I can always—'

'Yvonne, we'll be fine,' Frank interrupted. 'And I really need to close the door before this cold air gets on my chest.'

'Go on, then, get yourself inside,' she said. 'I'll see myself out.' Then, realizing what she'd said, she chuckled. 'Oops! Silly me, I'm already out, aren't I?'

Frank gave a strained smile, then nodded goodbye and waved her off before closing the door.

Irena was pacing the floor, but she abruptly stopped when he came back to the kitchen.

'What happen?'

'I told her you're my niece, and you're staying a few days while you recover from an accident.'

'Did she believe?'

'I think so.'

'And she will not tell anybody I am here?'

'I doubt it. She doesn't have family, as far as I know, and we don't get a lot of passers-by up here, so there's no one for her *to* tell, apart from her animals.'

'Thank you, Frankie.' Irena breathed out loudly and returned to her seat.

Frank turned away from her without answering and picked their plates up off the table. Maureen was the only person who had ever called him Frankie before, and the memory had brought unexpected tears to his eyes. Blinking them away as he tipped the uneaten food into the bin, he washed the plates and then dried his hands on the tea towel.

'Right, I need to nip out for a bit,' he said turning to Irena. 'Will you be all right till I get home?'

'You are not go to police?' she asked warily.

'No, of course not,' he assured her, lifting his coat off a hook on the back of the door. 'I'm going to the shop to pick up a few bits, that's all. If anything happens while I'm out – which I'm sure it *won't* – my mobile number is on the pad next to the phone in the hall.'

* * *

Frank's phone started ringing as he was pulling into the car park behind the supermarket, and he smiled when he saw his daughter's name on the screen.

'Hello, love. I've not heard from you in a while. How's it going?'

'You tell me?' Jo replied sharply. 'Yvonne sent me a message telling me you've caught some kind of bug, but I'm not to worry, because your *niece* is looking after you.'

'Yvonne?' Frank frowned. 'I didn't know she had your number.'

'I gave it to her before we left, so she could let me know if anything happened to you,' said Jo. 'And I'm glad I did, or I'd never have found out about this. So who is this mysterious cousin I seem to have acquired overnight, because this is the first *I*'ve ever heard of her.'

Aware that she would react badly if she heard he'd invited an illegal immigrant with a violent trafficker on her tail into his home, Frank said, 'She's just a lass who got lost on a night out with her mates. I caught her trying to break into the barn in the early hours, and it was freezing, so I let her spend the night in your room.'

'Are you crazy?' Jo spluttered. 'What if she'd let someone in when you went to sleep and they'd murdered you in your bed?'

'I doubt she'd have risked that after having my gun aimed at her head.'

'Oh, my God, Dad, why have you still got that? I thought you said you were getting rid of it when you retired? What if they'd wrestled it off you and *you'd* got shot?'

'She was on her own, and I only took it out as a precaution,' Frank said, wondering why she always jumped to the worst-case scenario. 'And I told Yvonne she was my niece because I didn't want her getting hold of the wrong end of the stick and spreading silly gossip around the village.'

'Well, I hope you've sent her on her way?' Jo asked. 'It's all very well being a good Samaritan, but you're not fit enough to be taking in waifs and strays.'

'She's gone,' Frank lied. 'I dropped her at the station ten minutes ago.'

'Good.' Jo sounded slightly mollified. 'Are you on your way home now?'

'I will be soon as I've done a bit of shopping,' said Frank. Then, changing the subject, he said, 'Oh, I meant to tell you, I popped round to your place to fix the boiler yesterday. Evan rang and said the letting agent told him it was on the blink.'

'Did you fix it?'

'Yeah, it only needed refilling and relighting.'

'I wish you hadn't,' Jo grumbled. 'The cheeky buggers have been living there for months, and we haven't had a single penny off them yet.'

'That's not good,' Frank said, climbing out of the car and locking the door. 'Do you want me to call the letting agent and find out what's going on?'

'No, it's OK.' Jo sighed. 'I sent him a message yesterday and told him he's got till the end of the month to sort it or I'll let someone else handle it. If I have to evict them, will you go round and make sure they don't take anything of ours?'

'Of course,' Frank agreed. 'And I'm sure Evan would come with me to add a bit of muscle.'

'Thanks, Dad,' Jo said gratefully. Then, at the sound of her daughter calling out to her in the background, she said, 'Sorry, I've got to go. We're taking Emily to choose a dog from the rescue centre, and she's really excited.'

'You're getting a *dog*?' Frank asked, but Jo had already gone.

In the shop, he thought about the implications of Jo getting a dog as he made his way around the aisles. It seemed odd that she'd take on that kind of responsibility if she was only going to be in Australia for another eighteen months or so. Or had they already decided they weren't coming back, and she was waiting until nearer the time to break the news to him?

Saddened by the thought that they might never come back, he paid for his items and drove home.

6

Irena was asleep on the sofa, but she woke with a start when the front door opened.

'Oh, Frankie, thank God is you!' she gasped when he popped his head into the room. 'I was scared is Nikolai.'

'Sorry, didn't mean to startle you,' Frank apologized, holding up the shopping bags. 'Lamb chops OK for dinner?'

'Anything you choose is good,' Irena said, getting up and following him into the kitchen. 'Would you like for me to make?' she offered. 'I enjoy cook, but Nikolai did not allow us to make food.'

'Us?' Frank gave her a questioning look as he took milk and butter out of one of the bags and carried them to the fridge.

'He has four girl in house,' she explained as she started emptying the second bag onto the worktop. 'There is one more when I arrive, but she get sick, so he take her away and we never see her again. Now I, too, am gone, he will need to fill empty room. I only pray he does not go to my village to find more girl, or he may hurt Karel to punish me.'

'I'm sure he won't do that,' Frank said, although he had no idea what this Nikolai man might be capable of.

'I hope you are right,' Irena murmured.

She gazed up at Frank when he came to unload more food, and he looked quickly away when he noticed her eyes were the same vivid blue as Maureen's had been before age and illness had robbed them of colour and vitality.

'I, um, thought we might take a look online after dinner,' he said. 'See if there's anyone we can contact about your situ—'

'No,' Irena interrupted. 'I have already decide what I am to do. Before I come to this country, I hear about place call London. They say is plenty work there for woman like me, and if is far away, Nikolai will not find me and I will be safe. Is good idea, yes?'

Frank pursed his lips thoughtfully. He still thought she ought to report this man to the police to prevent him from enslaving any more girls – which would also give her the chance to apply for asylum, so she wouldn't have to spend her life looking over her shoulder in fear of being caught and sent home. But it was her call to make, not his, so he shrugged.

'If that's what you want to do, I won't try to dissuade you. But you'll need money for the train and somewhere to stay when you get there.'

'Oh . . . I did not think of this.' Irena frowned. Then, raising her chin, she said, 'Is OK. I will find way.'

'How?' Frank asked. 'I'm not trying to put a dampener on

your plans, love, but you don't know anybody in this country apart from me and that man.'

'I will walk,' she said.

'It's more than two hundred miles,' Frank pointed out. Then, sighing when he saw the hope fading from her eyes, he said, 'Don't worry, I can help you.'

'No.' She shook her head. 'I cannot take your money.'

'Seems to me it's your only option,' Frank said bluntly. 'But if it makes you feel better, we'll call it a loan. I just want to know you'll be safe.'

Irena chewed on her lip and stared at the floor. Then, giving a tiny nod, she said, 'OK, I will accept loan. But I will repay as soon as I have find job.'

'No rush,' Frank said, already praying that his kids never found out about this, because they would think he'd lost his mind.

Later that evening, when they had finished eating, Frank and Irena moved into the living room, where she took a seat on the sofa with a glass of wine in her hand, while he sat in his chair, a glass of whisky in his.

'Tell me about your family,' she said, making herself comfortable.

Smiling, because she looked so relaxed, Frank said, 'Where do you want me to start?'

'I would like to hear about your wife,' she said. 'Where did you meet her?'

'At a disco,' said Frank. 'We were both there with our mates, and her friend came over and told me she wanted to dance with me.'

'This is very brave for girl.'

'She didn't actually know anything about it until I walked over to her,' Frank said, chuckling at the memory. 'And she wasn't too happy when I told her what her friend had done, but she was too polite to refuse, so we had a few dances.'

'Then what happen?'

'She had to be home by ten, so I walked her to the bus stop.'

'And you kiss her?'

'Not that night, no. But I remember telling my mate that I was going to marry her. And two years later, I did. That was her on our wedding day.' Frank indicated the photograph on the mantelpiece.

Irena looked up at it, and smiled.

'She was very beautiful.'

'Yes, she was,' Frank agreed. 'And our daughter, Jo, looks a lot like her.'

'And your son, he look like you?'

'Yep.' Frank nodded. 'Unfortunately for him.'

'No, you are handsome man, Frankie,' Irena chided. 'Like film star I saw in old film.'

'Rubbish,' Frank scoffed.

'Is true,' Irena insisted.

Embarrassed, Frank threw her question back to her: 'So who do you take after? Mother or father?'

'Karel look like our mother, with same dark hair and eyes,' Irena told him. 'But I resemble fa—'

She abruptly stopped speaking when a bright light arced over the closed curtains, and she looked at Frank when she heard a car pulling onto the drive.

'Is come here?'

'It's probably Yvonne,' Frank said, putting his glass down on the table and standing up. 'Stay here while I get rid of her.'

It wasn't Yvonne, it was Evan, in a battered old Land Rover Frank had never seen before.

'All right, Pops,' Evan said, jumping out of the driver's seat and blowing on his hands as he trudged across the snow. 'Kettle on?'

'What are you doing here?' Frank asked. 'Did your sister send you?'

'No.' Evan pulled a face, as if he didn't know what Frank was talking about. 'I haven't heard from her in weeks. I was passing and thought I'd pop round to see how you're doing.'

Frank didn't believe that for one minute, but he could hardly turn him away, so he stepped aside and waved for him to come inside.

Evan cast a quick glance around the hallway as he shrugged his coat off.

'Looking for something?' Frank asked, closing the door. 'Or should I say some*one*? That *is* why she sent you, isn't it? To make sure my guest has really gone?'

'Guest?' Evan repeated, maintaining the innocent act. 'I haven't got a clue what you're on about.'

57

Quickly stepping in front of the living room door when Evan walked toward it, Frank said, 'Go and put the kettle on. I'll be with you in a minute.'

Evan gave him a bemused look and headed into the kitchen, and Frank went into the living room.

'It's my son,' he told Irena quietly. 'I'm going to have a cup of tea with him, and then I'll get rid of him. Do you want to stay in here, or would you rather go upstai—'

'Any biscuits to go with this brew?' Evan asked, popping his head around the door.

Sure that he'd done it on purpose, Frank scowled at him. But Evan was too busy staring at Irena to notice.

'Well, hello,' he purred, edging past Frank and holding out his hand. 'I'm Evan. And you are . . . ?'

Conscious that his son had no idea of the life Irena had escaped and probably thought she would be flattered by his attentions, Frank shoved him back out into the hall, saying, 'She's not feeling too well, so let's leave her in peace, eh?'

'Wow, what a beauty,' Evan said when Frank pulled the door shut. 'Bit young for you, though, isn't she?'

'Don't be so disrespectful,' Frank scolded.

'Joke.' Evan held up his hands.

'Not funny,' Frank snapped, herding him into the kitchen. 'And now you've seen what you came to see, you can have your drink and go home.'

'Marie's at bingo, so I'm in no rush,' Evan said, flopping onto a chair. 'So who is she?' He jerked his head at the door. 'And what's with the bruises?'

'Her name's Irena, and she got separated from her mates on a night out and had a fall,' Frank said, merging the lies he'd already told Yvonne and Jo in case they compared notes. 'I found her out by the barn and brought her in to get warm – exactly as your mother would have done.'

'Chill out, Pops, I wasn't accusing you of anything.' Evan smirked. 'I know you'd never cheat on Mum. Although, technically, it wouldn't be cheating now she's gone, would it?'

'Nothing's going on, so get it out of your head,' Frank said gruffly as he finished making the teas his son had started.

'Never say never,' said Evan. 'You're still young enough to start again, and Mum would want you to be happy.'

Frank didn't reply to that. It was true that Maureen wanted him to find love again, because she'd told him so on numerous occasions during her last few weeks. But he wasn't ready to think that far ahead, so he changed the subject, asking: 'How's Marie getting on with her Christmas preparations?'

'Don't ask.' Evan rolled his eyes. 'She seems to think she's in competition with Mum, and she's been writing lists of all the ingredients she's going to need. I told her not to bother, 'cos she'll never compare to Mum, and she proper went off on one.'

'What did you expect?' Frank asked, handing a cup to him before taking a seat on the other side of the table. 'You should never compare your wife to your mother, and if you want a stress-free life you'd better go home and tell her you were joking.'

'Stress-free – with Marie?' Evan pulled a face. 'Are you kidding me?'

'You chose to marry her.'

'Yeah, well, I wish someone had talked me out of it.'

'What's that supposed to mean? Are you two having problems?'

'Nothing a quick visit to a divorce lawyer wouldn't fix,' Evan snorted.

'Surely it's not that bad?'

Evan looked at Frank and pursed his lips as if he wanted to confide something. Then, seeming to think better of it, he shrugged.

'Nah, we're all right. I'm just fed up of her ramming all this Christmas stuff down my throat. If I had my way I'd cancel it, 'cos it won't be the same without Mum.'

'You're not wrong there,' Frank agreed, gazing over at the Aga and picturing Maureen standing there in her pinny with a paper crown on her head – her Christmas uniform, as she'd called it.

A tap at the door brought him out of his reverie, and he gave Irena a questioning look when she looked in.

'Are you all right, love?'

'I am tire, so I think I will go to bed,' she said. 'Is OK if I take shower first?'

'Of course.' He stood up. 'Let me get you a fresh towel.'

Evan gazed up at Irena when his father headed into the utility room and tipped his head to one side.

'Nice accent. Where are you from?'

'Prague,' she replied shyly.

'Cool place,' he said. 'I went over there with some mates for a stag weekend a few years back. Can't remember the name of the town where we stayed, but the locals were really friendly.'

'Some are nice, some not so.'

'And what brought you here? Only, I can't imagine it was our crappy weather that attracted you.'

'I came look for work,' Irena said, smiling at Frank when he came back with a towel. Nodding at Evan, she said, 'Goodnight, Even. It is nice to meet you.'

'It's Evan, and the pleasure's all mine,' he drawled, leaning back in his chair to watch as she walked out into the hall and up the stairs. Whistling softly through his teeth when she'd gone, he turned back to Frank.

'Christ, that accent's sexy. She doesn't sound much like the birds I met when I went over there, though.'

'Probably from a different region,' said Frank. 'Anyway, it's snowing again, so you'd best drink up and get going.'

'I might stay over,' Evan said, taking a swig of tea.

'No, you won't,' Frank countered firmly.

'Oh, aye?' Evan grinned. 'Cramping your style, am I?'

'No, I just don't want you getting stuck out here if the weather gets any worse.'

'I've got the works' fourby for the week, and it can handle a bit of snow.'

'You're not staying, and that's the end of it.'

Evan's smirk told Frank that his son suspected he had an ulterior motive for wanting him gone. He was right, but not for the reasons he clearly thought. Frank had never particularly taken to his daughter-in-law, but Evan had married her, and if they were having troubles, he needed to tackle them head-on instead of running away. And staying here, in the company of a woman he was obviously attracted to, would not help him to do that.

Relieved when Evan drank his tea without further argument, Frank saw him out and then locked and bolted the door before going into the living room to damp the fire and collect the glasses he and Irena had used. She'd finished her wine, but his glass was still half-full, so he quickly drained it before carrying them both into the kitchen.

Heading upstairs after washing up and switching the lights off, he reached the landing as Irena was coming out of the bathroom. She had the towel wrapped around her body, and her wet hair was dripping onto her bare shoulders.

'Thank you for let me shower,' she said, gazing shyly up at him from beneath her lashes. 'It feel nice to be clean.'

'You're welcome,' he said, edging past her when he picked up the scent of the mango shampoo Maureen had used. 'Night.'

'Night,' she replied, watching as he headed into his room and closed the door.

7

Up and outside early the next morning, Frank knew he was going to struggle to get the car out when he saw how deep the snow was. Even out here in the wilds, where the weather conditions were always much harsher than in the city, it was unusual for it to snow before December – and even more unusual for it to stick. But he'd promised Irena he would drive her to the station, so he took a spade out of the shed and set about trying to clear a path.

After digging for twenty minutes to no avail, he paused to wipe the sweat off his brow and noticed Irena standing at the living room window. Nodding when she held up a steaming cup, he stamped the ice off his boots and went inside.

'It's rock solid,' he told her when she came out into the hall. 'But I'll take another crack at it in a bit, when I've got the feeling back in my hands and feet.'

'Take off coat and go sit by fire,' she ordered, holding on to the cup when he reached for it. 'I do not want for you to get sick.'

Reminded of the lie he'd told Yvonne when she'd called round the previous morning, Frank frowned as he shrugged his coat off and hung it up. He was still annoyed with her for reporting him to Jo, but at least he wouldn't have to see her today, because there was no way she'd risk driving, or try to walk over in this weather.

Shivering when he went into the living room and the heat from the fire seeped into his bones, he sank down on his chair and held out his hands to thaw them. Smiling when Irena placed the cup on the table beside him, he said, 'Thanks, love.'

'You have nice smile,' she said, taking a seat on the sofa. 'It shows in your eyes, which means you have good heart.'

'Ah, that reminds me . . .' Frank said, pushing himself back up to his feet and walking round to his desk.

'What is this?' Irena asked, watching as he took a foil strip of tablets out of the drawer and popped one into his mouth.

'I had a heart attack a couple of years ago,' he explained after washing it down with a swig of tea. 'And I have to remember to take one every morning to keep my blood pressure in check.'

'Ah . . . this is like my brother. His is for head, not heart, but he need medication every day to stop him be sick.'

'You worry about him, don't you?' Frank said, catching the wistful look in her eyes.

'Always.' She sighed. 'But I will send for him when I have reach London and find job.'

'Why don't you call him?' Frank suggested. 'He's probably been wondering why he hasn't heard from you.'

'He does not have phone, and I cannot call house in case Father answer,' Irena said. 'But he can see email when he use computer at library.'

'Send him a message then,' Frank said, leaning down to turn his computer on. 'It's not very fast, because the signal's pretty weak out here, but it gets there in the end.'

'Thank you,' Irena said gratefully, coming over and taking a seat in front of the screen.

'You're welcome,' Frank said, patting her on the shoulder. 'I've got a few things I need to do, so I'll leave you to it.'

Irena nodded without turning her head, and Frank left the room, pulling the door shut to give her privacy. He hadn't thought to ask how long she had been in the country, so it could have been a long time since she'd had any contact with her brother. He only hoped the lad replied quickly, because that would make Irena feel a lot better, he was sure.

Smiling when he heard the clackity-clack of her fingernails hitting the keyboard, Frank went into the kitchen and took a roll of bin-bags out of the cupboard before heading upstairs. After going through Maureen's clothes the previous morning to find something for Irena to wear, he decided he might as well finish the job and get the rest packed up.

It took a couple of hours to clear Maureen's wardrobe and drawers, and Frank had filled five bin-bags by the time he was done. He'd selected a few skirts, blouses, and dresses that Maureen had kept from her slimmer days, and he carried those downstairs to see if Irena wanted them. She'd finished with the computer by then, and he found her in the kitchen. There was flour all over the worktop, vegetable peelings in the sink, and a lovely aroma coming from the Aga.

'That smells nice,' he said, placing his bundle on the table.

'I hope you do not mind?' Irena turned to face him and wiped her hands on Maureen's apron. 'I want to prepare nice dinner for you, so I take chicken from freezer and make Czech dish. Is my mother's special recipe.'

'I look forward to it,' Frank said, hoping it tasted as good as it smelled. 'Did you manage to send your message?'

'Yes, and now I must wait to see if he reply before I leave.'

'I don't think that'll be a problem,' Frank said, nodding at the window when he noticed it was snowing again. 'I know you're keen to get going, but if this doesn't let up you could be stuck here for another day or two.'

'You would not mind?'

'Of course not.'

'Thank you.' Irena smiled. 'Now go and sit in warm while I finish make food.'

Amused that she was doing the same thing Maureen had always done – kicking him out of the kitchen when she was cooking – Frank said, 'OK, I'll get out of your way. I just wanted to see if you'd like any of these?' He gestured toward the clothes on the table. 'But don't feel obliged to take them if you don't like them.'

Irena reached for the baby-blue cardigan that was sitting on top of the pile and held it up against herself before putting it back down.

'Is very beautiful, but is too expensive for someone like me.'

'Don't be daft,' Frank argued, saddened to think that her self-esteem was so low she didn't consider herself deserving of nice things. 'I want you to have it – and Maureen would, too. It's only going to go to the charity shop if you don't take it, and someone'll end up getting it for a couple of quid, so it's not that expensive if you look at it like that.'

'I do like very much,' Irena said, touching the soft material again.

'Then it's yours,' Frank said, pleased that she liked it because it had been one of Maureen's favourites. 'There's another five bags upstairs if you want to have a root through them, as well. But they're all bigger, so they might not fit you.'

'These are enough,' Irena said. 'Now go,' she shooed him toward the door. 'I need finish cook.'

The meal was every bit as delicious as it smelled, and Frank guiltily admitted – to himself, but not to Irena – that it was as good, if not better, than anything Maureen had ever made for him. When they'd finished eating, Frank washed the dishes and Irena dried them, and then they moved into the living room and settled in front of the TV; Frank drinking his whisky, while Irena finished the bottle of wine he'd opened for her the previous night.

A storm had rolled steadily in during the evening, and by

midnight, when they decided to head up to bed, gale-force winds were battering the farmhouse from all sides. After two decades of living through these extreme weather snaps, Frank had no trouble falling asleep with the wind howling down the chimney and the windows rattling violently in their frames. Tonight was no exception, and he dropped off as soon as his head hit the pillow, only to be woken a short time later by the sound of crying coming through the wall. Guessing that Irena must have been spooked by the storm, he got up and pulled his dressing gown on before padding down the landing and tapping on her door.

'Are you OK, love?' he asked through the wood.

'No,' she whimpered.

He eased the door open and peeped in. With the light from the landing behind him, he could see Irena sitting upright in the bed, her knees pulled up to her chest, her face streaked with tears.

'I am sorry for wake you,' she apologized, swiping at her cheeks with the back of her hand. 'But I am so scared.'

'Bad dream?' he asked.

'It was not dream,' she insisted. 'I hear noise outside, and I think Nikolai has find me.'

Frank went over to the window and peered out into the blizzard. There were no footprints or animal tracks in the snow on the ground, so he closed the curtains and turned back to Irena.

'There's no one out there, love,' he assured her. 'And no cars have come past, because I'd have heard them, so try to relax and get some sleep, eh?'

'Will – will you stay with me?' Irena asked, her voice so quiet Frank thought he'd misheard her.

'Sorry?' He tipped his head to one side.

'I see monster every time I close my eyes,' she sniffled. 'But I will feel safe if you are with me. *Please*, Frankie.'

Frank stuffed his hands into his dressing gown pockets. He dreaded to think what people would make of this if they ever found out, but he had a feeling that *neither* of them would get back to sleep if he left her alone with her demons.

'OK,' he said. 'If it'll help, I'll stay with you until you fall asleep.'

'Thank you,' she said gratefully, shuffling over to the other side of the bed. 'It will help very much.'

Relieved to see that she was wearing the old nightgown of Maureen's he'd given her, Frank climbed onto the bed and sat stiffly back against the headboard, his legs stretched out before him.

Beside him, Irena sighed and closed her eyes, murmuring, 'Goodnight, Frankie.'

'Night,' he said, stifling a yawn.

8

'Are you awake?' Maureen's soft voice worked its way into Frank's dream.

'No,' he replied sleepily, his eyes still closed. 'S'up?'

'I can't sleep,' she said, her warm breath caressing his cheek.

'Sshhh . . .' He rolled over and placed his arm over her.

She wriggled closer and slid her hand up under his pyjama top, and Frank groaned when she raked her fingernails through the hairs on his chest before slowly trailing them down over his stomach.

'Make love to me, Frankie,' she whispered, sliding her hand inside his pyjama bottoms.

His eyes snapped open, and he jerked away from her in horror.

'Oh my God, I'm so sorry,' he spluttered. 'I was dreaming, and I thought – I thought you were Maureen.'

'Please don't stop,' Irena begged, sitting up and taking his face in her hands. 'I want you, and you want me, too – I know you do.'

BRUTAL

'I can't do this,' he croaked, leaping out of bed. 'I'm so sorry,' he apologized again, glancing back at her as he stumbled to the door and yanked it open. 'Please forgive me.'

9

Frank was too embarrassed to meet Irena's eye when she came downstairs the next morning. She had suffered nothing but abuse since arriving in this country, and now, albeit unwittingly, he had almost abused her, too.

'You are angry with me?' she asked, perching on the edge of the sofa.

'No, of course not,' he said, reaching for the poker and jabbing at the coals in the fire.

'Then why you cannot look at me?'

'Because I'm ashamed.'

'Why? You must know I have feeling for you.'

'No you don't. You're only being kind because you know how bad I feel.'

'You are wrong,' Irena insisted, sitting forward and clasping her hands together between her knees. 'You are nicest man I have ever meet, and I like you very much. But I know you are still sad for wife, so I should not have ask you to stay in bed with me.'

'This is my doing, not yours,' Frank countered. 'You were scared, and I was supposed to be making you feel safe. I just don't understand how . . . *that* happened.'

'I welcomed your touch,' Irena said. 'But I know you do not feel the same, so I will go.'

'You can't go yet,' Frank said, placing the poker back into its holder. 'I was watching the local news earlier, and they said all the trains and buses have been stopped.'

'Then I will stay in daughter's room so you do not have to see me.'

Frank felt guilty all over again when she stood up. She'd gone through hell to escape from a house where she'd been forcibly confined to a bedroom, and now, because of his inability to control his semi-conscious body, she was going to voluntarily confine herself to Jo's. It wasn't fair, and he couldn't allow it.

'You don't have to do that,' he said, forcing himself to look at her. 'Please, love . . . this is my fault, and I don't want you to feel awkward around me.'

'You are sure?' Irena hesitated.

'Positive,' he said, getting up. 'Sit down. I'll make us a cup of tea.'

'I will stay,' Irena agreed, holding his gaze. 'But only if you promise to stop feel bad about last night. I want it to happen, and I thought you did, too. I was wrong, and I am sorry.'

'Please stop apologizing.' Frank sighed. 'Let's just forget about it and start again, eh?'

'OK.' Irena smiled. 'I would like this.'

In the kitchen a few minutes later, Frank had boiled the kettle and was pouring water into the cups when he heard his mobile phone ringing faintly. Tracing it to the pocket of his coat in the hall, he pulled it out and saw that it was Jo – and he'd already missed three calls from her.

'About time!' she said when he answered. 'I've been trying to reach you for hours. Why haven't you been answering your phone?'

'Sorry, I didn't hear it. You should have tried the landline instead.'

'I did, but I got the dead tone. What's going on?'

Wandering back into the kitchen, Frank glanced at the house-phone on the worktop and tutted softly when he saw that its screen was blank.

'The storm must have knocked the line out,' he said, wedging the mobile under his chin so he could add sugar to the cups.

'Evan said it was a bad one. Has it done any other damage?'

'I don't know yet. I'm going to take a look around when I've had my brew.'

'You couldn't pop over to Yvonne's while you're at it, could you?' Jo asked. 'I tried ringing her when I couldn't get hold of you, but she's not answering, either.'

In no mood to see his nosy neighbour, Frank said, 'Her phone will have been affected, as well. We're on the same line, don't forget.'

'And her mobile?' said Jo. Then, her clipped tone telling him that it wasn't so much a request as an order, she said, 'Just do it, Dad. She was kind enough to check on *you* after Mum passed away, and being a good neighbour is a two-way street, you know?'

'Fine, I'll go over there,' Frank conceded.

'Make sure you do,' Jo said. 'And let me know how she is.'

'Will do.'

'Right, well, I've got to go. I'm supposed to be helping Emily with a school project.'

'How's she getting on?' Frank asked.

'She loves it,' said Jo.

'Ah, that's good. Give her my love, and say hi to Sam.'

Immediately that call was finished, Frank's phone started ringing again, and this time it was Evan.

'Morning, Pops. How did you get on with the storm?'

'I'm going to check when I've had a brew. How about you?'

'A couple of slates came down, but nothing major. Has Jo managed to get hold of you yet? She rang me in a flap, reckons she's been trying to call you all morning.'

'I was talking to her before you rang,' Frank said, stirring milk into the drinks. 'I take it you didn't tell her about Irena still being here?'

'Course I didn't,' said Evan. 'But, while we're on the subject, is she still with you? Only I was thinking I wouldn't mind going back to Prague one day, and I wanted to ask if she could recommend any good hotels.'

'Too late, she's gone,' Frank lied, seeing straight through the excuse. 'Her friend picked her up this morning.'

'Oh, that's a shame.' Evan sounded disappointed. 'I don't suppose she gave you her number before she went?'

'No, she didn't,' said Frank. 'And if that's all you're ringing for, I need to get off. Yvonne's not answering her phone and Jo's worried about her, so I said I'd go and check on her.'

'You'd better hope she's not dead,' Evan snorted. 'Can you imagine having to sit with her corpse while you wait for the roads to clear up enough for someone to come and get her?'

'I'd rather not imagine it, if you don't mind,' Frank said, eager to get off the phone when he heard Irena coming out of the living room. 'I'll speak to you later. Bye.'

Turning when Irena came in, he handed one of the cups to her.

'Thank you.' She smiled and took a seat at the table. Then, giving him a curious look when he sat down and reached for his boots, she asked, 'Are you go out?'

'Yeah, I promised my daughter I'd go round and check on Yvonne,' he said. 'And then I need to do a walkabout to see if the storm caused any damage, so you'll have the house to your-self for a while.'

'Is OK if I look on computer to see if my brother has answer email?'

'Help yourself,' Frank said, taking a couple of swigs of tea. 'See you in a bit.'

Evan hadn't long finished talking to his dad when his wife walked into the room, and he narrowed his eyes when she huffed her way past him and slumped heavily down on the already flattened cushion of her armchair. She'd never been a raving beauty, but at least she'd always looked presentable in the past. Now, she spent the majority of her time slopping around in baggy T-shirts and over-stretched leggings, and it pissed him off that she'd stopped making an effort for him. He'd defended her when Jo had slagged her off, but some of his sister's comments had hit a nerve. Marie complained that her legs swelled up if she had to stand for too long, but she was quite capable of sitting at a desk or working a till. She just didn't want to, because she'd got used to doing nothing. And that was a waste, because she wasn't stupid by any means. But she'd already given up on herself, and he couldn't be arsed arguing about it any more.

'What's up with you?' Marie demanded when she noticed him staring at her.

'Nothing,' he muttered, tearing his gaze away. They'd been bickering about her Christmas plans for the last few days, and that was another thing he couldn't be arsed with any more. Her food and gift lists were growing by the day, and he dreaded to think how much it was going to end up costing him. This would be the first time in six years that they had hosted it, or spent the day with her family instead of his, and he wasn't looking forward to it at all.

'Who was that on the phone?' Marie asked, patting her thigh.

'My dad,' Evan said, grimacing when the dog leapt onto her lap and licked her mouth. 'D'you have to do that?'

'He's my baby,' she replied. 'And he likes kissing his mummy – don't you, Bubby Boo Boo?' She addressed the dog affectionately. Then, voice back to normal, she said, 'Who's the woman you were asking about?'

'His neighbour, Yvonne.'

'What's she got to do with Prague?'

'For fuck's sake,' Evan snapped, irritated to think that she'd been eavesdropping. 'Were you out there with a glass pressed against the door, or what?'

'No, you've just got a big gob,' Marie replied curtly. 'So what was it about?'

'If you must know, we were talking about Prague last time I saw her,' Evan lied. 'And I was thinking of taking *you* there for a holiday, so I wanted to know if she could recommend a good hotel.'

'Why would I want to go to a filthy place like that?' Marie pulled a face.

'You're talking through your arse, it's gorgeous over there,' Evan said, snatching his phone up off the table. 'And if you want to talk about filthy, take a look at this place, 'cos I can't remember the last time you dusted or ran the Hoover round.'

'I'm not the only one who lives here,' Marie reminded him. 'And you had two hands last time I checked, so do it yourself if it's bothering you.'

'I work twelve hours a day.'

'Yeah, and so did I before I got ill. And you've got the week off, so quit bellyaching and get on with it.'

Evan opened his mouth to argue that the mess was all hers, because she never put anything away after she'd used it, but he couldn't be bothered.

'Where are you going?' Marie asked when he stood up.

'I told Billy Hicks I'd give him a lift to hospital to see his missus.'

'*Again?* That's three times in the last two weeks, and I bet you haven't asked him to help out with petrol, have you? You must think we're made of money.'

'Says her who thinks nothing of blowing thirty quid on bingo twice a week.'

'That comes out of my disability allowance, so it's got nothing to do with you.'

'And petrol comes out of my wages, so ditto.'

'You'd best be back before twelve,' Marie called after him when he walked out into the hall. 'You're taking me shopping, don't forget.'

'Drive yourself,' Evan called back. 'Or, better still, try walking and shift some of that fat off your arse!'

He stalked out at that, and jumped into the Land Rover he'd borrowed from work while his own car was in the garage.

Marie came out onto the step as he fired the engine, and yelled, 'You'd best come back to help me with the shopping, or don't bother coming back at all! I'm not joking, Evan . . . I'm doing this for your dad as well as my—'

Evan turned the radio up full-blast to tune her out, and reversed out of the driveway. Glancing in the rear-view mirror before turning the corner, he released a heavy sigh when he saw Marie, shoulders slumped, making her way back into the house. He shouldn't have chucked her weight in her face like that, and he'd had no right to get angry with her when he was the one who'd lied. She had her faults, but so did he, and he'd put things right when he got home. Hell, he'd even clean the house after they'd been shopping if it meant that much to her. But, right now, he needed a drink and some time alone to cool his hot head down.

10

Yvonne's cottage was half a mile from the farm, and Frank would ordinarily have walked it in ten minutes flat. But, today, with the snow and ice turning the lane into a skating rink, it took him twice as long, and his thighs were aching by the time he got there.

Yvonne's rusted old Fiat was parked on the drive, so he figured she must be home. But after knocking several times and getting no answer, he began to wonder if Jo might have been right to be concerned about her.

He made his way down the side of the cottage to try the back door, and was alarmed to find it standing ajar, its lock shattered, the wood splintered. Cautiously stepping inside, aware that the intruder might still be in there, he called Yvonne's name as he scanned the gloomy kitchen.

A faint groan came from the other side of the table, and his heart lurched when he saw Yvonne lying on the floor. He rushed over and squatted down beside her.

'Yvonne, it's Frank . . . are you OK?'

Her eyes fluttered open and she squinted at him for a few seconds before recognition set in.

'Oh, thank God it's you,' she croaked, her voice as dry as sandpaper. 'I thought I was never going to be found.'

'What happened?' he asked, shoving several mewling cats out of the way when they ran in from the other room and started trampling over her to get to him.

'I'm not sure,' she said. 'I came to get a drink, and next thing I knew, I was lying here with a sore head.'

Frank dipped down to take a look, and winced when he saw dried blood on her hair and the tiles beneath.

'Who did this to you?' he asked, sliding his phone out of his pocket. 'Did you see their faces?'

'I'll have tripped over something,' she said. 'My daft old legs aren't as strong as they used to be, so it wouldn't be the first time.'

Frank suspected she had disturbed a burglar and been whacked before they'd made their escape. But she obviously hadn't seen them, and he didn't want to frighten her, so he decided not to tell her about the door.

'How long have you been lying here?' he asked instead.

'I don't know?' she said, her brow creasing deeply as she tried to remember. 'It was the night I came to your place, I think.'

'Christ, that was a couple of days ago,' Frank said, thinking she was lucky she hadn't frozen to death. 'Are you hurt anywhere else?'

'My back doesn't feel too good,' she said, closing her eyes and swallowing loudly. 'And I can't really feel my leg.'

Shocked by how old and frail she looked without the garish make-up she'd been wearing the last few times he'd seen her, Frank said, 'OK, let me find something to cover you with while I call an ambulance.'

'There's a blanket on the sofa,' she told him.

Nodding, he got up and dialled 999 as he walked through to the living room.

'Ambulance, please,' he said, tugging a cat-hair-matted crocheted blanket off the sofa. 'And I think we might need the police as well,' he added quietly. 'I came round to check on my neighbour, and it looks like someone's broken in and attacked her. I found her on the floor with a nasty cut on the back of her head, and she says her back's hurting and she can't feel her leg . . . Yes, it's Yvonne Caldwell, and she lives at Rose Cottage on Marsh House Lane . . . In her sixties, I think. Give me a sec while I ask her.'

'Seventy-six,' Yvonne told him when he went back to the kitchen.

Surprised, because he hadn't realized she was that old, Frank relayed it to the operator and thanked her when she told him that help would be with them soon.

'She reckons they'll have trouble getting an ambulance up here in this weather, so they might have to send a helicopter,' he told Yvonne.

'Oh, what a lot of fuss for nothing,' she said guiltily. 'You should have told them to leave it till it clears up.'

'Don't be daft, you need looking after,' he said, laying the blanket over her. 'That better?'

'Mmmm.' She gave a weak nod and licked her cracked lips. 'Don't suppose you could get me some water, could you?'

'Course I can.'

Frank turned to the sink and froze in horror. He hadn't noticed the state of the place when he first came in, because his focus had been on Yvonne, but now he could see that the sink was piled high with dirty crockery, and the worktops were covered in dozens and dozens of cat-food tins – most of which still contained mouldy chunks of meat. Yet more rotten food festered in the numerous saucers and bowls that were scattered around the floor and ledges, and the contents of two over-flowing litter trays were undoubtedly contributing to the stench he had suddenly become aware of.

'Sorry about the mess,' Yvonne said sheepishly.

'It's fine, love,' Frank said, snapping himself out of it. 'I was looking for a cup.'

'Second cupboard,' she said.

Shuddering when he opened the cupboard and saw a family of cockroaches run for cover, Frank grabbed a cup and quickly closed the door. He had to lift a stack of plates out of the sink to get at the tap so he could rinse the cup before filling it and carrying it over to Yvonne.

She craned her neck forward when he held it to her lips, and took a big gulp.

'Thanks, pet. I was gasping.'

'No problem. Let me know if you want any more.'

She nodded and closed her eyes, and Frank sat on a chair

and watched her as she drifted in and out of sleep for the next forty minutes.

Relieved when, at last, he heard the distinctive sound of an approaching helicopter, he went outside. It was hovering low over the cottage, and he shielded his eyes to protect them from the ice and debris its blades were whipping up. Yvonne's garden was a good half acre in size, but her late husband's tractor and other rusted pieces of farming equipment were still standing where he'd left them, so the pilot was forced to land in the field beyond.

As the thunderous roar died down, Frank heard squeals coming from the far side of the garden. It was so long since he'd been here he'd forgotten that Yvonne kept pigs, and he wondered how she'd been managing to look after them when she was clearly struggling to take care of herself. Them, *and* the damn cats, which might well have started eating her if she'd been lying there for much longer.

Grimacing at the thought, Frank waved to the paramedics when they hopped out of the helicopter and climbed over the low fence.

'Mind where you put your feet on this side, lads,' he warned as they trudged across the snow. 'There could be anything buried under this lot.'

Evan had driven straight to the pub where he always had lunch when he was working. He had the week off, but he was hoping one of his workmates might come in and give him a bit of banter to cheer him up.

He was sitting at a table in the corner, enjoying his second pint, when the door opened and a cloud of perfume wafted in. Looking up, he recognized the woman who walked in as one of the receptionists from the car showroom next door to the plant-hire company where he worked. He nodded hello when she glanced his way, and then watched as she walked toward the bar. Her name was Lesley, or maybe Lisa, and they'd passed the time of day a few times over break-time fags. She was a big girl, but unlike Marie who tried – and failed – to disguise her size with baggy clothes, this girl accentuated her curves with tight-fitting clothes and high heels. Evan didn't fancy her, because he preferred slim girls – like the one who'd been staying at his dad's place; but he admired her for embracing her size.

Losing sight of her when a group of builders walked in and obstructed his view, Evan took a swig of his pint and pulled his phone out of his pocket when it pinged. It was a message from Marie asking where he was. The beer had mellowed him to the point that he knew he'd been too hard on her, but he wasn't in the mood for shopping yet, so he put his phone away without replying.

'Mind if I join you?'

Looking up at the sound of the voice, Evan saw the receptionist standing over him, a glass of wine in her hand.

'Yeah, sure,' he said, waving for her to take a seat.

'Thanks,' she said, sitting down and dropping her handbag onto the floor. 'How come you're not at work?'

'Week off,' he said, taking another swig of beer. 'What about you?'

'Same,' she said, casting a glance around the crowded room as she sipped her wine.

'Waiting for someone?' Evan asked, trying not to stare at her enormous breasts. She was usually wearing a coat whenever he was this close to her, so he'd never really noticed them before, and he couldn't help wonder how she'd managed to find a bra big enough to hold them.

'I'm supposed to be on a date,' she told him, looking at her watch. 'I'm half an hour late, so I've either missed him, or he's stood me up.'

'His loss if he has,' Evan said, raising his glass to his lips.

'Too right it is,' she agreed. 'I've seen his last girlfriend, and I'm a definite upgrade.'

'I don't doubt that.' Evan grinned.

'Ah, well, at least I've got you to keep me company, so I don't have to sit here on my own like Milly No Date,' she said. Then, putting her elbow on the table, she rested her chin on her fist and peered at him. 'Haven't you got lovely eyes?'

'You reckon?'

'Yeah, they've got a proper cheeky twinkle.'

'That'll be the beer,' Evan snorted.

'Had a few, have you?' She smiled.

Evan felt her knee press against his and drew his head back. 'Are you flirting with me, Lesley?'

'It's Laura, and what if I am?' She held his gaze. 'Not scared, are you?'

Amused, Evan said, 'Should I be?'

'Nah, I'm a pussy cat,' she said, giving a teasing smile.

Eyebrows shooting up when he felt her hand on his thigh, Evan said, 'Aren't you worried your date might walk in? If he got held up in the traffic, he could be here any minu—'

'What the *fuck* is going on?'

Jumping at the sound of Marie's voice, Evan snapped his head round.

'All right, love.' He smiled guiltily. 'I didn't see you coming in.'

'Oh, I bet you didn't,' she hissed. 'You were too busy drooling over this slapper.'

'Oi, who you calling a slapper?' Laura protested.

'The tart who's trying it on with my husband, *that's* who!' Marie spat, turning the glare onto her. 'Buy you this, did he?' She snatched up Laura's glass. 'Well, have it, then!' She tossed the contents into her face.

'Hey, come on, pack it in,' Evan said, jumping to his feet when Laura reared up out of her seat and grabbed Marie by the hair.

'Get your fuckin' hands off me,' Marie yelped, trying to claw Laura's face with her nails. 'And you can keep 'em off my husband, an' all, you trashy little slag!'

'What's going on?' the landlord bellowed, appearing behind the bar.

'Nothing, mate, I'm sorting it,' Evan said, pulling the women apart and shoving Marie toward the door.

'Get off me,' she snarled.

'Pack it in and get outside,' he ordered. 'There's nothing going on. She's only a mate.'

'If I wanted him, I'd have had him by now,' Laura called after them loudly.

Enraged, Marie turned on her heel and used her weight to barge past Evan. Two girls who'd been watching the fight from a nearby table almost fell off their seats in their haste to move out of the way when she snatched Evan's pint glass up off the table and lunged at Laura.

Throwing his arms around her to prevent her from smashing it over Laura's head, Evan manhandled her out of the door, saying, 'Calm down before you give yourself an asthma attack, you daft cow.'

'Let go, you cheating bastard!' she snarled, her chest heaving.

'I'm not cheating,' he insisted. 'I told you, she's just a mate.'

'So why did she say she could have you if she wanted you?'

'She was winding you up.'

'I don't believe you,' Marie said angrily. 'And how do you know her, anyway?'

'She works near me,' Evan told her truthfully. 'She'd not long come in when you got here, and *she* bought that drink you chucked over her, not me.'

'Why were you sitting together?'

'Because she's waiting for her date and didn't want to sit on her own. What was I supposed to do? Tell her to piss off?'

'*Yes!*'

'God, you're so paranoid, it's not even funny any more,' Evan snapped, losing patience.

'If I'm paranoid, maybe it's because you keep lying to me,' Marie spat. 'Remember Billy, do you? The mate you were supposed to be taking to hospital to visit his wife today? The one I rang soon as you left, who told me he hasn't seen you in *weeks*? So where *have* you been going? And it'd better not have been with that *tart* in there!'

Laura came out of the pub before Evan could respond. She paused and looked Marie up and down, then shook her head, a sly smile playing on her painted lips.

'What are you looking at, you fat slag?' Marie roared, struggling to break free again.

'*You're* calling *me* fat?' Laura snorted. 'Have you looked in the mirror lately, sweetheart?'

'I look a damn sight better than *you*!' Marie retorted furiously.

Laura laughed at this, and Evan, fearing that he wouldn't be able to restrain Marie for much longer, said, 'Just go, will you? You're making it worse.'

'Oh, don't worry, I'm going,' she said. 'But now I understand why you're always eyeing me up, if *that's* what you're married to.'

She raised her chin at that and marched over to her car, and Evan held on to Marie until she'd driven out of the car park.

'Don't think this is the end of it,' Marie said, straightening her clothes when he let go of her. 'And don't bother coming back to the house, or I'll have you arrested.'

'For what?' Evan asked incredulously. 'I haven't done anything.'

'You're a *liar*,' Marie hissed, shoving past him and waddling over to her car.

Watching as she climbed behind the wheel and reversed out of the space, Evan threw his hands up in a gesture of defeat. He could probably get to the house before her if he put his foot down, but what was the point? She thought she'd caught him out, and he really didn't fancy spending the night in a cell if she kicked off and called the police to have him removed from the house.

11

Irena was sitting at the kitchen table nursing a cup of tea when Frank let himself into the house, and he saw the fear in her eyes as she jumped to her feet.

'What happen? I see helicopter, and I am scared you are hurt.'

'It was for Yvonne,' he said, slipping his coat off and hanging it up before joining her in the kitchen. 'Her back door was open when I got there, and it looks like someone broke in and attacked her.'

'Oh, no!' Irena covered her mouth with her hand. 'I hope she is not hurt badly?'

'She's got a nasty cut on her head, and they think she might have broken her hip, but they'll know more when they get her to hospital. I've been talking to the police – that's why I was so long.'

'The police?' Irena's eyes widened. 'You did not tell them about me?'

'No, of course not. They were asking if I'd heard anything suspicious, or seen any strangers hanging around – stuff like that.'

'Will they come here?'

'Maybe.' Frank shrugged and flopped down on a chair. 'They'll talk to everyone from roundabout, but I'm the closest and I didn't hear anything, so I don't hold out much hope of them catching whoever did it. And Yvonne doesn't remember anything, so she'll be no help, either.'

'She did not see who did it?' Irena asked, taking a cup off the draining board to make him a drink.

'Nope.' He shook his head. 'She remembers going into the kitchen to get a drink, then waking up on the floor. She'd been there for a couple of days, and she was frozen stiff when I found her. I'm surprised she survived, to be honest.'

'She is very old?'

'A lot older than I thought,' said Frank. 'And she's been struggling for a while, judging by the state of her place.'

'Is bad?'

'Terrible. And it's swarming with mangy cats, and starving pigs.'

'Ah, she have pigs . . .' Irena said. 'This is what I can smell.'

'Sorry,' Frank apologized. 'They're pretty clean creatures, by and large, but I don't think they've been mucked out in a while.'

'Is very strong.' Irena wrinkled her nose.

'I'll take a bath and get changed,' Frank said. 'I'll ring Jo first; let her know what's happened. She tried to call me when I was talking to the police, but I had to ignore it.'

'Ah . . . I mean to tell you,' Irena turned round and gave him a sheepish look. 'Phone ring while you are out.'

93

'Really?' Frank raised an eyebrow. 'It wasn't working this morning, so they must have fixed the line. That was fast.'

'It was after I hear helicopter, and I think might be you, so I answer,' Irena went on. 'But is your daughter, and she is angry when she hear my voice. She ask why I am still here, and I do not know what to tell her, so I say you will call when you are home. I am sorry if I have cause problem.'

'You haven't,' Frank said, scraping his chair back. 'She was questioning me about you being here the last time we spoke, and I didn't want to tell her what was going on so I said you'd left. Don't worry, she'll understand when I explain it to her.'

'I hope so,' said Irena.

Me too, Frank thought as he made his way upstairs and started the bath running before going into his bedroom to make the call.

Jo answered on the second ring and launched straight into him, demanding to know why Irena was still at the house when he'd told her she had left.

'And what do you even know about her?' she went on before he'd had the chance to answer her first question. 'She could be a con woman, for all you know. I hope you haven't left any money lying around, because she's probably already got her eye on that. And if she so much as *touches* anything of my mum's, I swear I'll—'

'If you've quite finished,' Frank cut in. 'I'm not an idiot.'

'Well, you're doing a bloody good impression of one. And how do you think Mum would feel about you inviting a strange woman into her house and letting her walk around as if she owns the damn place?'

'Your mother is dead,' Frank reminded her bluntly. 'But if she *was* still here, she'd be doing exactly what I'm doing, because she would never turn her back on someone in need.'

'Oh, I see,' Jo replied sarcastically. 'This woman's fed you a sob story, and you've fallen for it. Come on, then . . . what's she after? Has she lost her passport and needs money to get back to wherever she came from? Or is one of her relatives desperately ill, and she needs to pay for their treatment?'

'She hasn't asked for a penny, as it happens,' Frank said truthfully. 'But if I decide to help her out, it'll be my choice – just like it's my choice who stays at *my* house.'

'Then why lie about it?'

'I've got my reasons, and I expect you to respect that.'

'Well, I'm sorry, but I can't. It's obvious you're hiding something, and if I find out you've betrayed my mother, I will never speak to you again!'

Irritated when she disconnected as soon as she'd had her say, Frank tried to call her back. It went to voicemail, but before he could try again, a tap came at the door.

'*Yes?*' he barked.

'You forget tea,' Irena said, eyeing him nervously when she came into the room.

'Thanks,' Frank muttered, tossing the phone onto the bed. 'And sorry for snapping.'

'It did not go well with daughter?'

'Not really, no.'

'She does not like me be here, but I understand this. She is worry about you.'

'More like she's annoyed because she can't jump in her car and come over here to boss me about,' said Frank. Then, tutting softly, he shook his head. 'Sorry, love. I shouldn't be involving you in this. It's between me and Jo.'

'But is *because* of me, so I am already involve,' said Irena. 'Maybe I can speak with her and tell her I am leave soon.'

'Believe me, it wouldn't make any difference,' Frank said wearily. 'She's as stubborn as a mule when she gets something into that daft head of hers. But there's nothing I can do about it while she's ignoring my calls, so I'm just going to have to wait for her to contact me again.'

'I hope is soon,' Irena said, reaching out and touching his shoulder. 'I do not like to see you upset.'

Frank had a flashback of her lying naked beneath him the previous night, and he backed away from her when he felt his cheeks start to burn. His and Maureen's sex life had pretty much gone on hold after his heart attack, but it had completely died out after her cancer diagnosis. And he'd been absolutely fine with that, so he didn't understand why his sleeping body had responded so strongly to Irena's touch – or why his stomach was fluttering now.

'Drink your tea before it get cold,' Irena said, backing toward the door. 'I will go and see what I can make for dinner while you have bath. Let me know if you need help to wash your back.'

'Sorry?' Frank snapped his head up.

'I say let me know if you need help with neighbour's cat.' She smiled. 'I grew up near farm, and I am good with animal.'

'Oh, right,' he murmured. 'Sorry, I misheard you.'

'You are tired, and this can cause confusion,' she said. 'Take bath and try to relax.'

'I'll try,' he agreed, returning her smile as she left the room.

When he'd heard her going downstairs, he headed into the bathroom and locked the door before turning the taps off and getting undressed. Exhausted by the walk to and from Yvonne's – and everything that had happened since – he stepped into the water and released a blissful sigh as the heat soothed his tense muscles.

In the kitchen, peeling potatoes to go with the lamb chops she had placed in the Aga, Irena snapped her head around when she heard a car pulling onto the drive. Afraid that it might be the police, she dropped the peeler and rushed into the hall to look through the spyhole in the front door. Relieved to see Evan climbing out of a vehicle that was parked behind Frank's car, she opened the door.

'Well, this is a nice surprise.' Evan gave a lopsided grin. 'The old man told me you'd gone.'

'I forget something and come back,' she lied, stepping aside to let him in before quickly closing the door. 'Your father is in bath. I will tell him you are here.'

'You couldn't make us a cuppa first, could you?' Evan asked as he slipped his jacket off. 'I'm absolutely freezing. Here, feel...'

He reached out and touched her face with the back of his hand.

'Oh, is like ice,' she exclaimed.

'You'd best get the kettle on to warm me up, then, eh?'

Irena nodded and walked back into the kitchen. Following, Evan took a seat at the table and watched as she switched the kettle on.

'You're looking better than last time I saw you,' he said. 'Those bruises are fading pretty fast.'

'Yes, is healing well,' she agreed. 'Your father has take good care of me.'

'Oh, I bet he has,' Evan replied slyly.

Frank woke with a start. The bath water was cold, and the sky outside the window was dark, so he figured he must have been sleeping for a while. Shivering, he sat up and leaned forward to pull the plug out, but froze at the sound of muffled voices coming from down below. Afraid that Irena's abuser had found out she was here and forced his way in while he'd been sleeping, he leapt out of the bath and quickly pulled his clothes on before rushing to his bedroom to get the cricket bat.

His heart was thudding as he crept down the stairs, and he took a deep breath to calm himself before barging through the kitchen door.

Evan and Irena were sitting at the table, and they both jumped in alarm.

'Christ, Dad, what are you playing at?' Evan squawked, wiping spilled tea off the front of his T-shirt. 'You scared me to bleedin' death!'

'What are you doing here again?' Frank demanded. 'And why did you answer the door?' he added to Irena. 'It could have been anyone.'

'I see him from window, and he is your son so I think is OK,' she said.

'All right, Pops, chill out.' Evan frowned.

'Sorry,' Frank apologized, placing the bat in the corner. 'I wasn't expecting anyone, that's all.'

'Is something going on here that I need to know about?' Evan asked, suspicion in his eyes.

'No.' Frank shook his head and raked his fingers through his damp hair.

'So what's with the Rambo act? Have you got the bailiffs after you?'

'Don't be daft.'

'Well, *something's* got you spooked.'

Aware that his son wasn't going to stop digging until his curiosity was sated, Frank said, 'If you must know, Irena's recently escaped from a violent relationship, and she's scared he'll come after her.'

'Ah . . .' Evan drew his head back. 'I guess that explains the bruises, then?'

'Yes,' said Frank. 'And the less people who know she's here, the less chance there is of him finding her, so you need to keep this to yourself.'

'Fair enough,' Evan agreed. 'But you'd best tell our Jo what's going on, because she called me when I was on my way over, and she's really pissed off with you.'

'I know. I spoke to her earlier, and she hung up on me.'

'She call when your father is out, and I answer phone,' said Irena. 'I think she is angry when she hear my voice.'

'You're not wrong there.' Evan chuckled. 'Think yourself lucky she's on the other side of the world, 'cos she'd be bloody livid if she could actually see you.'

Irena gazed blankly back at him.

'I do not understand.'

'No girl wants her dad to hook up with someone who's better looking than them,' he explained, grinning.

'That's enough,' Frank chided. 'I've already told you there's nothing going on.'

'If you say so.' Evan winked at Irena.

Scowling at him, Frank said, 'I need to go to Yvonne's, so hurry up and drink your tea. You can drop me off on your way home.'

'Weren't you supposed to be going over there this morning?' Evan asked, reaching for his cup.

'I did, and I found her on the floor,' said Frank. 'It looks like someone broke in and whacked her.'

'You're joking?' Evan's eyebrows shot up. 'And there was me going on about you finding her dead. Is she going to be all right?'

'Your father call helicopter and they take her to hospital,'

Irena said, gazing at Frank as if he'd done something heroic. 'And he has offer to take care of animal until she come home.'

'Are you sure you're up to that with your dodgy ticker?' Evan asked Frank. 'I can do it, if you want?'

'I'm perfectly capable of feeding a few pigs and cats,' Frank said, snatching his coat off the hook. 'Let's go.'

'Actually,' Evan said sheepishly, 'I was going to ask if I could stay for a couple of nights.'

'Why? What have you done?'

'Nothing! Why do you always assume it's me?'

'Because it usually is.'

'Yeah, well, not this time,' Evan grunted. 'Me and Marie had a barney earlier, so I went out for a pint.'

'And?'

'And she followed me and kicked off when she saw me chatting to a mate.'

'Really?' Frank said knowingly. 'And was this mate female, by any chance?'

'Yeah, but that shouldn't make any difference.' Evan pulled a face. 'Mum wouldn't have made a holy show of *you* for talking to another bird, would she?'

'No, because she knew she could trust me,' Frank said piously. 'So what happened?'

'Her and the lass had a fight, and she told me not to bother going home.'

'Did you try talking to her?'

'Yeah, course I did, but she wasn't having any of it. And she threatened to have me arrested if I tried to get back in the house. So can I stay, or what?'

Frank shook his head in despair. Then, tutting, he said, 'Fine, you can stay tonight. But, first thing tomorrow, you go home and sort this out.'

'Sure thing, Cap'n.' Evan saluted. Then, jumping to his feet, he said, 'Let's go and sort these animals out, then. Coming, Irena?'

'No.' She shook her head. 'I offer to help Frankie, but if you are go with him, I will stay here and finish cook.'

'A stunner *and* a domestic goddess.' Evan looked at her with fresh appreciation.

'Get moving,' Frank said, pushing him out into the hall.

Between them, Frank and Evan made short work of feeding Yvonne's pets. The stench inside the cottage helped, because neither wanted to be in there for any longer than absolutely necessary. As shocked by the state of it as Frank had been, Evan almost threw up when he saw one of the cats munching on the pool of congealed blood.

'It's like being on the set of *Texas Chainsaw Massacre*,' he complained, dragging the collar of his T-shirt up over his mouth and nose. 'How the hell has she let it get this bad?'

'She's seventy-six,' said Frank, as if that were explanation enough.

'Well, you're not that far off, and you still keep the house clean,' said Evan.

Frank gave him a withering look and herded him out through the door, leaving the cats to fight over the food he'd shared out.

'We'll go back tomorrow and do some cleaning,' he said as Evan drove back up the lane. 'Fix the door, and make things a bit nicer for when she gets home.'

'She needs putting in a home, if you ask me,' Evan replied bluntly. 'I'm not being funny, Dad, I know she was Mum's friend, but come on . . . who lives like that?'

'Old people who care more about others than they care about themselves,' said Frank, feeling guilty again for the way he'd snubbed Yvonne.

Once they'd eaten the dinner Irena had prepared, they all moved into the living room, where Frank sat on his armchair, while Evan made himself comfortable beside Irena on the sofa. Evan turned the TV on and scrolled through the channels until he found an old comedy film he wanted to watch. Frank had seen it before, and he'd enjoyed it, but he struggled to concentrate this time, because he was distracted by Evan playing up to Irena. He'd had words with him while they were out, telling him to quit leering at Irena and focus on sorting his marriage out. But his words had clearly fallen on deaf ears, because Evan was acting as if they were on a date and no one else was present.

Finally, unable to bear any more of it, Frank slammed his whisky glass down on the table and stood up.

'I think it's time for bed.'

'Night,' Evan said without looking at him.

'I meant you, as well,' said Frank. 'You need to get up early so you can go home and talk to Marie.'

'I'm not tired,' Evan argued. 'You go up. I'll turn off down here when we're finished.'

Frank gritted his teeth. Evan was a grown man, so he couldn't order him to go to bed. And Irena was still watching the film, so he had no choice but to leave them to it.

12

Evan was up, dressed, and sitting at the kitchen table when Frank went downstairs the next morning. Hoping it was a sign that his son had taken his advice on board and intended to go home early to sort things out with Marie, his heart sank when Evan told him he'd spoken to her earlier and she'd accused him of spending the night with the girl from the pub.

'What did you expect?' Frank sighed, taking a seat facing him. 'She already thought she'd caught you cheating, so she was bound to think that's where you'd gone when you didn't go home.'

'She told me not to,' Evan reminded him. 'And you don't know what she's like when she gets jealous. She'd probably have tried to stab me if I'd gone back, or set the stupid dog on me.'

Sure that he was exaggerating, because, while his daughter-in-law was undoubtedly moody, he'd never witnessed her being violent in any way, Frank said, 'So what are you going to do? Avoid going back and let her think she's right?'

'I don't know.' Evan slumped back in his seat and laced his fingers together behind his head.

'Do you want me to talk to her?' Frank offered. 'She might calm down if she realizes you were here.'

'There's no point. She'll only think I've asked you to cover for me.'

'Well, you've got to do *something*,' Frank persisted. 'Marriage is a commitment, so you can't just walk away from this.'

'That's exactly what I feel like doing,' Evan grunted. 'I've stuck it out for six years, but I honestly don't know how much more I can take.'

'You can't blame it all on her,' Frank said. 'Me and your mum had our fair share of fights over the years, and there were plenty of times when I could have given up and walked away. But you work your way through these things, if you're willing to put the effort in.'

'I've made plenty of effort,' Evan replied wearily. 'But I can't seem to do right for doing wrong these days.'

'So, that's it?' Frank raised an eyebrow. 'You're giving up?'

'I don't know.' Evan shrugged. Then, sighing, he lowered his arms, and said, 'I'll talk to her again when she's had time to calm down, but it might take a few days.'

'What about work? You can't risk driving to Manchester every morning in this weather.'

'I'm not in again till Monday, and my boss said I can keep the fourby till I get my own car fixed, so I'm sorted.'

'OK,' Frank relented. 'You can stay for a few more days. But you need to figure out a way to get your marriage back on track while you're here, and I don't want you making a nuisance of yourself with Irena.'

'As if,' Evan scoffed.

'I mean it,' Frank said, lowering his voice when he heard footsteps on the floor above. 'She's had a rough time, and she doesn't need you coming on strong and making her feel uncomfortable.'

'She was fine last night,' Evan reminded him, giving him a questioning look. 'Are you sure it's not *you* who's uncomfortable, because you've taken a shine to her?'

'For the last time, there is nothing going on between me and Irena,' Frank hissed, aware that she was on her way down the stairs and would be here within seconds. 'I just don't want you putting your marriage in jeopardy because you think you've got a chance with her. She'll be gone as soon as the snow clears, and you'll have lost everything – your wife, your house, possibly even your job, for *nothing.*'

Evan looked at him as if to say *That's what* you *think, old man,* but Irena walked in at that moment, so Frank was forced to drop the subject.

'Morning.' Evan greeted her with a grin, as if he'd already forgotten – or dismissed – every word Frank had said. 'Sleep well?'

'Yes, I have nice sleep, thank you,' she said, returning his smile before turning to Frank. 'Shall I make tea?'

'Sorry, I meant to put the kettle on, but we got talking,' Frank said, pushing his chair back.

'Is OK, I will do,' she insisted.

Following her with his eyes as she carried the kettle to the sink, Evan said, 'That cardigan really suits you. The colour matches your eyes.'

'Your father has let me wear,' Irena said self-consciously. 'But I will give back when I leave.'

'You might as well keep it,' Evan said. 'My mum's never going to wear it again, and it'll probably only end up in the bin when the old man gets around to clearing her stuff out.'

'I've already told her to keep it,' said Frank. 'And the rest will be going to the charity shop in the village, not the bin.'

'Want me to drop it off for you?' Evan offered. 'Irena can come with me and see if there's anything a bit more fashionable there for her.'

'No!' Frank said sharply. 'I've already told you, the less people who know she's here the better, so she can't be seen out with you. Anyway, don't bother making plans, because you'll be helping me today.'

'Doing what?' Evan asked, still eyeing Irena.

'Fixing Yvonne's place up,' said Frank.

'I can clean, if you like?' Irena offered.

'It's OK, love, we'll manage,' Frank said.

'Aw, come on, Pops,' Evan drawled. 'How can you refuse that pretty face?'

'I said no,' Frank repeated. 'It's daylight, and we can't risk anyone seeing her.'

* * *

Yvonne's cottage was in an even worse state than Frank had remembered, and it took him and Evan several hours to make a dent in clearing out the rubbish. Leaving it at that for the day, they went back to the farm, where Frank called the hospital to ask how she was doing.

'How is she?' Evan asked when he'd finished the call.

'Her hip's definitely broken, and they reckon she's got a chest infection, so she could be in there for a while,' Frank told him, dismayed at the prospect of having to go back and forth to the cottage twice each day for God only knew how long to feed her pets. And it wouldn't end there, because she'd undoubtedly need help once she came home, as well. 'I think I'd best have a word with her and see if she'll agree to let me get them rehomed.'

'Good luck with that,' Evan said, plucking cat hairs off his jeans. 'Even if she said yes, you'll have trouble getting those moggies out of there without losing a couple of fingers, 'cos they're wild as fu—'

'Yes, all right, I get your point,' Frank interrupted, conscious that Irena was in the room. 'But she'll have to do something, because I can't keep doing this forever.'

'If I was to stay, I could do for you,' Irena said over her shoulder as she looked in the freezer to see what she could use for dinner. 'But I am to leave soon, so I cannot.'

'Thanks, love,' Frank said. 'But this is going to be a long-term problem, and Yvonne needs to make some serious decisions.'

'You can take the fourby if you want to visit her,' Evan suggested.

'No, it's OK,' Frank replied, noting that his son hadn't offered to drive, meaning that he'd intended to stay here with Irena. 'The nurse said she's doped up, so I'll leave it till she's a bit stronger.'

'Well, the offer's there if you change your mind,' said Evan.

'I won't,' Frank said with finality, letting him know that he was on to his game.

13

The few days Frank had said Evan could stay stretched into a few more, and the stress of trying to keep his son and Irena from spending too much time alone together was sending his blood pressure through the roof. The daylight hours weren't too bad, because there were plenty of jobs to keep Evan occupied, both at the farm and the cottage. But when night came around, and the three of them settled down to watch TV, his irritation kicked in all over again.

Fed up by the end of the week, he waited until he and Evan had gone to feed the animals, before asking, 'Don't you think this has been going on for long enough, Son?'

'Marie will let me know when she's ready to talk,' Evan replied unconcernedly. 'But I still haven't decided what I want to do.'

'Well, you'd best make your mind up soon,' Frank said. 'Either go back and make it work, or man up and tell her it's over.'

'And if I break it off, can I move back in with you?' Evan asked.

'No.' Frank stood firm. 'I'm sorry, but I'm not giving you an easy way out of this.'

Evan gave a sly smile, saying, 'You mean you're not giving me an easy way *in*? I've seen the way you look at Irena, and I reckon you're jealous that we're getting on so well.'

'Don't be ridiculous,' Frank protested. 'I'm only trying to stop you from throwing your marriage away.'

'Why? You don't even like Marie.'

'I've never said that.'

'You didn't need to, Dad, it's obvious. Just like it's obvious you fancy Irena.'

'I do *not* fancy Irena.'

'Then you won't mind if I take a crack at her if I decide to split from Marie, will you?'

Frank didn't answer, but Evan's words stayed in his mind for the rest of that day. The near-miss he'd had with Irena on the night of the storm had stirred something inside him that he'd thought was long dead, and, as hard as he'd tried to fight it, he couldn't deny that he was attracted to her. She was beautiful, intelligent, and kind, and he'd enjoyed the few quiet evenings they had spent together before Evan had come to stay. So was his son right? he wondered. *Was* he jealous?

Confused by these unfamiliar feelings, and disgusted with himself for viewing his son as a rival, Frank headed up to bed earlier than usual that night – even though it meant leaving Evan and Irena alone for the first time in days.

Since that first night he'd been forcing himself to stay up until they went to bed, and, more often than not, it wasn't until the early hours of the morning. Determined to catch up on the sleep he'd been missing, he changed into his pyjamas and climbed into bed. But sleep wouldn't come, and after tossing and turning for the best part of an hour, he flopped onto his back and stared at the shadows on the ceiling. Something was bothering him, but he couldn't quite put his finger on what it was. He could hear the TV down in the living room, but that was all he could hear – and that was unusual, because Evan had an annoying tendency to give a running commentary on whatever they were watching.

Unable to ignore what his instincts were telling him, Frank got up and pulled his dressing gown on before making his way downstairs. If Evan and Irena wanted to be together, so be it. But not like this. Whether Evan liked it or not, he was a married man, and he needed to do the decent thing and break it off with Marie before he started a relationship with Irena.

He'd reached the hallway and was about to knock on the living room door to announce his presence, when he heard a little squeal, followed by Irena screaming: '*FRANKIIIEEEE . . . Help me!*'

Her voice became muffled, but Frank had heard enough, and he burst into the room to see what was going on. His blood ran cold when he saw Evan on top of Irena on the sofa, his hand covering her mouth.

'What the bloody hell are you *doing*?' he bellowed.

'It isn't what it looks like,' Evan yelped, jumping up. 'She came on to me, then flipped out when I kissed her.'

Irena had shuffled into the corner of the sofa, tears streaming down her cheeks. The terror in her eyes when Frank glanced at her told him everything he needed to know.

'Go to your room,' he ordered Evan.

'But I haven't done anything,' Evan protested. 'I was ready to go to bed, but she pulled me down and started kissing me.'

'Is not true,' Irena sobbed. 'I do not touch him.'

Evan snapped his head round and stared at her in disbelief.

'Why are you lying? You've been flirting with me all week, so don't make out like I was trying to force myself on you. You're the one who started this, and you should have told me if you changed your mind.'

'Go to your room,' Frank repeated. 'We'll talk about this in the morning.'

Refusing to leave it at that, Evan said, 'Tell him the truth, Irena. What the hell's up with you?'

'That's enough,' Frank said sternly, shoving him out into the hall. 'You know what she's been through, and I've been telling you all week to leave her alone, but you just wouldn't listen, would you?'

'But she started it,' Evan insisted. 'She was all over me the minute you went to bed. Why would I lie?'

'You're the one who's been doing all the chasing, as far as I can see,' said Frank. 'And the booze has clearly gone to your head and made you think she feels the same. But you're wrong.'

'Christ, you believe her, don't you?' Evan gaped at him. 'You hardly even know her – and I'm your *son*, so why are you taking her word over mine?'

'I know what I saw,' Frank said. 'And I'm not discussing this with you while you're drunk, so go to bed before you do any more damage.'

Evan's cheek muscles twitched, and he balled his hands into fists. For a split second Frank thought he was about to be punched, but then Evan shook his head and took a step back.

'You know what, she ain't worth it. I don't know what her game is, but if you swallow that bullshit, you deserve everything that's coming to you.'

'What are you doing?' Frank asked when Evan turned and yanked his jacket off the hook. 'You can't drive, you've been drinking.'

'So?' Evan tugged the jacket on and pulled his keys out of his pocket.

'I'm not letting you put yourself and anyone else who might be on the road in danger,' Frank said, putting himself between Evan and the door. 'Now go to bed and stop being stupid.'

'I've only had a couple of glasses,' Evan said, easily pushing him out of the way. 'And don't bother talking to me again until you're ready to apologize for calling me a rapist.'

'I didn't say that,' Frank protested, following him out onto the step.

'As good as,' Evan shot back, marching over to the Land Rover.

Frank tried again to reason with him, but he jumped behind the wheel, fired the engine, and reversed angrily out onto the lane before taking off with a screech of rubber.

Irena was still huddled on the sofa when Frank went back into the living room.

'Are you OK?' he asked, perching on the cushion beside her.

'I don't know what happen,' she said, gazing tearfully up at him. 'Film was finish, so I tell him I am go to bed. Then . . . then he start kiss and touch me. I tell him stop, but he say I am ask for it. And when I shout for you, he cover my mouth and I feel like I am suffocate.'

'I'm so sorry,' Frank apologized, placing his hand over hers. 'He had no right to do that to you, and I'm sure he'll be disgusted with himself when he wakes up tomorrow and remembers what he's done. But he's gone now, so try to put it out of your mind.'

'I will try,' Irena agreed, resting her cheek on his shoulder.

Disturbed when his body instantly reacted to the nearness of her, Frank jumped to his feet.

'I, um, think we both need some sleep,' he said, shoving his hands into his dressing gown pockets. 'I'll see you in the morning.'

'Goodnight, Frankie,' Irena said quietly.

Nodding his reply, Frank left her and went back to his room.

14

Evan careered around the twists and bends of the lane at break-neck speed, his teeth so tightly clenched his jaw started to throb. Conscious of the alcohol in his bloodstream, he forced himself to slow down before he reached the village and released the tension on a long exhale. He couldn't believe what Irena had done, and he was furious with his dad for automatically siding with her. Yes, he'd flirted with her, but she'd been giving him secretive little looks and smiles all week, so he'd genuinely thought the attraction was mutual. But was it possible that he'd misread it, as his dad had suggested? Had the booze deceived him into thinking she was giving him the come-on, when, in fact, she was only being friendly? If so, it was no wonder she'd reacted the way she had. She'd already suffered abuse at the hands of her husband, and it must have been terrifying to have one of the only two people she trusted do something like that to her.

Except he *hadn't* actually done anything. It was *her* who had kissed *him*.

Torn between feeling guilty for allowing himself to get sucked in by her, and angry with his dad for thinking he was the kind of man who would force himself on a woman, Evan decided to go home to try to sort things out with Marie. He only hoped she'd missed him enough to let him in, because it was too late to turn up at any of his mates' houses, and way too cold to spend the night in the car. Then, tomorrow, when he'd had some sleep and calmed down, he would go back to his dad's and apologize – even though he genuinely didn't believe he'd done anything wrong.

Marie's car was parked on the drive when Evan reached the house an hour later, and he could see a light flickering behind the bedroom curtains. Guessing that she must have fallen asleep watching TV when he rang the bell a couple of times and got no answer, he slotted his key into the lock.

He'd half expected her to have changed the locks, or at least put the bolt on, so it came as a surprise when the door opened. Evan stepped inside and wrinkled his nose as the stench of dog hit him in the face. Almost immediately, the landing light came on, and Marie appeared at the top of the stairs, her hair all over the place, her sleep-swollen eyes wide with fear.

'Who is it?' she yelled.

'It's me,' he said. 'Sorry. I didn't mean to scare you.'

'Who said you could let yourself in?' she demanded, clomping down the stairs. 'In case you've forgotten, you don't live here any more.'

'I rang the bell, but you didn't answer,' Evan said, pushing the dog's snout away when it rushed down behind her and started sniffing his legs.

'I was sleeping.' She glared at him. 'It's two o'clock in the fucking morning, so what the hell are you doing here? Did you think you'd catch me with another man and use it as an excuse to take the house off me, or something?'

'I'd never do that,' he assured her, closing the door. 'I want to talk, that's all.'

'Oh, I see . . .' Her eyes narrowed and she gave him a knowing look. 'She's kicked you out, hasn't she?'

'There is no *she*. I've been at my dad's.'

'So *you* say.'

'It's true. And he's spent the entire week telling me to stop being stupid and come home.'

'As if!' Marie gave a snort of disbelief. 'He hates my guts, so he'll have been made up that you left me.'

'I didn't leave, you chucked me out,' Evan reminded her. 'And he doesn't hate you, he just doesn't like the way we treat each other – and neither do I.'

'That's your fault, not mine,' Marie said huffily. 'Every time I try to talk to you, you criticize me and put me down. It's like I can't do right for doing wrong, and I'm sick of it.'

Evan could have argued that it was the total opposite, in his opinion: *he* tried to talk, while she nagged and bitched. But that would go down like a lead balloon, and he didn't want to argue, so he held up his hands.

'OK, you're right . . . it's all me. I'm a selfish prick, and you deserve better.'

'Yes, you are, and I do,' Marie agreed. 'So what do you want?'

'To sort things out,' said Evan. 'I know I've treated you badly, but I love you, and I want to make it right.'

'How do I know you're not just saying that to worm your way back in here because you've got nowhere else to go?' Marie asked. 'You say you've been at your dad's, but I've only got your word for that. You could have been with that tart, for all I know.'

'Do you want me to ring him so you can ask him yourself?' Evan slid his phone out of his pocket – praying that she wouldn't make him go through with it.

Marie tutted and rolled her eyes.

'You know damn well I wouldn't make you disturb him at this time of night. Anyway, he'd only lie for you, so what's the point?'

'You're wrong about that,' Evan said. 'If you'd heard the way he's been going on at me this week, you'd know he's on your side, not mine.'

Marie pursed her lips, but her expression had softened a little, and Evan could see that she wanted to believe him.

'I shouldn't have stayed away so long, and I totally get why you're mad at me,' he said. 'But I'm home now, so can we sit down and talk?'

'Fine, we'll talk,' she agreed. 'But don't make yourself too comfortable, 'cos I haven't decided what I'm doing yet.'

She turned at that and stomped into the kitchen with the

dog on her heels, and Evan shook his head as he looped his jacket over the newel post. This was as much his house as it was hers – more so, in fact, considering he'd paid all the bills since she packed her job in. But she had the moral high ground, so he was going to have to take whatever she threw at him and hope she'd agree to let him stay. He'd sleep in the spare room or on the sofa if he had to, he honestly didn't care as long as he could get his head down for a few hours.

'Why are you still standing there?' Marie asked, walking out of the kitchen with a can of beer in one hand and a glass of wine in the other. 'Thinking of taking off again?'

'No, of course not,' Evan said, his gaze dipping to her backside as he followed her into the living room. She was wearing pyjamas he'd seen her in a million times before, but they didn't seem to be as tightly stretched as usual. 'Have you lost weight?'

'Half a stone,' she said, shoving the can into his hand before sinking down on her chair. 'It's a side effect of not knowing where your husband is – or *who* he's with,' she added, flashing him an accusing look.

'I'm sorry,' Evan apologized, perching on the sofa. 'But I honestly wasn't with another woman.'

'Yeah, well, you probably did me a favour,' Marie sniffed. 'I've been having a great time without you. I can watch what I want, go where I want, and see who I want without you pulling your face and making me feel like shit.'

'I'm not that bad,' Evan protested, tearing the tab off his can and taking a swig of ice-cold beer before resting his elbows on his knees.

'Yeah, you are,' Marie countered, holding her glass up in the air so the wine didn't spill when the dog clambered onto her lap. 'So what now?' she asked. 'You come back with your tail between your legs, and I'm supposed to forgive and forget, am I?'

'I haven't done anything,' Evan said wearily.

'You're obviously forgetting that I caught you with that tart,' said Marie. '*And* you lied about taking Billy Hicks to see his wife in hospital, when he reckoned he hadn't seen you in weeks.'

'I was telling the truth about the woman,' Evan insisted. 'But I admit I was lying about Billy.'

'I knew it! So, go on, then . . . where were you really?'

'The pub.'

'With that slapper?'

'No, on my own.'

'Yeah, right.'

'It's true. You can ask the landlord if you don't believe me.'

'Why would you do that?' Marie frowned. 'Sit in a pub on your own, when you could have stopped in with me and had a few cans?'

'I needed time out.'

'From what?'

'You,' Evan said bluntly. '*Us*,' he added to soften the blow. 'And *that* . . .' He nodded at the dog, which was on its back licking the underside of her chin. 'I know you don't mind it, but it makes me heave.'

Shoving the dog's head away, as if she hadn't even noticed what it was doing until then, Marie said, 'They've got antiseptic tongues.'

'They eat shit and lick their own arses,' Evan countered. 'Can't you see how disgusting that is?'

'It's only as disgusting as you scratching your sweaty balls when you think no one's looking.'

'I'll do you a deal . . . I'll stop doing that, if you stop letting the dog lick your face.'

'And what about the lies?' Marie asked. 'It's like you can't help yourself. You open your mouth and bullshit pours out.'

'OK, no more lies,' Evan promised. 'From now on, we'll be completely honest with each other.'

'I already am,' Marie said piously. 'You're the one who's always sneaking around being secretive. And that's another thing . . . why do you always go out of the room when your Jo rings? I know she's your sister, but I'm your wife, and you shouldn't let her come between us like that.'

Considering the on-off relationship he had with his sister, Evan didn't think he *had* let Jo come between them. But she had been calling him a lot more often than usual since finding out about their dad and Irena, and he hadn't discussed the situation with Marie, so he supposed his wife had a point.

'We're not hiding anything from you,' he assured her. 'She's only been ringing to have a moan, 'cos she's got a bee in her bonnet about the woman my dad's taken in.'

'Woman?' Marie repeated, frowning. 'You never told me he had a woman living with him.'

'She's not actually living there,' Evan backtracked. 'He's letting her stay till she finds her own place.'

'Was she there while you were staying?'

'Yeah, but I didn't spend any time with her, so you've got nothing to worry about,' Evan lied. 'I stayed in my room and left them to it.'

'Left them to what? Is he seeing her, or something?'

'He reckons not, but who knows?' Evan shrugged and took a swig of beer.

'What's she like?'

'I haven't really spoken to her, but she's dog ugly, and skinny – like a junkie.'

'Why would Frank go for someone like that?' Marie's frown deepened. 'I know he's getting on a bit, but he's a good-looking bloke, so he could easy get someone better.'

'No idea.' Evan shrugged again. 'But our Jo's told him she's having nothing to do with him till he gets rid, so I doubt he'll keep her there for too much longer.'

Marie's eyes had narrowed again, and she peered at him with suspicion.

'Is that why you've come back? Did he kick you out because you and Jo don't like his girlfriend?'

'No.' Evan shook his head. 'I'm not gonna lie, we did have words, but that's not why I left. I came back because this has been going on too long and I wanted to come home.'

Marie took a swig of wine and stared down at the rug for several seconds, as if mulling everything over. Then, releasing a weary breath, she said, 'OK, I suppose you can stay. But things have got to change, 'cos we can't go on like it was before.'

'Absolutely,' Evan agreed.

'I mean it,' she said. 'No more lies, and no more putting me down.'

'We *both* need to make more effort,' he replied evenly.

'Yes, well, we'll talk in the morning and set some ground rules,' Marie said, shoving the dog off her lap and putting her glass down on the table. 'I'm going to bed. Are you coming up, or stopping down here?'

Surprised, and grateful, because he hadn't expected to be allowed back into their bed so quickly, Evan said, 'I'll be up in a minute, love.'

15

The sun was shining when Frank came back from feeding Yvonne's animals the next morning, and the snow had started to melt, revealing patches of green. Certain that Irena would be pleased, because he imagined she must be desperate to get away after the events of the previous night, Frank smiled when she joined him in the kitchen as he was making them both a cup of tea.

'Looks like you'll be able to get going soon,' he said, nodding toward the window, through which the sunlight was streaming. 'I checked earlier, and the trains and buses are running again, so I'll take you to the station when you're ready.'

'I think this will make you happy,' Irena murmured. 'But I will miss be here with you.'

'We can stay in touch, if that's what you want?' Frank said, handing one of the cups to her when she took a seat at the table. 'But London's a huge city, and you'll soon forget about me when you make new friends.'

'I do not want to make new friend,' she replied quietly, her gaze fixed on the steam rising from the cup.

'I thought you were looking forward to moving on?' Frank said. Frowning when Irena gave a tiny shake of her head and pulled a tissue out of her pocket, he sat beside her. 'Is this about last night? I know you've been treated badly in the past, and I'm really sorry for what Evan did, but I honestly don't think he meant to hurt you.'

'This is not about *Evan*.' She spat the name out. 'I do not care about him, I care about *you*, and I am sad to know that I will not see you again. I am sorry if this make you uncomfortable, and I know you do not feel same, but is how *I* feel.'

Sighing, Frank reached for her hand.

'Love, you don't want me. You've been through a terrible experience, and you're bound to be feeling vulnerable, but—'

Before he could go on, Irena leaned forward and kissed him. Instantly aroused, Frank leapt to his feet.

'You can deny, but I *know* you feel something for me,' Irena said, her gaze intense as she too stood up. 'You have guilt because of wife, but she is gone and I am here, so please do not push me away.'

Frank raked his fingers through his hair and backed away from her. He had given himself a good talking to before going to sleep last night, and he'd truly thought he had got his emotions under control when he woke this morning. Irena was beautiful and, at thirty-six to his sixty, the age-gap wasn't so great as to make a relationship completely unthinkable. But her being here had caused a rift between him and his children, and he had to put them first.

'Frankie, look at me,' Irena urged, cupping his cheek in her hand. 'I did not expect to feel love when I meet you, but it happen, and I cannot leave without tell you this. If there is chance you can ever feel same, let me stay for few more days. If you do not want me after this, I will leave and you will never hear from me again.'

Frank squeezed his eyes shut. *You've got to stop this*, he told himself. *Why?* another voice argued. *She wants you, and you want her, so what's the problem?*

When he still hadn't spoken a few seconds later, Irena sighed and dropped her hand.

'Is OK. Your silence has answer for you.'

'Wait,' Frank said when she turned to walk out.

She paused and gazed back at him.

'Yes?'

'Don't go,' he said. 'Not yet, anyway. You're right, I *do* feel something. I've tried not to, I really have, but it's not working. And I know we haven't known each other long, and my kids will probably never speak to me again, but—'

'Stop talk,' Irena said, walking up to him and looping her arms around his neck. 'You have already say everything I need to hear.'

Their lips connected, and Frank went into an immediate state of turmoil: his body craving the intimacy after two – or was it closer to three? He honestly couldn't remember – years of celibacy; his head warning him that his already damaged relationship with his children would undoubtedly disintegrate even further if he went ahead with this.

His touch-starved body won and, no longer trying to resist, he walked Irena backwards through the hall and into the living room, their lips still locked together, their hands unbuttoning and unzipping their clothes as they went.

Lying on top of her on the rug in front of the fire a few seconds later, Frank hesitated, and asked, 'Are you sure about this?'

'I thought I tell you to stop talk,' she replied huskily, pulling him into her.

'Was good?' Irena asked, gazing into Frank's eyes as she played with the hairs on his sweat-slick chest a few minutes later.

'Uh huh,' he murmured, his heart beating too hard for him to form complete words.

'Is good for me, too,' she purred, her soft breath tickling his throat. 'I have dream of this since night of storm when you sleep in bed with me.'

Breathing out loudly when his pulse began to slow at last, Frank put his arm around her and pulled her closer. He hadn't lasted very long, but she didn't seem to mind, so he obviously wasn't as rusty as he'd thought. Next time would be better – if she didn't change her mind in the meantime.

They had been lying in each other's arms for a few blissful minutes, when the doorbell rang, shattering the peace that had descended over the room.

'Do not answer,' Irena urged when Frank sat up. 'If is important, they will come back.'

Another peal echoed through the hallway, and then a shadow crossed the window. Conscious that the curtains were open, Frank glanced round, and his blood ran cold when he saw Evan peering in. Their eyes met, and Evan jerked back as if he'd been burned.

'Oh, shit!' Frank muttered, scrambling to his feet.

'What is wrong?' Irena asked, snatching her clothes up off the floor to cover herself when he dragged his jeans on. 'Where are you go, Frankie?'

He ran out into the hall without answering, and opened the front door in time to see Evan striding to the Land Rover.

'Evan, wait!' he yelled, pausing to pull a coat on to cover his bare chest before going after him.

'For what?' Evan asked angrily. 'So you can tell me that wasn't what it looked like? Ironic, eh? That's exactly what I said to you last night, only in *my* case it was true.'

'I can explain,' Frank said breathlessly, putting his hand on the roof of the car to steady himself when stars began to pulse behind his eyes.

'Don't bother,' Evan said coldly. 'I saw everything I needed to see. I just can't believe you're being such a fucking hypocrite. And when did it start – before or after I came to stay? I mean, I knew you had a problem with me cracking on to her, but if I'd known it was because you were already screwing her, there's no way I'd have touched her.'

'That was the first time.'

'Do me a favour! It was obvious you had the hots for her,

and I even tried to tell you I'd be OK with it, but you flat out denied it.'

'It's true,' Frank insisted. 'And I was going to tell you next time we spoke.'

'Well, I guess that's one awkward conversation we don't need to have now, isn't it?' Evan replied coolly. 'But whether it was the first time or the millionth time, you need to ask yourself why she tried to cop off with me the minute your back was turned last night.'

'You were drunk and you misread the situation,' Frank argued. 'I'm sure you didn't mean for it to go as far as it did, but, come on, Son . . . you can't keep blaming Irena.'

'Bullshit!' spat Evan. 'I didn't misread a damn thing! She started it, and I reckon she heard you coming down the stairs and put that show on for you 'cos she didn't want you to see her for what she really is. The only thing I did wrong was put my hand over her mouth. I shouldn't have done that.'

'Well, that's a start,' said Frank. 'And I'm sure Irena won't hold it against you if you apologize.'

'Are you for real?' Evan's eyebrows knitted together in disbelief. 'I'm not apologizing to that conniving bitch. I was going to, for *your* sake, but you can both fuck off.'

He climbed into the car with that, and Frank was forced to jump back to protect his bare feet when Evan slammed his foot down on the accelerator and reversed out onto the lane.

Irena was standing in the hall when he went back inside the house.

'Was bad?' she asked.

'Awful,' he muttered. 'I need a drink.'

'I will get,' she said. 'You go sit down. Your face is very pale.'

Frank didn't argue. His heart was still pounding, and he knew his blood pressure must be sky high, so he went into the living room and took his medication before sinking down on his chair.

Irena came back a few minutes later and handed him a cup of tea. Thanking her, even though he'd meant that he needed an alcoholic drink, Frank was about to take a sip when his mobile phone started ringing, and he said, 'That didn't take long,' when he saw Jo's name on the screen.

'Is daughter?' Irena asked, still standing beside the chair. 'Would you like for me to talk to her?'

'No, definitely not,' said Frank. 'Give me a minute, eh?'

Irena nodded and left the room, and Frank took a deep breath before answering the call.

'Hello, love.'

'Evan just rang me, and I can't believe what he told me,' Jo launched straight in without returning the greeting. 'I'm absolutely disgusted.'

Sighing, Frank said, 'I know it looks bad, but he'd had a lot to drink, and I'm sure he didn't mean to—'

'I'm not talking about *him*, I'm talking about *you*,' Jo interrupted. 'You're his father, and you've known him his entire life, so how could you accuse him of something as vile as that?'

'I didn't accuse him of anything,' Frank replied evenly. 'I

caught him. But, like I told him, I'm sure he got his wires crossed and misread the situation.'

'She *threw* herself at him. There's nothing to misread in that.'

'With respect, love, you're not here, and you haven't seen the way he's been behaving around her.'

'So he flirted with her – big deal. He's a man. That's what they do when they're attracted to someone.'

'Not all of us.'

'Oh, come off it, you're no saint. Mum knew exactly what you were like, and it used to really piss her off when you turned on the charm for other women.'

'I never cheated on your mother,' Frank protested. 'I loved her.'

'So why are you disrespecting her memory by screwing that bitch in her house?' Jo demanded. 'And why would this woman even *want* to have sex with you if Evan tried to force himself on her? Rape is one of the most traumatic things a woman can go through, and there's no way she'd have got over it that fast.'

'I know what I saw,' Frank said, rubbing his temples when they started throbbing. 'Evan was lying on top of her with his hand over her mouth when I walked in, and she was absolutely terrified.'

'She put it on because she heard you coming down the stairs,' Jo said, repeating Evan's theory. 'But if you'd given him the chance to tell you what actually happened, you'd know she'd offered to give him a blow job immediately before that. And

I'm sorry if that offends you, but you need to know the kind of woman you're dealing with.'

Patience wearing thin, Frank said, 'Irena has done nothing wrong, and I don't appreciate you talking about her like this when you haven't even met her.'

'No, I haven't met her, and I don't bloody *want* to, because I'd be tempted to rip her lying face off,' Jo retorted defiantly. 'How *dare* she worm her way into my mother's house and cause trouble like this!'

'This isn't really about her, is it?' Frank asked perceptively. 'It wouldn't matter who she was, or where she'd come from, you just can't bear that she's here. But your mum's gone and she's never coming back, so it's about time you accepted it.'

'I can't believe you said that,' Jo gasped. 'You might want to forget about Mum, but I *never* will.'

'Neither will I,' said Frank. 'And you know damn well that isn't what I meant. I'll never stop loving your mother, and I wish to God she was still here. But she isn't, and nothing's ever going to change that.'

'Well, I hope you're very happy with your new life,' Jo said bitterly. 'But don't expect me and Evan to accept that . . . *woman* into the family, because it's never going to happen!'

She hung up at that, and Frank slammed his phone down on the arm of the chair. He shouldn't have said that about Maureen being gone, because Jo had been very close to her, and that remark had clearly stung. But she'd been out of order, too. Both she and Evan had made choices he'd disagreed with in the past, but they were adults, so he'd figured they were entitled to make their own decisions. It was disappointing they weren't willing to extend the same respect to him, though.

Irena tapped on the door, and Frank guessed from the wary expression on her face when she entered the room that she'd heard him raise his voice.

'Is OK?' she asked.

'Not really,' he admitted. 'But it's my problem, not yours, so I don't want you worrying about it.'

'Is my fault,' she said dolefully. 'I should leave.'

'It is *not* your fault,' Frank argued. 'If you want to leave, that's your decision, but I won't have you chased out of here because my children can't accept that I'm moving on. I know they think it's too soon, but I reckon they'd feel the same if this had happened next year, or in ten years, so there's no point waiting for their approval.'

'So you do not want me to leave?' Irena asked.

'No.' Frank reached for her hand. 'Nothing's changed as far as you're concerned.'

'Then I will stay,' she said, smiling as she walked over to him. 'And we will prove son and daughter wrong – yes?'

Frank rested his cheek on her sweet-smelling hair when she slid onto his lap. He had no idea if this was the beginning of something special or the biggest mistake he'd ever made, but Maureen had wanted him to be happy, so he owed it to her, and himself, to at least try to make a go of it.

16

Frank didn't hear from Evan or Jo again in the run-up to Christmas, but he tried not to dwell on it, reminding himself that he'd done nothing wrong, and it was down to them to make the first move to build bridges.

It hadn't snowed again since that last bad spell, and bright sunlight was streaming through the partially open curtains when he woke on Christmas morning. It brought him no joy, and he felt like dragging the quilt over his head and staying there until it was all over. This had always been the one day of the year when Maureen would get up a couple of hours before him, and she'd have made a start on the cooking by the time he went downstairs and would be pottering around making sure the house was ready for when the kids and their families arrived. But, today, with Maureen gone, and Jo and Evan still giving him the cold shoulder, there would be none of the usual noise, laughter, and present swapping.

He caught the lyrical strains of Irena singing along to the radio in the kitchen, and sighed as he shoved the quilt off his legs. He might not be feeling particularly festive, but she'd been looking forward to spending Christmas here with an almost childlike excitement, so, for her sake, he would make the effort to shake off the gloom. It wasn't going to be easy, but she'd tried so hard to cheer him up these past few weeks, he figured he owed her the same consideration.

After washing and dressing, he made his way downstairs and paused in the hallway when he saw Irena swaying her hips to the music as she peeled vegetables at the kitchen sink. The ugly bruises that had marred her face when she'd first arrived had completely disappeared, and her confidence had grown as the terrible fear she'd been feeling lost its power over her. She regularly went with him in the evenings to feed Yvonne's animals, which was nice, but she still wasn't quite brave enough to go out in daylight in case someone spotted her. Still, she seemed content to stay behind and take care of the house whenever Frank had to go out, and the place was as spotless as Maureen had always kept it.

Irena turned round at that moment, and jumped when she saw him standing there.

'Oh, Frankie, you scare me,' she chided, her hand on her breast. 'I did not hear you come down the stair. How long have you been stand there?'

'Sorry,' he apologized, grinning sheepishly as he walked into the room. 'Only a minute.'

'You cannot come in here,' she said. 'This is very special day and dinner must be perfect, so go find something else to do and give me peace.'

Frank didn't see why she was making such an effort when it was only going to be the two of them eating, but he raised his hands and backed away, saying, 'OK, I'll keep out of your way. But can I at least make myself a brew first?'

'Don't you need to go feed animal?' she asked.

'Bloody hell, you do want rid of me, don't you?' he chuckled.

'Yes, I need concentrate,' she said, shooing him out into the hall.

'Fine, I'll make myself a brew while I'm there,' he conceded.

'Good,' Irena said, handing his coat to him. 'And don't come back until two o'clock. Surprise will be ready by then.'

Wondering what on earth she had planned, Frank left her to it.

After he'd seen to the animals and finished his coffee, Frank still had a few hours to kill, so he decided to drive over to Leeds and pay Yvonne a quick visit. It was almost a month since she'd been admitted to hospital, and – to his shame – this would be the first time he'd been to see her. He'd been meaning to go for ages, but he never seemed to have the time – or the energy. Still, Irena wanted him out of the way, and he had nowhere else to go since Evan wasn't talking to him and he'd pretty much lost touch with his and Maureen's old friends, so he figured it was as good a time as any.

It was outside of visiting hours when he arrived at the hospital, but he located Yvonne's ward on the board and took the elevator up to the second floor, holding the box of chocolates he'd bought for her from a garage on the way.

The nurses' station was unmanned when he reached the ward, so he rested his elbow on the ledge and waited. Several minutes passed with no sign of any staff members, but just as he was about to go and look for someone, he spotted Yvonne lying in a bed at the far end of the ward and decided he might as well go over.

The patients in the other beds he passed were all deathly pale, and there was a peculiar odour in the air which reminded him of the smell he'd noticed in his and Maureen's bedroom during her last hours. Yvonne's eyes were closed when he reached her, and he was shocked to see how much older she looked than the last time he'd seen her. But being stuck in here, surrounded by these barely breathing skeletons, would have that effect, he supposed.

'Yvonne . . . ?' He touched her shoulder gently. 'Are you awake, love? It's Frank.'

At the sound of his voice, Yvonne opened her eyes and rolled her head over on the pillow. His heart sank when she gazed up at him as if she'd never seen him before, but then a spark of recognition flared in her eyes, and she gave a weak smile.

'Hello, pet. What are you doing here?'

'I came to see you,' he said, pulling a chair up to the side of the bed. 'To wish you happy Christmas and give you these.' He placed the chocolates on the bedside table.

'It is Christmas?' She frowned.

'All day.' He grinned. 'So, how are you, love?'

'Better now I've seen you,' she said, her voice dry and whispery.

'But you didn't need to put yourself out on a day like this. You should be at home with Mo and the little 'uns.'

Assuming that she mustn't have woken properly yet, Frank said, 'Maureen's gone, love. Don't you remember?'

'Gone?' Yvonne repeated, her wispy eyebrows creeping together. 'You don't mean she's left you? Oh, love, I'm so sorry. What on earth happened?'

Alarmed to realize that she thought Maureen was still alive, Frank wondered if the blow to her head had caused some kind of damage in there. If so, and he told her the truth, it might upset her, so he decided to play along instead.

'Everything's fine, love. Her mum's not too well, so she went to stay with her for a few days, that's all.'

'Oh, right.' Yvonne looked relieved. 'Sorry if you've already told me, I've been forgetting things left right and centre. Must still have baby brain, eh? So, you'll be having dinner over there with them, will you?'

'Yeah, I'm driving over soon as I leave here,' Frank said, wondering what she'd meant by baby brain.

'I don't suppose you could ask Mo to make up a plate for Don, could you?' Yvonne asked. 'He popped in to see me last night, and I don't think he's been eating properly.'

'Course I will,' Frank agreed, even more concerned that she thought her late husband was still alive – *and* that he'd visited her last night – considering it was a good ten years since he'd died.

'Thanks, love,' Yvonne said gratefully. 'I feel bad for leaving him on his own, 'cos he falls to bits when I'm not there. But I can't go home till Johnny's strong enough to come with me.'

Frank had never heard any mention of anyone called Johnny, so he wasn't sure who she was talking about.

'The poor little mite was crying all night,' Yvonne went on quietly. 'But that miserable bugger, Matron, wouldn't let me keep him in here in case he woke the other babies.'

'And, um, where is he now?' Frank asked, trying to remember if he'd ever heard mention of Yvonne and Don having a son.

'They took him to the nursery to give me a break,' Yvonne said, pulling a face as she added, conspiratorially, 'More like *they* wanted a break. But it's not his fault he's poorly, is it?'

'No, it's not,' Frank murmured, thinking this was all getting a bit surreal. 'I hope he gets better soon.'

'He'll be right as rain once I get him home,' Yvonne said. Then, giving a surreptitious nod in the direction of the desk, she said, 'Uh, oh . . . Matron's just walked in, and she doesn't look best pleased to see you.'

Frank glanced back over his shoulder and stood up when he saw a nurse striding toward them.

'I'd best get going,' he said, leaning down to kiss Yvonne's paper-thin cheek. 'I'll try to come and see you again soon.'

'I'll probably be home in a few days, so there's no need,' Yvonne said. 'But it was lovely of you to take time to see me today. And don't forget to make up that plate for Don.'

'I won't,' he promised. 'Take care, love.'

The nurse had reached them by then, and she said, 'You

shouldn't be in here. It's an acute care unit, and visiting hours are strictly regulated.'

'Sorry, but there was no one around to get permission from,' Frank apologized as she ushered him toward the door.

'We're on skeleton staff because of the holidays,' she replied curtly. 'You should have waited.'

'Sorry,' he said again. Then, hesitating when they reached the door, he said, 'Is Yvonne OK? Only she was saying some pretty weird stuff.'

'Are you a relative?'

'No, I'm her neighbour.'

'Then I'm afraid I can't discuss this with you.'

'I know you can't go into detail, but I've never seen her like this before,' Frank persisted. 'She's usually as sharp as a tack, but she was talking about people from the past as if they're still alive. She thinks my late wife is at home waiting for me, and she told me her husband visited her here last night, even though he's been dead for years. And she said you took her baby off her last night because he wouldn't stop crying. Do you think it might be related to the head injury?'

'She's being closely monitored,' the nurse replied. 'But it might help if one of her relatives came to see her, so maybe you could give them a nudge if you get the chance?'

'I've never actually met her family,' said Frank. 'I didn't even know she had a child, and I've known her for twenty-odd years.'

'Well, I suppose that explains why she's had no visitors since she was admitted,' the nurse said.

It felt like an accusation, and Frank's cheeks reddened as he said, 'I've been meaning to come in for ages, but I've got a lot on, so I haven't had the time.'

The look the nurse gave him told him that she'd heard a million such lame excuses from the friends and relatives of the close-to-death patients in her care, and he felt even more ashamed of himself.

At the sound of a buzzer, the nurse said, 'Sorry, I need to go and see to that.'

'Yeah, course,' Frank said, stepping out into the corridor. 'Happy Christmas,' he added, but she'd already closed the doors.

Sighing, he rode the lift back down to the ground floor and walked outside. If Yvonne had suffered some kind of trauma to the brain, he hoped it wasn't permanent, because he doubted she'd be allowed to go home while she was so far out of touch with reality. She would need looking after, and Social Services would probably step in and have her moved into a care home. Yvonne would absolutely hate that, but there would be nothing Frank or anyone else could do about it if her family couldn't be traced.

Making a mental note to have a little nose around in the cottage when he went to feed the animals that afternoon, to see if he could find an address for the mysterious Johnny, Frank climbed into his car and set off for home.

17

The bumper of a car was sticking out from the behind the wall at the back of the house when Frank pulled onto his drive, and his heart leapt as he wondered if Evan had decided to pay him a surprise visit. Quickly parking up, he unlocked the front door and smiled when he heard the low murmur of voices coming from behind the closed kitchen door. A male laugh rang out as he was slipping his coat off, and he paused and tipped his head to one side. It hadn't sounded anything like Evan's laugh, and he frowned as it occurred to him that it might not be his son, after all. But if it wasn't Evan, who was it? Irena would never have opened the door for someone she didn't know.

Nikolai . . . The name leapt into his head.

Had the man tracked her down and forced his way in?

Shaking now, Frank was looking around for something to use as a weapon when Irena's tinkling laugh drifted out to him. She didn't sound scared, so maybe it was Evan.

He opened the kitchen door with a half-smile on his lips, but it slipped when he saw Irena sitting at the table with two men he'd never seen before: one blond, with a tattoo of three teardrops running down from the corner of his eye; the other with jet-black hair, dark eyes, and heavily tattooed hands.

Irena spotted him and leapt to her feet.

'Ah, good, you are home.'

'What's going on?' he asked, warily eyeing the men.

'Is my surprise,' she said, placing her hand on the shoulder of the dark-haired one. 'Karel has arrive to spend Christmas with us. Is fantastic, yes?'

'Sorry?' Frank was thrown. 'I thought he was supposed to be in Prague? And how did he know where to find you?'

'I tell him address in email,' Irena said, her smile faltering. 'What is wrong? I think you will be happy for me.'

Something about the way the brother was looking at him made Frank feel uneasy. Irena had never mentioned his age, but from the way she'd spoken about him, Frank had assumed him to be a child. This man, however, appeared to be around the same age as her, if not older.

'Could I speak to you for a minute?' he asked Irena, backing out into the hall.

About to do as he'd asked, Irena hesitated when the man grasped her wrist and pulled her down to whisper into her ear. Frank's mind was spinning. He'd had no idea she was planning to invite her brother over, and it upset him that she hadn't thought to ask if he minded before going ahead. And where had she found the money to send for him, because Frank certainly hadn't given it to her?

Irena was the first to speak when she came out.

'Why are you behave like this?' she hissed, pulling the door shut behind her. 'I have tell them you are good man and will make them feel welcome, but you are treat them like stranger.'

'That's because they *are* strangers to me,' Frank replied quietly, guiding her into the living room, conscious that the men might be able to hear them. 'You should have told me he was coming and given me time to prepare, but I didn't even know he'd replied to your email.'

'You tell me to help myself to computer, so this is what I do. I think you would be happy for me.'

'I'd have been happier if you'd discussed it with me first. And who's the other one?'

'He is friend.' Irena folded her arms. 'He help bring Karel into country.'

'And are you expecting me to let them *both* stay?'

'Is this not my home, too, Frankie?' Irena frowned. 'Did you not ask me to stay and share your bed – like wife without ring?'

'Yes, but this isn't about you,' Frank argued. 'I know he's your brother, and you've been worried about him, but—'

The door opened before he could go on, and Karel strolled in.

'There is problem?' he asked, his accent even thicker than Irena's.

'No, there is no problem,' Irena said, her gaze fixed on Frank as if pleading with him to back her up.

For her sake, he smiled and extended his hand.

'It's nice to meet you, Karel.'

The man grasped his hand and gave it a vice-like squeeze. Sensing that it was deliberate, Frank willed himself not to react – and he resisted the urge to rub his crushed fingers when Karel released him.

'Sorry if I seemed a bit off when I came in,' he said, shoving his hands into his pockets to keep them safe. 'I've just come back from visiting my neighbour in hospital, and I'm a bit worried about her.'

'Is she get better?' Irena asked.

'It's hard to tell,' said Frank. 'She was saying some pretty weird stuff while I was there, but the nurse told me they're keeping an eye on her, so I'm hoping they'll find out what's wrong and fix it.'

Conscious of Karel's piercing stare as he spoke, Frank wondered if it was a symptom of the mental problem Irena had alluded to. She'd said their father found him difficult, and he was beginning to understand why, because the man had a decidedly menacing air about him.

The blond man walked into the room just then, and looked from Karel to Irena.

'What's happening? I'm starvin' me arse off out there while youse lot are having a chit-chat.'

Frank's eyebrows rose in surprise when he heard the man's Mancunian accent.

'Oh . . . you're British?'

'Yeah, *and*?' the man replied churlishly.

'Not now, Nick,' Irena murmured, flashing the man a hooded look.

A chill skittered down Frank's spine. Nick . . . Or *Nikolai*?

He'd been right. The man *had* tracked her down, and he'd forced his way in and made Irena lie about who he was so Frank wouldn't get suspicious. But why was her brother going along with that if he knew his sister was being abused?

Still studying Frank's face, Karel's eyes narrowed, and a sly smile lifted the corner of his thick lips.

'Is something wrong, *Frankie*?'

Confused to hear that the man's heavy accent had disappeared, Frank took a step back, saying, 'I know who you are, and you need to get out of my house right now.'

'Oh, dear . . . looks like we've been rumbled,' Nick chuckled.

'I mean it,' Frank barked, fumbling his phone out of his pocket. 'Get out, or I'm calling the police.'

Nick lunged at him before he had a chance to press any numbers and smacked the phone out of his hand. Watching as it skittered across the floor, Frank turned and snatched the house-phone out of its stand on the computer table. He jabbed his finger on the 9 button, but it was dead, and he realized they had disconnected it when he saw the wire on the floor.

Nick grabbed him by the front of his jumper and dragged him out from behind the chair before shoving him forcefully down onto the seat.

'Now be a good boy and you won't get hurt,' he said, placing a hand on each of the chair's arms and staring into Frank's eyes.

A surge of adrenaline brought Frank back up to his feet, and he slammed his hands into the man's chest and propelled him toward the door, yelling, '*GET OUT OF MY HOUSE!*'

Unfazed, Karel looked pointedly down at his friend's hand, and said, 'I'd calm down if I was you, old man.'

Frank hesitated and followed his gaze. Shocked to see that Nick was holding a gun, he raised his hands and backed slowly away, smashing his knee against the corner of the coffee table before falling heavily back onto his chair.

'What do you want?' he asked.

Karel looked at Irena and raised an eyebrow.

'Do *you* want to tell him, or shall I?'

'Tell me what?' Frank croaked.

'He still don't get it,' Nick sneered, slotting the gun into the waistband of his jeans.

'Yes, I do,' said Frank. 'You're the ones who held her prisoner and beat her senseless when she refused to sleep with the men you lined up to abuse her. She told me *everything*.'

'Don't tell me you actually fell for that shit?' Nick snorted.

Sweat was seeping from Frank's pores, and he felt it run down the side of his face when Karel mimicked Irena, saying: '*Oh, Frankie, help me. The bad man has brought me into the country and forced me into prostitution.*'

Unable to believe she was playing a voluntary role in whatever this was, Frank looked to her for answers, but she wouldn't – or couldn't – meet his eye.

'Aw, jeez, look at the muggy twat's face,' Nick jeered. 'She must have done a *proper* job on him.'

Karel grasped Irena's chin in his hand and turned her face toward him.

'How far did you go?' he asked, his voice deceptively soft.

'I already tell you I did not do anything with him,' she replied, coolly returning his gaze. 'He want to, but I tell him I am good Catholic girl and must wait till I am marry.'

'You'd better not be lying,' he said, putting his arm around her waist and pulling her toward him.

Shocked when the man gave her a decidedly *un*brotherly kiss, Frank gaped at them in disbelief.

'Ahhh, look at the lovebirds making up for lost time,' Nick crooned. 'Makes you feel all mushy, don't it, Frankie boy?'

Desperate to get these people out of his house, Frank remembered the money he'd withdrawn from the bank during one of his shopping trips a few weeks earlier. He'd intended to give it to Irena to pay her way to London and afford her a couple of nights in a hotel while she looked for work, but then they had decided to give their relationship a go, so she hadn't needed it.

'If it's money you're after, there's five hundred in an envelope in my bedroom,' he said. 'Just take it and go.'

Karel released Irena and wiped his mouth on the back of his hand.

'You think you can pay us off with five hundred poxy quid?'

'That's all I've got. There's some jewellery you might be able to get a few quid for, but please don't take my wife's wedding ring.'

'You can shove your jewellery up yer arse,' Nick said, coming up behind the chair and yanking Frank's head back. 'We know how much you've got in the bank, matey.'

Unable to move his head because the man had a tight grip on his hair, Frank looked at Irena out of the corner of his eye.

'You leave detail on computer, so was easy to see,' she said.

A bitter taste flooded Frank's mouth as he realized Jo and Evan had been right about her. They'd tried to warn him, but she'd flattered his ego, and – stupid old fool that he was – he'd lost his mind.

'Come on, now, Granddad, don't be stressing out and having another heart attack,' Nick purred down his ear, letting Frank know that they knew about his health problems as well as his account balance. 'We need you alive and kicking for what we've got in mind, so you just sit there and chill while we have some scran, then we'll bring you up to speed. And if you promise to be good, Reeny'll make you a nice brew to calm you down – yeah?'

Frank nodded and then held his breath as the three left the room. Chair legs scraped loudly on the kitchen floor tiles, and he could hear Irena taking plates out of the cupboard and cutlery from the drawer. They were going to sit and eat the food she'd been cooking when he'd left that morning – the food Frank had bought at her insistence, because – she'd claimed – she wanted to make this Christmas the most perfect one ever. It had all been a lie, because she'd known all along that these men would be here.

But she'd also lied to them, he realized, when she'd told Karel – if that was even his name – that nothing had happened between her and Frank. So maybe she wasn't that willing a participant, after all, and was only going along with this because she was terrified they would hurt her if she didn't?

His mobile phone suddenly started ringing, and he looked around, desperately trying to locate where it had landed. Just as he'd spotted it sticking out from under Maureen's chair and was about to go for it, Karel walked in holding Frank's shotgun.

'Don't even think about it,' he said, aiming the gun at Frank's head as he walked over to retrieve the phone. Picking it up, he glanced at the name on the screen and grinned. 'It's your son. Maybe he wants to make friends for Christmas, eh?'

'He'll get worried and come round if I don't answer,' Frank croaked.

'You'd best hope he doesn't, 'cos he won't be leaving again if he does,' said Karel. 'Now, answer it, and tell him to stay away. And don't say anything to make him suspicious, or I'll kill you and then go after him.'

'What am I supposed to say?' Frank asked when Karel tossed the phone onto his lap. 'He's not stupid; he'll be able to tell something's wrong.'

'Don't fuck with me,' Karel barked, smashing the gun into

the side of Frank's head. 'I told you what to do, so *do* it. And put it on loud-speaker so I can hear.'

The blow had cut Frank's temple, and blood trickled down the side of his cheek and dripped onto his sweater. Irena walked in carrying a cup of tea, and he was gratified to see a flash of alarm in her eyes. She might not love him, as she'd professed, but she couldn't have spent all this time alone with him and not feel anything, so if he could get through this call and make Karel believe he was co-operating, maybe he'd be able to talk to her on her own at some point; convince her to persuade the men to take whatever they wanted and leave.

'About time,' Evan said when, at last, Frank answered. 'I was about to give up.'

Acutely aware of the danger he'd be placing his son in if he screwed this up, Frank forced a cold edge into his voice, and said, 'Well, maybe you should have, because I've got nothing to say to you.'

'Come on, Pops.' Evan sighed. 'It's Christmas, and this has gone on for long enough. We both said and did things we didn't mean, so let's forgive and forget and start over, eh?'

'I've done nothing I need forgiving for,' Frank said, squeezing his eyes shut as he added, 'And attempted rape isn't so easy to forget, so I don't know what made you think I'd be willing to brush it under the carpet. I gave you ample time to apologize to Irena, and I tried to build bridges with you, but you didn't want to know, so that's that.'

'*Seriously?*' Evan sounded both hurt and angry. 'You still believe her about that?'

'Yes, I do,' said Frank. 'And I'm guessing you don't want Marie to find out about it, so I suggest you get on with your own life and leave me and Irena to get on with ours.'

'Is that a threat?'

'Take it however you like. But I love Irena, and I won't have you ruin this for me, so stay away.'

'Are you out of your fucking mind?' Evan yelled. 'You've only known her a few weeks, and look what she's done to us already with her lies. Mum would be rolling in her grave if she coul—'

Frank abruptly disconnected the call and breathed in deeply to calm his racing heart when Karel snatched the phone out of his hand. He'd dealt Evan a low blow by threatening to tell Marie about the accusation Irena had made against him, and he could only hope that his son would forgive him if he ever got the chance to explain. But it was the only thing he'd been able to think of to stop him from coming round.

Karel was staring at Irena when Frank looked up.

'What's this about rape?'

'Is nothing.' She returned his gaze as boldly as when she'd lied about her and Frank earlier. 'He came to stay, and he would have interfere with plan, so I accuse him of try to rape me to make Frank send him away.'

Karel put his hand around the back of her neck and pulled her face close to his.

'If you're lying . . .'

He left the rest unsaid, but Frank could tell by the frozen look on Irena's face that she knew exactly what he meant.

Seeming to decide that he believed her, Karel released his grip and turned to the door, saying, 'Give him his drink, then come and serve dinner.'

When the man had left the room, Irena placed the teacup on the table beside Frank. He grasped her by the wrist before she could turn away, and whispered, 'I know you're not as involved in this as they're making out, and if you help me get out of here, I promise I'll help you to escape as well. Close the kitchen door when you go back in there, and I'll be able to sneak out without them seeing me.'

For a moment, the Irena he'd thought he knew peered back at him. But then, shaking her head, she yanked her arm free and walked out without saying a word.

18

Marie's family had made short work of the huge Christmas dinner she'd cooked, and were now cracking each other up over a drunken game of charades. After all the worrying she'd done that week, stressing out about every little detail, wanting everything to be perfect, she was made up that it was going so well and the house was filled with laughter.

Evan wasn't so happy, though, and she could tell his heart wasn't really in it, even though he'd been making an effort to join in. He'd had no contact with his dad since coming home, and she knew it was getting him down, especially today, but he was too stubborn to make the first move. So, after dinner, she had forced his hand by ringing Frank and passing the phone to him.

He had gone into the kitchen to talk in private, and she'd hovered in the hallway, praying that it would go well and he'd cheer up. It didn't sound like it had, though, and when he went quiet, she went in and found him sitting at the table with a glum look on his face.

'How did it go?' she asked, as if she hadn't been listening.

'He wouldn't talk to me.' Evan sighed. 'Told you it was a waste of time.'

'I'm sorry.' Marie squeezed his shoulder. 'I only rang him because I know you're missing him, and I thought he'd be missing you.'

'Clearly not.'

'Don't let it get you down, love. It'll get sorted eventually.'

'I hope so,' Evan said miserably. 'Hearing his voice made me think of all the good times, and I don't want to lose him over a stupid misunderstanding.'

'Want to talk about it?' Marie asked, hoping that he wouldn't clam up like he usually did when she tried to broach the subject.

'Nah.' Evan shook his head. 'I'll go over tomorrow and talk to him face to face. But let's not go on about it today. You've put a lot of hard work into this, and I don't want to ruin it for you.'

He smiled, but Marie could tell it was forced, and she said, 'Why don't you go over there now, love? He's probably sitting on his own feeling as miserable as you, so go talk to him.'

'No, tomorrow will do,' Evan insisted, getting up and taking a can of beer out of the fridge.

Outside, the dog had heard Marie's voice and started whining and scratching the door.

'Pack it in!' Marie yelled.

'Let him in,' Evan said, tearing the tab off the can.

'You sure?' Marie gave him a dubious look. 'He'll only start begging for leftovers and sniffing crotches.'

'Good,' Evan said, leaning down to add, in a whisper: 'It might make your lot push off faster.'

'Don't be so mean,' she scolded.

'Only kidding,' he grinned. Then, taking a swig of beer, he wiped his mouth on his sleeve, and said, 'Right, come on, you. It's Christmas, so let's give that family of yours a party to remember.'

Happy that he'd decided not to let the situation with his dad cast a cloud over the day, Marie let the dog in and followed Evan into the living room.

PART TWO

19

'So, here's the plan . . .' Karel said.

He, Nick, and Irena had eaten, and they were now in the living room with Frank: the men lounging on the sofa with glasses of Frank's whisky in their hands; Irena perched on the arm beside Karel, a large glass of wine in hers.

'You're going to marry Irena.'

Conscious of Maureen smiling down at him from the photo on the mantelpiece, every fibre of Frank's being revolted, and he couldn't prevent himself from blurting out a horrified, '*No!*'

'You what?' Karel narrowed his eyes.

'I can't,' Frank spluttered, thinking on the spot. 'She's in the country illegally; we'd never get away with it.'

'Is she fuck illegal,' Nick snorted, picking a piece of turkey out of his teeth with his fingernail and examining it before eating it again.

'I don't understand.' Frank switched his gaze onto Irena. 'You said he'd taken your passport.'

'She says a lot of things, but it doesn't mean any of it's true,'

Karel said, placing a proprietorial hand on her knee. 'Now as I was saying . . . you'll marry her, and then you'll make a will leaving everything to her.'

'My kids would never accept that,' Frank said, guessing that they planned to kill him as soon as they got their hands on his money. 'My daughter used to work for a solicitor, so she'd definitely contest it. And there's nothing here of any value, anyway.'

'Your daughter is on the other side of the world, and by the time she hears about this it'll be too late,' Karel countered smoothly. 'And there's plenty of value here.' He waved his hand, indicating that he was talking about the house.

'And plenty of privacy, an' all, now we've got rid of that nosy old bint from the cottage,' Nick added.

'She's not dead,' Frank muttered, sickened to think that these thugs had attacked that defenceless old woman in her own home.

'Ah, well, you know what they say,' Nick smirked. 'If at first you don't succeed . . .'

It was clear to Frank that these people had targeted him in order to take his house off him, but why choose this crumbling old wreck when there were so many better farmhouses in the area?

Because the others are still active farms, he answered his own question. And they're all staffed by strapping young farmhands, with customers to supply, and firms to take regular deliveries from – all of which would make it hard, if not impossible, for anyone to launch a take-over and get away with it. Frank, on the other hand, was a sitting duck. His wife was dead, his daughter was in Australia, and he and his son were at logger-heads, so he had no one to fight for or with him. The lane finished in a dead-end, so there was little danger of passers-by witnessing anything strange and reporting it. And now these men had effectively got rid of Yvonne, there were no neighbours close enough to interfere with their plans.

'There's no way out, old man,' Karel said, grinning slyly as he pulled his phone out of his pocket and brought a photograph up on the screen. 'You'll do as you're told, or you won't be the only one who suffers.'

He turned the phone round and leaned forward, and Frank's blood ran cold when he saw a shot of Evan and Marie coming out of their house.

'There's more,' Karel said, quickly scrolling through the photos to find the one he wanted.

This time the image was of Jo's house, and Frank felt the blood rush to his head when he spotted his granddaughter at the living room window, which told him that the photograph had been taken before the family had left the country.

'As you can see, we've been planning this for some time,' Karel said, slotting the phone back into his pocket. 'And don't make the mistake of thinking your daughter's safe because she's in a different country, 'cos she'll be home soon, and we'll be at the airport to meet her and Miss Emily if you don't do as you're told.'

The sound of his granddaughter's name leaving the man's mouth caused Frank to almost throw up. Aware that he had no choice but to go along with it – for now – he said, 'OK, I'll do whatever you want. But you've got to leave my kids out of it.'

'Oi, Billy Big Balls, *we're* giving the orders, not you,' Nick scoffed.

'He look pale,' Irena said quietly to Karel. 'I think he need eat so he does not get sick. Can I get him plate?'

Looking at Frank, Karel said, 'Yeah, go on, then.'

Touched that, despite her involvement, she still had some level of compassion for him, Frank thanked her with his eyes when she glanced at him before making her way to the door – but he didn't allow himself to smile, for fear that it would enrage Karel and make him question her again.

Irena came back a few minutes later with a plate of food, and Frank picked at it as she took a seat on the sofa between the men. Karel draped his arm around her and reached for the TV remote, and all three settled down to watch the film he chose.

Out of the corner of his eye, Frank studied Irena's face as she watched the on-screen antics of a baby-faced boy trying to outwit two hapless burglars. Her entire demeanour had changed since the arrival of the men, and he could see no trace of the contented girl he had left a few short hours earlier. He didn't know which version was the real Irena – or how she had managed to fool him so completely. The bruises had definitely been real, though, because he'd seen them up close and had watched them fade. But had she voluntarily taken a savage beating in order to make her story more realistic, or had these men beaten her to force her into doing it?

He so wanted it to be the latter, but seeing her like this, sitting between the man she had said was her brother, and the one she'd claimed had held her prisoner and forced her into prostitution, Frank had to accept that it had all been an act – and he had fallen for it hook, line and sinker. And, worse, he'd fallen for *her*, destroying his relationship with his children in the process.

Too disgusted with himself to stomach any more food, Frank put his fork down and cleared his throat.

'I need to go to the toilet.'

'You'll have to wait,' Nick said without taking his eyes off the TV.

'Take him,' Karel ordered at the same time.

'I don't need an escort,' Frank said, standing up. 'I'm hardly going to do anything stupid and put my family in danger, am I?'

'Better safe than sorry,' Karel replied, clicking his fingers at Nick.

Grumbling that he didn't see why he had to do it, Nick grudgingly got up and, pulling his handgun out of the waistband of his jeans, jammed the barrel into Frank's back and shoved him out of the room.

Upstairs, Frank hesitated when Nick made to follow him into the bathroom.

'I wouldn't if I were you,' he said, rubbing his stomach.

'My gut's churning, and I reckon it's going to be pretty disgusting.'

Nick pulled a face and took a step back.

'Get on with it, then. But don't try anything, 'cos I'll be out here listening.'

Frank nodded and closed the door. Alone at last, he leaned his back against the wood and inhaled deeply, soaking up the familiar scents of the soap and the pine toilet cleaner in an effort to clear the smell of the cigarettes and the men's combined body odours out of his nostrils.

'Oh, Maureen, what have I done?' he whispered, squeezing his eyes shut. 'What the *hell* have I done?'

'Who you talking to?' Nick barked, rattling the handle. 'You'd better not have another phone in there, or I swear to God I'll blow your fuckin' head off!'

Frank quickly unlocked the door and held up his hands to show that he didn't have a phone.

'I was talking to myself,' he said, falling against the door frame when the man barged past him and scanned the room. 'And it was force of habit to lock it, but I'll leave it open this time.'

'Nah, I ain't taking chances,' Nick said. 'Do what you gotta do, and hurry up.'

Frank couldn't pretend that he needed to sit down with the man watching him, so he unzipped his fly and tried to urinate instead. But nothing happened.

Losing patience, Nick booted him in the back of his thigh.

'I told you to hurry up, dickhead!'

'I can't go with you watching me,' Frank croaked, putting his hand on the wall to keep his legs from buckling.

'You trying to tell me you've never had a slash in front of another bloke?'

'Not one who's aiming a gun at me, *no.*'

'Right, fuck this,' Nick said, pushing Frank back out onto the landing. 'You've had your chance, so don't bother asking me to fetch you up again.'

Evening crawled into night, and Frank's body stiffened as he sat rigidly in his chair while the others watched a seemingly endless stream of Christmas films. Irena had nodded off, her head resting on Karel's chest, and Frank guessed that the men, who were halfway through their second bottle of whisky, wouldn't be too far behind if their drooping eyes were anything to go by.

Karel had placed the shotgun on the coffee table, and a plan began to form in Frank's mind as his gaze drifted to it. It was closer to them than it was to him, and Nick still had the handgun stuffed in his waistband. But if both men closed their eyes, even for a second, he could easily grab it and use it to secure his escape. And once he was safely out of here, he would warn Evan and Marie to get out of their house and then call the police.

Karel suddenly stretched and sat up straighter, killing Frank's hopes of getting his hands on the gun.

'I'm going to bed,' he said, nudging Irena awake before

standing up. 'Go and get it warm for me. We're having the big room at the front.'

'That is Frankie's room,' she told him quietly as she sleepily rose to her feet.

'It's ours now,' he said, narrowing his eyes as he added, 'Unless there's a reason why you don't want to sleep in there with me?'

'His wife die in bed,' she said. 'And I do not want to sleep with death.'

'I'll have that one, then,' Nick said, covering a yawn with his hand as he, too, stood up.

'What about him?' Irena nodded in Frank's direction.

'He's going in the cellar,' Karel said, gesturing for Frank to get up.

'Is too cold,' Irena argued.

Karel narrowed his eyes.

'Why do you care if he's cold?'

'I do not care about him,' she replied evenly. 'But if he freeze, we lose everything. I have wait long time for you to leave prison and join me here, and I have suffer, so I do not want to risk him die before he sign papers.'

Karel pursed his thick lips thoughtfully. Then, nodding, he said, 'OK, he can sleep with his dead wife. Nick'll stay with him and keep an eye on him.'

'You can fuck that *right* off,' Nick protested.

If Frank had been in any doubt as to who was in control, Karel made it clear when he seized his friend by the throat and stared into his eyes.

'Who's the boss here? Me or you?'

'You,' Nick spluttered.

'Dead right,' Karel said, releasing his grip and patting the man's cheek none too gently. 'And don't forget it again, or you know what'll happen.'

'I still don't see why I've got to kip with him,' Nick muttered, rubbing his throat, on which the imprints of Karel's fingertips were blossoming. 'Give him some shit to knock him out if you're scared he's going to escape.'

'Right, here . . .' Karel took a small clear plastic bag containing tablets out of his pocket and tossed it to him.

'You don't have to do that,' Frank said. 'I've already told you I'm not going to try anything.'

'And I've already told you it's better to be safe than sorry,' Karel relied smoothly, putting his arm around Irena's waist and picking up the shotgun before ushering her out of the room.

'Just you and me now, Frankie boy,' Nick grinned, shaking four of the tablets out of the bag before sliding his gun out of his waistband. 'Here you go.' He handed the tablets over. 'Take them, then open your gob so I can make sure you've swallowed 'em.'

'I can't swallow them dry,' Frank said tersely. 'I need water.'

'Get 'em down your fuckin' neck,' Nick barked, swinging his arm back.

'OK!' Frank conceded, ducking his already injured head. 'I'll take them.'

'Good lad,' Nick sneered, watching as Frank stuffed the tablets into his mouth. 'Keep this up, and you an' me are gonna get along all right.'

Frank flashed him a venomous look as he forced himself to swallow the foul-tasting tablets. Karel was a dangerous man, he'd already seen that, but Nick was a dangerous idiot, and Frank would have to tread very carefully with him if he was to stand a chance of getting through this.

20

Frank's head was throbbing when he woke up, and he was confused to see that he was still dressed when he sat up and caught sight of his reflection in the dressing-table mirror. Frowning when he noticed a trail of dried blood down the side of his face and an angry-looking scab on his temple, he gingerly touched it and winced. It was really tender, and he wondered if he'd had one too many whiskies last night and taken a tumble.

The distinctive beeping of a reversing vehicle coming from outside cut through the fog in Frank's brain, and he shoved the quilt off his legs and staggered over to the window when he heard male voices. Squinting in the bright daylight that assaulted his eyes when he drew the curtain aside, he frowned when he saw three men unhooking a shabby caravan from the back of a Transit van. About to open the window to ask them what the hell they thought they were doing, he hesitated when another man emerged from the porch below and pointed toward the back of the house. The man suddenly turned his head, and

Frank inhaled sharply when memories of the previous day rushed back to him at the sight of his face.

At the sound of the key turning in the lock behind him, Frank snapped his head round and stared at Irena when she walked in carrying a steaming cup.

'Oh, you are awake,' she said, hesitating by the door. 'How are you feel?'

'How the hell do you *think* I feel?' he snapped.

Irena's eyes widened. Immediately feeling guilty, Frank sank down on his chair and raked his hands through his hair.

'Sorry,' he apologized. 'I didn't mean to shout.'

'Is OK,' she said, eyeing him warily as she came further into the room and placed the cup on the bedside table.

'No, it's not,' Frank countered, gazing over at her. 'Nothing about this is OK, and I'm really struggling to believe you're doing this of your own free will. You said you loved me.'

'It was lie.' Irena shrugged.

'If that's true, why lie to Karel about us?' Frank asked. 'If you getting with me was part of the plan, he'd have been all right with it, but you denied anything happened when he asked you.'

'I do not need to explain myself to you,' Irena said, turning to the door.

'No, you don't,' Frank agreed. 'But I don't really need you to, to be honest, because I can see what's going on. Karel's forced you into this, because he controls you, same as he controls that other one – Nick, or whatever his name is.'

'You are wrong,' Irena insisted. 'Karel is passionate man, and you mistake this for control. But you know nothing.'

Frank could tell by the proud tilt of her chin that she didn't want to believe – or admit – that her relationship with Karel might not be everything she'd convinced herself it was.

'I'm not trying to upset you,' he said softly. 'But I don't believe that everything we had was a lie. You might have set out to trick me, but I think your feelings changed when you got to know me, and you started to enjoy being here. Am I wrong?'

'Yes,' she said, bluntly. 'Karel is only man I love.'

'Then why sleep with me, when you knew I'd have let you stay in Jo's room for as long as you needed without strings?' Frank asked. 'And why did you have to drag Evan into it? If the plan was to get in here and take the farm off me, why couldn't you leave him out of it?'

'He got in way,' Irena said. 'And I do not want to talk any more. Drink tea. I will bring food later.'

'I know you're scared I'll tell Karel what we did, but I'm not going to do that,' Frank said before she stepped out onto the landing. 'All I ask in return is that you think about what you're doing, and if there's any small part of you that still cares about me, please help me to get out of this before it goes any further.'

Irena glanced back at him and chewed on her lip as if she wanted to say something. But just as Frank thought he had got through to her, someone called her name, and she quickly left the room, locking the door behind her.

Frank turned back to the window and saw Irena walk outside a few seconds later and go over to Karel. Unable to watch when the man pulled her up against him and kissed her full on the lips, Frank got up off the chair and walked round the bed to get the drink she'd left for him. Now that he'd remembered the tablets Nick had forced him to take, he sniffed the steaming liquid before taking a tentative sip. It smelled and tasted normal, and he assumed they must be reserving the drugs for night-time use, to make sure he was incapable of escaping.

Confident that the tea was safe to drink, Frank carried the cup back to his chair and watched through the net curtain as the Transit van was driven away and the caravan was pushed out of sight down the side of the house.

When Irena headed back inside a short time later, and Karel and the other men disappeared from view, Frank gazed out over the barren landscape and wondered how the hell he was going to get through this. The idea of marrying Irena and making a new will in her favour was ludicrous, and he couldn't believe that Karel thought it was going to be that easy. But they knew damn well that he would do anything to protect his children, so there was nothing he could do to stop them.

'Yet.'

The word slipped out from Frank's lips and took him by surprise, but it reminded him that all was not yet lost. It took time to organize a wedding – even one where there would be no genuine guests to cater for. They would have to apply for a licence and book a slot at the registry office. And, while they waited, they would have to keep him alive – which would give him time to find a way out of this.

21

Frank was still at the window when the Transit van came back two hours later, and he sat forward in his seat when it reversed onto the drive. Nick walked into view and opened its back doors, and Frank's eyebrows rose when four young women climbed out and looked around as if they had no idea where they were.

Karel strolled out from the porch, and Frank saw that he was grinning as he approached the group. One of the girls smiled back at him, and Frank guessed she was trying to impress him when she flicked her long black hair over her shoulders and straightened her back.

Irena had obviously noticed, too, because she marched over to the group with a tense expression on her face and quickly ushered the girls inside.

Curious to know what was going on, Frank rushed to the door and pressed his ear against the wood.

* * *

176

Downstairs, Irena had lined the girls up in the hallway.

'Why are we here?' one of them asked, gazing around in confusion. 'This is not what I was promise.'

Nick walked in before Irena could answer, and said, 'OK, ladies, hand your shit over, then Reeny'll get you settled in.'

'I need to call my mother and let her know I have arrive,' another girl said, clutching the holdall she was carrying to her stomach.

'Don't worry, we'll let your folks know you got here safe and sound,' Nick said, holding out his hand. 'Come on . . . give it up.'

'I think there is mistake,' the first girl piped up. 'Alexander promise me apartment in city, so I am not stay here.'

Nick snapped his head round and stared at her through narrowed eyes.

'You'll stay wherever I say you're staying,' he said, all trace of joviality gone. 'Now shut your gob, and hand your bag over. Unless you want me to take it off you? In fact, why don't I do that anyway?'

'Get off me!' the girl protested, her voice high-pitched with fear as she clung on to her bag. 'I want see Alexander, or I will—'

Nick lashed her across the face with the back of his hand, and then grabbed her by the hair.

'Let's get one thing straight, bitch,' he spat. '*I'm* the boss here, and you'll do as you're told if you ever wanna see your family again.

'And that goes for you lot, an' all . . .' He looked at each of the others in turn. 'You owe us a shitload of money for fetching you over here, and you'll be working for us till it's paid off. Now quit your snivelling, and get your fuckin' arses upstairs before the rest of you get what *she's* about to get.'

At the sound of footsteps stumbling up the stairs, Frank pressed his ear harder against the door. He could hear crying and guessed that the girls were beginning to realize they'd been tricked. It sounded exactly like the scenario Irena had described when he'd found her that night, and it sickened him to think that she had drawn on the suffering of previous victims in order to fool him into taking pity on her.

The group reached the landing, and Frank listened as Irena ushered them past his door.

'What is happen to Viktorya?' one of the girls asked fearfully, at the sound of a muffled scream from down below. 'Why is that man hurt her?'

'Go into room, and do not make noise,' Irena replied quietly. 'She will be OK.'

A door opened and then closed, and Frank moved over to the wall that divided his and Evan's bedrooms. He could hear the girls whispering tearfully to each other on the other side, but he couldn't understand a word they were saying. Wherever they were from, it didn't appear to be the same country as Irena, because she'd addressed them in English. From the brief glimpse he'd had of them, they all appeared to be in their late teens or early twenties, and it broke his heart to think how scared they must be right now – and how worried their parents were going to be when they didn't hear from them.

Nick had taken the girl into the living room by the time Irena went back downstairs after locking the other girls into Evan's old room. The door was closed, but she could hear the slaps, threats, and screams as clearly as if she were in there with them. It was a harsh introduction to a life she had neither asked for nor expected, but the girl would quickly learn that these men tolerated nothing less than absolute obedience.

Cold air circled Irena's ankles when the back door suddenly opened, and she looked round as Karel walked in. Hesitating when he heard the girl scream, he said, 'What's going on?'

'One of the girls was argue with Nick, so he take her in there,' Irena told him.

Karel stalked past her and burst into the living room. The girl was on her back on the floor, her bottom lip was split, and both eyes were swollen. Standing over her, Nick raised his fist to deliver another blow, but Karel grabbed him before he had the chance to land it, and threw him across the room where he landed heavily on the sofa.

'What the *fuck*?' Nick squawked, leaping up to his feet.

'Who said you could touch her?' Karel roared, slamming him up against the wall.

'She was gobbing off, so I was teaching her a lesson,' Nick spluttered, his face flushed and sweaty. 'What was I supposed to do? Let her make a prick of me?'

'Look at the state of her . . .' Karel said angrily. 'How the fuck am I meant to send her out like that?'

'It ain't my fault,' Nick argued. 'She should've done as she was told.'

'*I* would have dealt with her.'

'You weren't here.'

As the men continued to argue, the injured girl hauled herself up onto her knees, and Irena could see the pain on her face when she clutched at her ribs. It reminded Irena of the beating Nick had given her before dropping her off at the end of the lane that night. He'd told her that it would make her cover story more realistic, but she had quickly realized that the violence was turning him on, and she remembered fearing that he was going to rape her. She had been saved by the intervention of one of the other gang members that night, just as this girl had been saved by Karel today. But others hadn't been so lucky – and there would be more of those in the future, she was sure.

Karel's mobile beeped, and he released Nick and pulled the phone out of his pocket. There was silence while he read the message on the screen, then he jerked his chin up at Irena, saying, 'Go and clean her up. I need to make a call.'

Irena helped the girl to her feet and led her into the kitchen. Livid bruises were blooming around her eyes, and her lip looked as if it might need a couple of stitches. But Karel would never allow her to be seen by a doctor at this early stage, so Irena sat her down at the table, then filled a bowl with warm water and added a liberal pouring of salt before taking a roll of cotton wool out of the drawer.

As she was about to get started, the girl grasped her hand, and sobbed, 'I want go home, lady. Please help me. *Please* . . . I beg you!'

'Don't speak,' Irena said, sliding her hand free and gently swabbing the blood off the girl's lip and chin.

'Is hurt,' the girl wailed.

'Sshhh,' Irena urged. 'The salt will make numb.'

Karel walked into the room, and Irena stepped aside and watched as he cupped the girl's chin in his hand and examined her face. His eyes were narrowed, and Irena guessed he was mentally assessing how long it would take before she'd be fit enough to be put to work. She was incredibly pretty, with long black hair and huge blue eyes, and Irena hadn't been impressed by Karel's reaction to her flirtatious smile outside. But she hadn't been brought here for Karel to toy with, and it seemed his mind was back on business when he took two small white tablets out of a bag and dropped them into her hand.

'Take these. They'll help with the pain until I can get something stronger.'

'Wh-what is it?' she asked, gazing warily up at him.

'Don't question me,' he said, his voice deceptively smooth as he stroked her cheek with the back of his fingers.

Frowning when the girl gave him a tiny smile, Irena poured a glass of water and handed it to her, trying to speed the process along.

'What's your name?' Karel asked.

'Viktorya,' the girl replied shyly, dipping her head – as if, Irena thought, she didn't want him to see her at anything but her absolute best.

'Beautiful name for a beautiful girl,' Karel smiled, seeming to have forgotten – or simply not caring – that Irena was standing right there. 'Now, take your tablets so we can make you more comfortable. Yes?'

The girl nodded and carefully slid one of the tablets between her damaged lips. Watching Karel as he watched the girl swallow, Irena forced herself to maintain a neutral expression. She wasn't sure what the tablets were, but the *something stronger* would probably be heroin, because that was what he usually gave them. And once she was hooked, he would no longer be interested.

When both tablets had been swallowed, Karel patted the girl's shoulder. Then, turning to Irena, he said, 'Take Viktorya to her room so she can get some rest, then make the men a drink and something to eat.'

'Will you be long?' Irena asked, but he walked out without replying.

Following him with her eyes, Viktorya looked up at Irena when he and Nick had left the house.

'He is your husband?'

Irena shook her head and walked over to the bin to dispose of the bloodied cotton wool.

'He treat you like wife,' Viktorya said, her voice sounding a little slurred.

'This is because he love me, and we *will* be marry,' Irena said, asserting her authority to let the girl know that there was no point flirting with him again. 'Now come . . .' She held out her hand. 'You need rest.'

'I do not feel good,' Viktorya said, swaying when Irena helped her to her feet.

Aware that the drugs Karel had given her were taking hold and she could fall unconscious at any moment, Irena opened the back door and called for one of the men who were outside cleaning the caravan to come inside.

'What's up?' Gaz Ahmed asked, wiping his hands on a dirty rag as he strolled in.

'I need help to take girl to bed,' Irena told him, nodding at Viktorya who was slumped in the chair, mouth open, eyes rolling in their sockets.

Gaz looked at the girl, and Irena saw anger flare in his dark eyes.

'Nick?' he said, more statement than question.

Irena nodded but didn't elaborate. All the men on Karel's payroll were capable of extreme violence, and that was why he kept them close and paid them so well. Nick aside, Irena had never seen any of them mistreat a woman, and Gaz, in particular, had always been polite and courteous. But, still, she would never make the mistake of badmouthing one of his friends to him, because she'd long ago learned that the men's loyalties lay firmly with each other.

'I will stay here to make drinks,' she said when Gaz scooped

Viktorya gently up off the chair. 'Leave her with other girls, and please do not forget to lock door.'

Nodding, Gaz carried Viktorya out as if she weighed little more than a feather. When he'd gone, Irena filled the kettle and placed bread under the grill while she waited for it to boil.

Gaz trotted back down the stairs a few minutes later.

'The farmer needed the loo, so I took him,' he told her. 'Now he reckons he needs his medication. He says you know where it is?'

'I will take to him once I have serve men,' Irena said, placing the plate of toast she'd just buttered onto a tray alongside the cups of tea she'd poured from the big pot.

'You're all right, I'll take it,' Gaz said, picking the tray up. 'You go see to him.'

He carried the tray outside, and Irena watched through the window as the other men climbed out of the caravan and sat down on the ground to eat and drink. Pouring another cup of tea from the pot, she carried it into the living room and fished Frank's tablets out of the pot on the mantelpiece before heading up to his room.

The girls would only be allowed water today, and – depending on Karel's mood when he came back – maybe a slice of toast later in the evening. He believed that depriving them of nourishment speeded up the spirit-breaking process, but Irena doubted they'd be able to stomach much anyway. And once he got them hooked on smack, food would be the last thing on their minds.

* * *

Frank was pacing the bedroom floor, but he abruptly stopped when the door opened. Irena walked in, and he saw that the deep shadows that had surrounded her eyes on the night they'd first met had reappeared. She was obviously under pressure, but it was of her own making, so he refused to feel pity for her.

'What happened to that girl?' he demanded. 'I asked your *friend*, but he wouldn't tell me anything.'

'Do not worry about her,' Irena said, holding out the cup and the foil strip of tablets.

'How can I not worry?' Frank snapped, snatching them from her hands. 'This is *my* house, in case you've forgotten, and it sickens me that this is happening under my roof. Aren't you ashamed of yourself? Can't you hear those poor girls crying in there?' He jabbed a finger in the direction of the wall. 'Or don't you care?'

'They will settle in time,' she replied, her gaze dipped.

Frank's eyebrows knitted together.

'Is that what you really think, or something you say to make yourself feel better about what you're doing? Because, I've got to tell you, I'm struggling to believe that the Irena I know and lo—' He choked on the word and swallowed it, before saying, 'This is pure evil – and *you're* evil for going along with it.'

'I am not evil,' Irena protested, colour flaring across her cheeks. 'I am try to protect them.'

'Bullshit! I heard what Nick did, and you didn't even *try* to stop him. Christ, Irena, what the hell happened to make you so cold?'

'There is only so much I can do. The rest is up to them.'

'*Them* being those girls in there, or those thugs you call your friends?'

'I cannot discuss this with you any more.'

'Can't, or *won't*?' Frank asked. Then, holding up his hand before she could answer, he said, 'You know what, I don't want to hear it. I thought I knew you, but I was wrong. So, well done, love, you fooled me good and proper. Now get out, because I can't bear to look at you.'

If he'd said this to one of the men, Frank had no doubt he'd have been given a taste of whatever Nick had done to that girl. But Irena merely nodded and left the room, locking the door behind her.

Alone again, Frank hurled the tea at the door and threw the cup onto the bed before marching over to the window. He'd seen Karel and Nick drive away in the Transit ten minutes earlier, but he knew at least one of the other lackeys was still here.

Right on cue, one of the men strolled around to the front of the house and lit a cigarette before leaning against the gatepost. Moving away from the window when the man glanced up at the house, Frank looked at the tea still dripping down his door and cursed himself for tossing it. His mouth was bone dry, and he needed to take his tablet to steady his racing heart, but he had a feeling that Irena wouldn't bring him another drink anytime soon after the way he'd spoken to her.

Whisky.

Remembering the bottle he'd brought up to his room the night Irena had arrived, he rushed over to the side of the bed and reached into the space between the bed-base and the bedside cabinet. He'd half expected it to have been removed, but it was still there, and he pulled it out and quickly unscrewed the cap. Neat alcohol wasn't ideal when he needed to keep his wits about him, but he was too thirsty to care right then. Anyway, he needed something to wash his tablet down.

The one swig he'd intended to take turned into several more, and he lay down on the bed and closed his eyes when he felt the tension lifting from his shoulders.

22

The sky was darkening when Frank woke up, and deep shadows were creeping across the room. Blinking the sleep from his eyes when he heard male voices and laughter drifting up through the floorboards, along with the clatter of crockery and cutlery, he glanced at the clock and guessed that Irena must have called the men in for dinner when he saw that it was 5 p.m.

Getting up, he went over to the window to check if the van was back. It wasn't, and he couldn't see anyone standing guard, so he cracked the window open and listened intently for sounds of movement or talking. When all he heard was wind and the evensong of birds, he leaned out a little further and looked down the lane. There was no sign of headlights in the distance, so he pushed the window all the way open. Clambering onto the ledge, he twisted his body round and dropped his legs down until he was hanging by his fingertips. It was a long way down to the gravel, and he squeezed his eyes shut and said a silent prayer before letting go.

He landed feet first, and gritted his teeth to prevent himself from crying out when an excruciating pain shot up his legs. Aware that he was on borrowed time, he hobbled over to the thick hedgerow that separated his garden from the lane. Ignoring the pain as the branches tore at his hands, he pushed his way into the hedge. Halfway through, he glanced back at the house. Nobody had appeared at the door or windows, so he pushed on through the hedge until he fell out onto the lane on the other side.

Driven on by pure adrenaline, Frank forced his aching legs to carry him into the field. There, he paused and looked around, trying to decide which route would be best to take. If he went forward through the field he'd have two miles to walk and a wide stream to cross before he reached Thornley's dairy farm. To the right, he'd be faced with trying to navigate his way around the disused quarry – and that was a treacherous enough job in daylight, never mind in darkness. To the left, he'd be able to get to Yvonne's place and use her phone to call for help before finding somewhere to hide.

The latter option would undoubtedly be quickest, but he would have to crawl through the field to get there, because he'd be spotted in an instant if those in the house discovered that he'd gone and came out to look for him. And it was also the first place they would come looking for him when they realized he'd gone.

Just as he'd decided it would be safest to go forward and head for Thornley's farm, Frank picked up the distinctive rumble of a diesel engine in the near distance, and when he looked round, he saw two faint orbs of lights coming over the rise some three hundred yards past Yvonne's place. Aware that it was the Transit when he picked up the repetitive bass beat of the awful music he'd heard playing when Karel and Nick had driven away from the house earlier, Frank threw himself down to the ground and slithered into a shallow trench.

Peeking over the edge of the dry soil, he watched as the Transit pulled onto his driveway a few seconds later, and his already pounding heart felt as if it might explode right out of his chest when Nick leapt out of the driver's seat, yelling: 'His window's open! The cunt's escaped! *Fuck!*'

There was more shouting, then Frank winced when Karel bellowed at Irena that it was her fault, followed by the sound of a sharp slap and a cry of pain.

'Shut the fuck up, you stupid bitch!' Nick joined in. 'I told him you couldn't be fuckin' trusted, and now look what you've done!'

'I'll deal with her,' Karel barked. 'You lot get out there and start looking for him. He's old and knackered, so he can't have gone far.'

From his hiding place, Frank watched the men come out onto the lane and head off in different directions. Aware that they would easily spot him if they came this way, he was trying to cover himself with soil and dead branches, when he heard Nick hiss, 'Someone's coming! Everyone back to the house.'

Releasing a shuddering breath of relief when he heard footsteps running in the opposite direction, Frank raised his head an inch when he heard the vehicle Nick had seen. It was still a fair way down the lane, but he could see the England flags attached to its roof-rack flapping in the wind, and his stomach flipped when he realized it was Evan's car. Aware that his son would get hurt – or worse – if the men got their hands on him, Frank scrambled to his feet and, dragging himself out of the trench, limped back to the house.

Karel and Nick were hiding behind the Transit when Frank staggered up the driveway, and he held up his hands when he saw they were both holding guns.

'Please don't hurt him,' he begged. 'It's me you're after, not him, so let me get rid of him and then I promise I'll do whatever you want.'

'Nah, mate, you've fucked us off, so now you're both gonna get it,' Nick spat, aiming the gun at him.

'If you kill us, you'll have to leave here and start over somewhere else,' Frank reminded him. 'Evan's wife will report him missing if he doesn't go home, and the police will come straight here. You said you've been planning this for ages, so are you really willing to jeopardize everything because you're pissed off with me?'

Evan was turning onto the drive by then, and Karel narrowed his eyes thoughtfully in the glare of the car's headlights.

'OK, get rid of him,' he said quietly. 'But, remember – I *will* kill him if you say the wrong thing.'

'Yeah, and then I'*ll* kill *you*,' Nick added nastily as he reluctantly stuffed his gun into his waistband.

Evan was out of the car and walking toward them. Thinking on his feet, Frank turned to face him.

'What are *you* doing here? I thought I told you to stay away?'

'We need to talk,' Evan said. Then, frowning when he noticed the blood on the side of his father's face, the dry leaves stuck to his sweater and the debris in his messed-up hair, he said, 'What's happened? You look like you've been dragged through a hedge backwards.'

'I fell over,' Frank lied, folding his arms. 'It's nothing.'

Unsure if he believed him, Evan eyed the other men and the van, and asked, 'Are you having work done on the house?'

'No, this is Irena's brother, and their friend.' Frank nodded at Karel and Nick in turn. 'Now, if you're finished with the inquisition, we've got things to do.'

Aware that he was being dismissed, Evan stood his ground.

'You're my father, and if you can put yourself out for this lot, don't you think I deserve the same consideration?'

'What's *this lot* supposed to mean?' Nick stepped forward aggressively. 'You some kind of fuckin' racist, or summat?'

Unfazed, Evan peered down into the smaller man's eyes, and said, 'No, I'm not. And this has got nowt to do with you, so why don't you back off and let me talk to my dad in private, eh?'

Aware that the guns could be brought out again as quickly as they'd been stashed away, Frank stepped between them, saying, 'It's OK, I'll deal with this.'

'There's nothing to deal with,' Evan said, tempering his tone as he turned to address his father again. 'I came to talk, not argue, so can't we—'

'No!' Frank interrupted sharply. 'I told you you're not welcome here, and I haven't changed my mind, so go home. *Now,*' he added, emphasizing the word with his eyes, praying that his son would pick up on the hidden message he was sending.

Evan stared back at him for several seconds, but just as Frank was beginning to fear that he wasn't going to give up, Karel walked over and clapped a hand on Evan's shoulder.

'Is sad when father and son disagree, and I can see this is upset you,' he said, adopting the same thick accent he'd initially used on Frank as he walked Evan back to his car. 'I will speak to him on your behalf, but I think is best if you respect his wishes and leave now. Yes?'

Evan breathed in deeply and pursed his lips thoughtfully as he looked back at his father. Then, nodding, he called, 'OK, Dad, I'm going. But I'm not to blame for any of this, and I'm not mugging myself off by apologizing for something I didn't do, so this is the last time you'll see or hear from me until you come to your senses.'

Frank's heart was breaking, but he held Evan's gaze, and shrugged.

'Fine by me.'

As soon as Evan had driven away, Nick aimed a savage kick at the back of Frank's thigh, sending him crashing to the ground.

'Don't touch his face!' Karel barked when Nick drew his leg back to kick Frank in the head. 'His son looked suspicious, and he might come back.'

Reluctantly dropping his foot, Nick pulled out the gun, and dragged Frank up to his feet.

'Inside, dickhead. And don't even think about trying to get away again, 'cos you won't be so lucky next time.'

As he drove away, Evan glanced in the rear-view mirror, but all he could see was the roof of the Transit above the hedge. Something had felt off back there, but he wasn't sure what his instincts were trying to tell him. He hadn't expected his dad to welcome him back with open arms given the tense conversation they'd had on the phone the previous day, but the coldness his dad had displayed toward him was totally out of character. And what was the deal with that gobby little twat who'd tried to front up to him? His dad had said he was a friend of Irena and her brother, but he was Mancunian, so it had to be someone she'd met during her marriage – in which case, why hadn't she gone to *him* for help when her husband started abusing her?

Those questions aside, the look his dad had given him when he'd told him to leave had been weird – almost, Evan thought, as if he'd been trying to warn him off. And then there was that cut on his head. It definitely hadn't been fresh, because the blood was dry, so why hadn't he washed it off?

As annoyed as Evan still was that his dad had taken Irena's word over his, Evan loved him and needed to know he was all right, so he stamped on the brake and did a quick U-turn. There was no point going back to the farm after the reception he'd received, and he doubted his dad would answer his phone if he tried to call him, so he decided to go to Yvonne's and ask *her* to call him instead. His dad wasn't overly fond of her, but she'd been his wife's best friend, so he would come round if she told him she needed help with something. And then Evan would be able to talk to him without Irena's brother and their runt mate listening in.

The cottage was in darkness when Evan pulled onto the drive a couple of minutes later, and Yvonne's rusty little car was parked exactly where it had been the last time he'd been there. He hadn't thought to ask his dad how she was doing, but he couldn't imagine they'd have kept her in hospital for this long, so he guessed she was probably sleeping.

Driving round to the rear of the cottage, in case someone drove past and alerted his dad that he was here, he parked outside the back door. The pigs started squealing and grunting when he climbed out from behind the wheel, so he went over to check on them before knocking on the door. Both troughs were empty, but he remembered where the feed was stored from when he'd helped his dad out that week, so he filled one with that and the other with water before going back to the cottage.

There was no answer when he knocked, and no signs of life when he peered through the windows, so he went round to the front door and rang the bell a couple of times before raising the flap of the letterbox. All he could hear were cats meowing, and the stench of ammonia turned his stomach, so he quickly dropped the flap and scratched his head thoughtfully. If Yvonne wasn't home, why hadn't his dad been round to feed the pigs? And if he hadn't fed them, he wouldn't have fed the cats, either.

Unless Yvonne *was* here, and she'd had another fall and couldn't get to the door.

Concerned, he walked round to the shed where Yvonne's late husband's tools were still stored, and, using the flame of his cigarette lighter, rooted out a crowbar. Using it to jemmy the kitchen window open, he climbed in and dropped down onto the tiled floor.

Yvonne's cats swarmed in from the hall when they heard him, and he almost lost his balance when they circled his ankles. The stench was even stronger in there, and he grimaced when he switched the overhead light on and saw little piles of shit dotted around the floor. Their bowls were empty, so he took a couple of tins of food out of the cupboard and quickly shared them out before making his way into the hall.

Yvonne's bedroom was at the front of the cottage, overlooking the lane. A heap of unopened letters was sitting on the hall table beside the front door, and he wondered if maybe Yvonne *had* been kept in hospital, after all. Deciding that he'd best check, just in case, he tapped on the door and slowly opened it, but the bed was empty, and the air smelled musty, as if no one had been in there for a long time.

Coughing when the dust he'd disturbed tickled the back of his throat, Evan closed the door and went back to the kitchen. The cats had finished eating, and the stench of fresh shit made him gag, so he rushed out through the back door, pulling it firmly shut behind him to prevent the cats from escaping.

23

The petrol station was still open when Evan reached the village, so he pulled in and filled his tank. Going inside to pay, he added forty cigarettes to the bill, and, on impulse, a wilting bunch of roses out of a bucket that was standing on the counter. It had taken a while for things to get back to normal between him and Marie, but they'd been getting on a lot better since they'd both committed to putting the effort in, and he figured she deserved a treat.

Back in the car, Evan laid the flowers on the passenger seat and lit a fag before starting the engine. About to set off, he hesitated when he spotted a white Transit van driving past. Sure that it was the one he'd seen parked outside his dad's place, he frowned when he glimpsed a girl's face through its grimy back window. It wasn't Irena, because she was blonde and the girl he'd seen had been dark-haired, and that made him wonder how many *more* strangers his dad had invited into his home.

Curious to know where the van was going, he hopped out of the car and removed the England flags before setting off after it. Whoever was in the van, he doubted they'd recognize his car if he stayed a few vehicles behind, but those flags would be a dead giveaway.

The Transit left the village and headed onto the motorway. Keeping it in his sights, Evan followed at a distance all the way to Manchester. At the exit, he usually took a right, but the van turned left, so he did, too. It drove through the city centre and on into the backstreets of Moss Side, before eventually coming to a stop on the driveway of a shabby, three-storey Victorian house in Whalley Range.

Evan pulled in behind an old camper van that was parked some way back and on the opposite side of the road from the house, and watched as the gobby Mancunian got out of the driver's side and walked round to the back of the Transit. A taller man with dark hair emerged from the passenger side, and Evan murmured, 'What the *hell* . . . ?' when they opened the rear doors and not one, but three young women climbed out. In the few seconds they were standing there before the men hustled them up the path, the girls' faces were illuminated by the sickly yellow glow of a streetlamp, and Evan thought they looked confused – as if they had no idea where they were, or what they were doing there.

A couple of minutes passed before the van's reversing lights came on, and Evan slid down in his seat when it backed off the drive and drove past him. Eyeing its tail-lights in the rear-view mirror, he almost jumped out of his skin when someone tapped on the passenger-side window, and he looked round to see a hooded man with sunken eyes and gaunt cheeks gesturing for him to lower the window. Wary, because he knew this area was a hotspot for muggings and car-jackings, Evan rolled it down an inch and jerked his chin up.

'S'up?'

'Five-O?' the man asked, his shifty eyes darting every-which-way.

'Eh?' Confused, Evan pulled a face. 'What you on about?'

'You ain't a fed, then, no?'

Understanding now, Evan shook his head.

'So what you lookin' for?' the man asked. 'Green, brown, or white? I ain't got nothin' on me, but I can go and get it if you give us the dough upfront.'

It was on the tip of Evan's tongue to tell him to fuck off, but, instead, he dipped his head to get better eye contact, and nodded toward the house where he'd seen the men take the girls.

'I don't suppose you know what goes on in there, do you?'

The man gave a sly grin, displaying heavily stained teeth.

'What's it worth?'

Evan slid his wallet out of his pocket and took out a fiver. He lowered the window another notch, and the man snaked his arm through the gap and made a grab for the note. Sensing that he'd take it and run without giving the info he was being paid for, Evan held on to it.

'It's a whore house, innit?' the man said, playing tug-of-war with the note. 'But if it's pussy you're after, I wouldn't go near that one, 'cos it's run by some proper psychos. There's a better one on Lloyd Street.' He jerked his head back to indicate the direction. 'Big white place – you can't miss it. My bird works there. Tell her TK sent you and she'll see you right.'

Muttering, 'Cheers,' Evan let go of the note and slid the window back up as soon as the man withdrew his hand.

The man scuttled away, and Evan narrowed his eyes as he turned his attention back to the house. So those girls were prostitutes, and the house was a brothel. But were those men the psycho owners the dealer had mentioned, or were they just drivers who dropped the girls off and picked them up? Either way, he doubted his dad knew about it, because the old man would never allow something like this to happen under his roof.

Determined to warn him, Evan tried to call his dad. It went straight to voicemail, but he didn't want to leave a message in case one of the other men heard it, so he tossed the phone onto the passenger seat.

There was definitely something dodgy going on, and the weird look his dad had given him was playing on his mind. He'd thought at the time that it seemed like some kind of warning, but had his dad actually been trying to communicate that *he* needed help?

No . . .

Evan shook the thought out of his head as he started the engine and pulled out of the space. His dad might be gullible and too generous for his own good, but he wasn't stupid enough to invite people into his home if he thought they posed a threat to him. So did he already know what they were doing, and was he – God forbid – involved in it?

His mobile started ringing on the seat beside him as he drove down the road, and he saw Jo's name on the screen when he glanced at it. He'd told her he was going to visit their dad today to try and build bridges, and she'd be calling to ask how it went. She was already up in arms about their dad copping off with Irena, and if she heard that the bitch's brother and those other men had now moved in, along with three prostitutes, she'd go off her nut and order Evan to call the police and have them removed. But he couldn't do that until he knew what his dad's involvement was, so he ignored the call and drove on.

Marie was watching TV when Evan arrived home, and she quickly shoved the dog off her lap when he walked into the living room. Evan acknowledged the action with a smile, and leaned down to kiss her on the cheek before presenting her with the flowers. Her babying of the creature had always grated on his nerves, and he appreciated that she was making an effort to curb the habit – in front of him, at least.

'Aw, they're lovely,' Marie said, admiring the lacklustre roses. Then, narrowing her eyes, she tipped her head to one side and gave him a mock-accusing look. 'What've you done?'

Feeling guilty, even though he knew she was joking, Evan forced a laugh, and said, 'I haven't done anything, you daft bat. I was trying to be romantic, but I can easy take 'em back if you don't want them.'

'Don't you dare!' Marie snatched them away when he held out his hand, and stood up. 'I'll put them in a vase.'

'Have we got any booze left?' Evan asked, shrugging his jacket off and looping it over the back of the sofa before sitting down. 'Or did your lot finish it all off yesterday?'

'There might be a couple of beers in the fridge.'

'Nothing stronger?' Evan kicked his trainers off and put his feet up on the coffee table.

'I think there might be a bit of vodka,' Marie said, slapping his feet down before picking the jacket up and walking out into the hall. 'How did it go with your dad?'

'Yeah, it was OK,' Evan lied. 'We had a good chat.'

'That's good,' she called back over her shoulder as she made her way into the kitchen.

Evan flopped his head back and raked his fingers through his hair. He wished he could tell her what was going on, but he couldn't risk her letting something slip if Jo rang while he was out.

Marie came back with the now-vased flowers and a glass of vodka and coke. Standing the vase on the mantelpiece, she sat down next to Evan and handed the glass to him.

'So what did you talk about?'

'Nothing major,' Evan said evasively, taking a swig of his drink. 'Work stuff, and cars, and that.'

'Was *she* there?'

Evan shook his head and swallowed another mouthful. Marie had no clue what the falling-out with his dad had really been about, and he had no intention of enlightening her. It had stung when his dad had not only rejected his olive branch, but also threatened to tell her about him and Irena.

But the real kick in the teeth had been his dad's declaration that he loved the bitch and didn't want Evan to ruin things for him. That was why Evan had driven over there today: to try and talk sense into him before he lost everyone and everything.

'So where was she?' Marie interrupted his thoughts.

'Not sure.' Evan shrugged. 'I think he said something about her staying with a friend.'

'Good,' Marie said approvingly. 'It's too soon for him to get involved with anyone, so it would never have lasted.'

Evan nodded his agreement, and said, 'Anyway, now we've broken the ice, I was thinking I might pop over there when I finish work tomorrow. Give him a hand fixing up his cars.'

'Ah, he'll like that,' Marie said. Then, giving a sheepish little smile, she added, 'I was actually going to ask you if you'd mind if I went to bingo tomorrow night? I saw Kelly and Liz earlier, and they said the jackpot's on its third rollover, so it's going to be huge. They're going to the karaoke bar straight after, but I'll give that a miss.'

'No, go with them,' Evan urged, glad that she'd made plans, because that meant he wouldn't have to rush home. 'And make sure you win that jackpot so we can retire and move to Spain.'

'I'll try,' Marie laughed, resting her head on his chest. Then, teasing his nipple through his T-shirt, she said, 'Fancy an early night?'

Evan took another swig of his drink and resisted the urge to sigh. He wasn't really in the mood for sex while he had all this shit about his dad rolling round in his mind. But Marie was making an effort, so he supposed he ought to, as well.

'Yeah, all right,' he said. 'But don't be expecting a long one, 'cos I'm wiped.'

'We'll see about that,' Marie grinned, springing to her feet and grabbing his hand to pull him up.

24

Viktorya Radu woke to find herself in a pitch-dark room. The painkillers she'd been given had knocked her out cold, and she'd dreamed she was at home with her mother. It had been so vivid, she wasn't immediately sure if *that* had been real and *this* was the dream. But the all-too-real pain that covered every inch of her body when she rolled over told her that she was far from the comforts of home.

As her vision began to adjust, she picked out the hazy outlines of unfamiliar furniture in the room. The bedsprings creaked when she sat up, and she gripped the edge of the mattress when a bitter taste flooded her mouth. Her head felt heavy and fuzzy, and she needed the toilet, so she dropped her feet to the floor and tentatively stood up.

Blindly feeling her way over to the door, she cried out in pain when she smashed her knee on the corner of a chest of drawers she hadn't noticed. Almost immediately, a tapping sound came through the wall, and she froze when someone whispered: 'Are you OK, love?'

It was a male voice with a British accent, and she began to tremble violently when a vision of the blond man with the teardrop tattoos flashed into her mind – along with the memory of the vicious beating he had given her.

'I know you must be scared,' the man behind the wall was saying. 'But I'm not one of them, I promise. My name's Frank, and this is my house. I'm locked in, as well, and I heard what they did to you, so I wanted to check you're all right?'

Viktorya stared at the wall, as if doing so would allow her to see right through it. The man sounded sincere, but she no longer trusted her own judgement. How could she when she'd allowed herself to be duped into coming to this country by someone who had convinced not only her, but also her entire family, that his friend ran a modelling agency in England and could make her a star?

Alexander had been handsome, charming, and extremely generous: insisting on paying her air fare, and promising to arrange for a limousine to pick her up at the airport and take her to a luxury apartment in the city centre.

It had all been a lie. The limousine had turned out to be a scruffy van with a filthy mattress in the back, upon which three other girls had already been sitting when she had climbed in. They all claimed to have been hand-picked by Alexander for catwalk stardom, and had chattered excitedly on the way here about the glamorous lives they were going to live now they were in England – the money they would be able to send home to their families.

That excitement had quickly turned to confusion when they'd found themselves at this house instead of the fancy apartments they had been promised. But when the dark-eyed man had walked outside and smiled at Viktorya, she had thought that maybe things were still on track, after all: that maybe he was the big-shot agent Alexander had told her about, and he'd had them brought here, to his home, so he could greet them personally before they were taken into the city.

She'd realized her mistake when the woman had brought them into the house and the blond man had followed them in and demanded they hand over their possessions before attacking her.

'Are you still there, love?' the man behind the wall asked, bringing her back to the present.

Afraid to reply in case it was some kind of trick, Viktorya backed away from the wall. The man had said that he, too, was locked in, so she guessed there was no point in trying the door. Instead, she felt her way over to the window and eased one of the heavy curtains aside. At first, all she could see was inky darkness, but then the moon emerged from behind a cloud and her face was bathed in its milky glow. And in the few seconds before it disappeared again, she saw that the window was nailed shut.

'I'm so sorry this is happening to you,' the invisible man was saying, his voice fainter now she'd moved away from the wall. 'But I'm going to get you and your friends out of here. I don't know how, or how long it'll take, but I'll find a way, I promise.'

Viktorya stared at the spot on the wall where the voice appeared to be coming from and covered her mouth with her hand when hot tears trickled from the corners of her swollen eyes and burned a path down her bruised cheeks. She so wanted to believe that he could help her, but if he was telling the truth about being locked in, he was clearly no match for these people.

On the other side of the wall, Frank held his breath and waited for the girl to respond. When she didn't, he sighed heavily and went back over to his bed. He had heard the fear in her voice when she'd cried out, and he'd hoped it might bring her some comfort if she heard that she wasn't alone. It obviously hadn't worked, and his heart ached when he thought about the terror she must be feeling. Her *and* her friends, who he'd seen Nick and one of the other men herd into the van shortly after Evan had left this evening. God only knew where they'd been taken, but Frank couldn't imagine they would be treated any better there than they were being treated here, and it sickened him to think that these animals were getting away with this. But he'd meant what he told that girl: one way or another, even if it meant sacrificing his own safety to achieve it, he was determined to save them.

25

Evan drove straight to Yorkshire after leaving work the following afternoon; his mountain bike, and a rucksack containing a flask of coffee, a sandwich, and a pair of binoculars in the boot. When Marie had questioned why he was taking the bike, he'd told her he was planning on persuading his dad to go for a ride, like they'd used to do in the old days: father and son, pedalling into the village to have a couple of pints and a game of darts at the pub. He'd also told her not to wait up in case it turned into a late one, but he knew she'd be plastered by the time she got home from the karaoke bar, so he doubted she'd even notice what time he got home.

The rush-hour traffic was heavy when Evan hit the motorway, and the drive took twice as long as usual. It was already pitch-dark by the time he got there, and he couldn't see a thing when he left the lights of the village behind and headed onto Marsh House Lane. Fortunately, he knew every pothole and bump like the back of his hand – and also knew the exact spot at which a vehicle became visible from his dad's place. When he reached that point tonight, he turned his headlights off and drove blindly on until he came to the tractor path at the perimeter of a disused field a mile back from Yvonne's cottage. Parking out of sight behind a hedgerow, he looped the rucksack over his shoulders before completing the journey on his bike.

Yvonne's pigs kicked up a fuss when he rode into the back garden and, guessing that they hadn't been fed again, he hopped off the bike and filled their troughs before climbing in through the window he'd jemmied open the previous day. Holding his nose when the stench hit him, he cursed under his breath when the cats swarmed in and snaked around his ankles. Batting one off when it started clawing its way up his leg, he used the light from his phone's torch to find and share out a couple of tins of food.

Leaving the moggies to fight over it, he took the binoculars out of the rucksack and looped them around his neck, then rooted through the drawers in search of the spare key his dad had left there after changing the broken lock. When he'd found it, he let himself out and hopped over the back fence, then waded through the field until he reached the low fence at the back of the farm.

As soon as he stopped walking, the back door opened, and Evan dropped to his haunches when a man stepped outside and lit a cigarette, activating the security light. Finding a gap in the fence, he trained the binoculars on the man's face, and frowned when he realized he hadn't seen this one before. Added to the three men he *had* seen, and the three girls, that totalled seven extra people in the house along with his dad and Irena. But there were only four bedrooms, so where the hell were they all sleeping?

The man suddenly moved away from the door, and Evan's question was answered when a second security light flared, highlighting a static caravan standing by the barn. The man walked round the back of it and, slotting the fag between his teeth, took a piss in the grass before climbing inside the caravan and switching a light on.

No longer able to see him, Evan turned his attention to the house. The kitchen blind was open, so he stood up and zoomed the binoculars through the window. Irena's brother, the blond man, and the dark-haired one were sitting at the table, along with two men he hadn't seen before. They were all counting piles of banknotes, and Evan muttered, 'You've got to be fucking joking,' when he noticed a white block wrapped in plastic in the centre of the table. Suspecting that it was cocaine, his hunch was confirmed when he scanned the tabletop and saw faint white lines and rolled-up banknotes among the cups, glasses, and overflowing ashtrays.

Shocked, he lowered the binoculars and tried to make sense of what he'd seen. His dad was so anti-drugs he'd threatened to report Evan to the police when he'd caught him having a sneaky spliff one time. And if he could do that to his own son over a bit of weed, why the hell would he allow these strangers to bring coke into his house? And he had to know about it, because the men certainly weren't trying to hide it.

Unless he'd had no choice in the matter?

A crevice formed in the centre of Evan's brow when he recalled the conversation he'd had with his dad the previous day. Frank had been uncharacteristically cold, and the look he'd given Evan when he'd sent him on his way had been odd, to say the least. That, added to the blond man's unwarranted aggression, and the smooth way Irena's brother had walked him back to his car, had made him think that something dodgy was going on. And after witnessing that scene through the kitchen window, he was even more convinced.

But was it possible that these people had forced their way into his dad's house and were holding him prisoner?

Evan shook his head slowly, unable to imagine his father being that vulnerable, that helpless. But the man who had brought him up would never willingly allow drugs to be brought into his house, so *something* must have happened to make him change his mind.

Irena.

His lip twisted into a sneer when her name entered his head. She'd caused nothing but trouble since turning up here that night, and he was sure she must have had a hand in whatever was going on in there. She'd claimed she had escaped her abusive husband and was in fear of her life, but what if . . .

Tutting when the hazy thought refused to solidify into something tangible, Evan raised the binoculars again and saw that the men at the kitchen table had finished counting the money, and the gobby Manc and Irena's brother were both sniffing thick lines of coke while one of the others bagged the neat wads of banknotes.

His mobile phone suddenly started ringing, the raucous strains of *Born To Be Wild* shattering the silence. Cursing himself for not thinking to put it on silent, Evan ducked his head and scuttled away from the fence when the man who'd gone into the caravan a few minutes earlier appeared at the door and peered in his direction.

His heart was pounding when he let himself into the cottage, and his pulse was thundering in his ears as he fumbled with the lock and the bolt. He stared out through the window when he'd managed it, searching the shadows for signs that he'd been followed.

When nobody appeared, he released the breath he'd been holding and slid his phone out of his pocket to see who had tried to call him. It was Jo, and he contemplated calling her back to tell her what he'd seen, but immediately dismissed the idea. His sister was headstrong, and if he told her what was going on she would get straight on the phone to their dad, and those men would know that he was spying on them. And, given what he'd just seen, if they came after him, he wouldn't stand a chance.

In need of a cigarette to calm his nerves, Evan picked his rucksack up off the table and carried it and one of Yvonne's kitchen chairs into her musty-smelling bedroom. Determined to find out what was going on, he lit up and settled at the window to keep an eye out for the Transit van. He didn't know if those girls he'd seen were staying at the farm along with the men, or if last night's excursion had been a one-off, but if the van went past tonight, he would give it a head start and then cycle back to his car and make his own way to the brothel. What he would do then, he wasn't quite sure. He would have to cross that bridge when he came to it.

As the minutes ticked past, his thoughts drifted back to Irena, and he wondered if she'd known her brother was involved in drugs and prostitution before she'd persuaded Frank to let him and his mates move in. If so, it didn't fit with the image he'd had of her at all. Jo had pegged her for a gold-digging scam-artist who'd homed in on a grieving widower with the intention of relieving him of his money, but after meeting her Evan had thought his sister dead wrong. Irena had seemed like a gentle, unassuming soul, and he'd been sucked in by her beauty. He still wasn't sure if it was the alcohol that had spurred him on to – almost – have sex with her that night, or if he'd done it purely to defy his dad. Either way, now he knew what she was really like, he was determined to get her and her scummy brother and friends out of there.

26

Karel had sent Nick and the other men out to check the field at the back of the house after Jacko told them about the blast of music he'd heard. They had also checked the lane at the front of the property, but had seen and heard nothing.

'Fucker's imagining things,' Nick jeered, elbowing Jacko in the ribs when they came back inside having found nothing. 'He'll be telling us he's seeing aliens next.'

'I'm sure I heard it,' Jacko insisted. Then, shrugging, he conceded, 'I suppose it could have been the wind. It's weird out here; does my fucking nut in.'

'You know where the door is if you want out,' Nick said over his shoulder as he opened a wrap of smack to prepare the girls' pre-work hits. 'But good luck getting a job that pays as well as this one for doing fuck all.'

'I never said nothing about quitting,' Jacko muttered, reaching into the fridge for a can of beer.

'Put that back,' Karel ordered before he had the chance to pull the tab. 'And you can all knock the gear on the head tonight,' he added, his gaze sweeping over the other men. 'There was probably no one out there, but I'm not taking chances while the gear's still in the house, so you can pair up and do half-hour walkabouts.'

The men nodded their agreement, and Nick gave a smug smile.

'Sure you can cope with that, Jacko? There's all sorts of shit roaming round out there at night, and we all know what a wuss you are. Here . . . maybe it was a fox you heard? I've heard they scream like a bitch getting shagged up the arse.'

'Maybe.' Jacko shrugged, no longer sure *what* he'd heard.

'Don't give 'em as much tonight,' Karel cautioned, watching as Nick started drawing the now-liquid heroin into one of the disposable syringes he'd laid out on the ledge. 'Big Shirl reckons she had complaints about them gouching out last night, and I haven't fetched them over to get nothing back.'

Nodding, Nick squirted some of the liquid back into the spoon before reaching for the second syringe.

The girls were fast asleep when Nick unlocked their bedroom door a few minutes later, and his dick sprang to life as he gazed at their naked young bodies sprawled on top of the duvet they were sharing. The clothes they'd arrived with had been stashed in the cellar, and their work underwear had been taken off them for washing when he'd brought them back to the farm in the early hours of that morning. But he reckoned they'd have stripped off even if they'd had clothes, because Karel'd had the heating on full-blast since he got here, and the room was as stuffy as hell.

Walking over to the bed, he admired the exposed tits and pussies before letting his gaze drift to Viktorya on the far side of the mattress. Karel had been dosing her up on Ketamine since Nick had battered her, and she'd been dead to the world every time he'd been in here. She was the prettiest of the girls, by far, and she'd shown she had spunk when she'd tried to fight him off – which was always a turn on. It was lucky for her that Karel had walked in when he had, or he'd have given her a damn sight more than a beating. But her time would come – he'd make sure of that.

Conscious that time was drawing on and he needed to get the other girls ready for work, Nick turned his attention back to them and slapped the arse of the one closest to him.

'Wakey wakey,' he said in a sing-song voice when her eyes shot open. 'Time for your medicine.'

Roused by their friend's cry of fear, the other girls woke up. Amused when they sat up and huddled together, covering their breasts with their hands, Nick grinned as he pulled his belt out of the loops of his jeans.

'Who wants to go first?' he asked, picking up one of the syringes.

'No, sir, please ...' one of them whimpered. 'We want go home.'

'You *are* home,' he purred, choosing her to take the first fix. 'Now be a good girl, and hold your arm out. Unless you want me to hit the wrong vein and make you bleed to death?'

Sobbing now, the girls held on to each other, and the terror in their eyes made Nick's dick throb even harder. If he'd had the time, he would have indulged in a nice little three-way blow job. But the search for Jacko's imaginary friend had put them behind schedule, so it would have to wait.

27

Evan had been sitting at Yvonne's bedroom window for over an hour, and he'd just lit his umpteenth cigarette and was contemplating going home when he heard the rumble of a diesel engine, followed by the glow of headlights strobing through the gaps in the hedgerow. The Transit van came into view a few seconds later, and he ducked his head and peered at it over the edge of the windowsill. It was too dark to see who was driving, and he couldn't see through its back windows when it trundled past, but it was only half an hour later than he'd seen it going out the previous night, so he figured it was probably heading to the same place – with the same cargo.

When the tail-lights had receded into the distance, Evan stood up and pulled his jacket on. Then, stuffing his flask and binoculars back into the rucksack, he let himself out of the cottage and cycled back to his car.

The Transit was a couple of miles ahead when Evan had joined the motorway ten minutes later, but there weren't many vehicles between them, so he eased his foot off the accelerator to avoid being spotted. Relieved to find that it had long gone by the time he reached the exit for Manchester, he took an alternative route to the brothel so he wouldn't cross paths with them.

Approaching the road where the house was situated from the opposite end to that which the van had arrived and left by the previous night, he parked a few hundred yards back and climbed out. He could see the van's back bumper sticking out of the gate-less driveway when he crossed over to the pavement on the other side, and he glanced at it out of the corner of his eye as he strolled past. There didn't seem to be anybody in it, so he switched his gaze to the house. At first glance it appeared to be the same as its neighbours, but then he noticed the steel gate covering its front door, and the metal bars across the upper windows.

A door at the side of the house suddenly opened, spilling light onto the path, and Evan quickened his step when the blond man and his friend appeared. Too far from either end of the block to duck into an alleyway, he crouched down behind a car when he heard the van doors slam shut and its engine fire to life. The beam of its headlights arced across the car's windows when the van reversed off the driveway, and Evan raised himself up an inch to watch as it drove past.

'Oi!' a rough voice barked. 'What you doin', ya little cunt?'

Evan jumped to his feet and held out his hands when a huge man in a stained vest ran out from the house behind him, setting off the security light.

'I said what you doin'?' the man repeated, marching over and seizing Evan by the collar of his jacket before slamming him up against the car. 'Tryin' to nick my fuckin' motor?'

'I'm looking for my cat,' Evan lied, blurting out the first thing that came into his mind. 'It's gone missing, and someone told me they saw one get hit by a car round the corner about an hour ago. You haven't seen it, have you? Big ginger thing.'

'No, I ain't,' the man said, releasing him, but still eyeing him with suspicion. 'But if it comes in my yard, my Staffies'll have it, so you'd best hope it don't come nowhere near.'

Muttering, 'Cheers,' Evan went on his way, making a show of looking around and calling out for the fictitious cat as he walked.

As he passed the brothel, an elderly man emerged from the shadows and looked both ways along the road before scuttling away. Guessing that it was a punter who lived locally and was scared of being seen by someone who knew him, Evan shook his head as he walked on. Old geezers like that ought to be at home with their wives, not sneaking around getting their kicks with girls who were young enough to be their granddaughters. But, then, who was to say the bloke's wife hadn't died, and this was the only way the poor bastard could get any?

Wondering if that was why his dad had allowed Irena to turn his head so quickly, Evan climbed into his car and lit a cigarette. He hadn't seen the girls tonight, but he figured they must have been in the van, because he couldn't see those men driving over here for nothing – and they wouldn't have had time to stop off on the way to pick them up.

Unsure what to do with that knowledge, Evan glanced round when a shadow crossed the passenger-side window. A man was walking past with the same furtive air about him as the old geezer, and Evan watched as he continued up the road before turning onto the driveway of the brothel. Yanking his keys back out of the ignition when an idea came to him, he hopped out of the car and took a last drag on the cigarette before flicking it away.

28

Frank was lying on top of his bed in his underpants. The heating had been on all day, and sweat was streaming off his body and soaking the duvet beneath him. But there was no way to escape the unbearable heat, because Karel had ordered his men to board his window up to prevent him from climbing out again, and the valve on his ancient radiator had snapped off when he'd tried to adjust it. And, to make matters worse, Irena hadn't brought him anything to eat or drink today, so he'd been taking rationed sips of whisky to quench his thirst.

The bottle was empty now, and Frank's mouth was bone dry. Earlier in the afternoon, desperate for the toilet, he'd banged on the door for almost half an hour. Nobody had come, so he'd been forced to relieve himself in an old vase of dried flowers Maureen had kept on the dressing table. Half-full now, the vase was standing in the furthest corner of the room. He'd placed one of his pillows over it in the hope of containing the smell, but it wasn't working, and the stench of hot piss, combined with the rancid odours of his sweat and sour breath, was almost as unbearable as the heat.

He was starting to wonder if this was what Hell felt like. Maureen had been brought up in a Catholic household, and she'd maintained her faith throughout their marriage, despite Frank being a firm non-believer. She'd attempted to drag him along to church on numerous occasions, but he'd stubbornly refused, unless it had been to attend a wedding, christening, or funeral. But these last few days, since coming home from visiting Yvonne and walking into this nightmare, he'd found himself praying fervently to the God he'd professed did not exist. The prayers hadn't been for himself, though; they were for those poor girls Karel was holding prisoner – and for his children.

At the thought of his son, Frank released a remorseful sigh. Evan was a smart cookie, and Frank had hoped he might sense that something was wrong and come back to check on him after his visit the previous day. He hadn't, and Frank had resigned himself to the thought that Evan, like his sister, had washed his hands of him. He could hardly blame them, given the way he'd behaved since meeting Irena, but it broke his heart to think that the recent bitter arguments would be their last memories of him if he didn't survive this ordeal.

A floorboard creaked outside his door, interrupting his thoughts, and Frank jerked upright, praying that someone had remembered to bring him a drink. Mouth already watering at the thought of it, he frowned when a shadow passed through the shaft of light under his door, followed by the sound of a key turning slowly in the lock of Evan's bedroom door. It wasn't Irena, because he'd heard her cry herself to sleep a couple of hours ago. And it wasn't Nick, because Frank had heard him driving the girls away from the house earlier, and the van hadn't come back yet. As far as he'd managed to ascertain, the other men slept in the caravan and never came any further into the house than the kitchen, so it wouldn't be one of them. That left Karel. But if it was him, why was he creeping into the room as if he didn't want anyone to know he was there?

Curious, Frank got up and crept over to the wall. Above the sound of bedsprings protesting, and a soft, feminine exclamation of confusion, Frank heard a deep, crooning voice, and his eyebrows rose sharply when he caught the words being spoken.

29

'Yeah?'

The woman who had answered the door stared out at Evan. She looked to be in her sixties, but her heavy make-up and tight-fitting clothes told him that she thought she looked much younger – glamorous, even.

Unsure what to say, he stuffed his hands into his pockets and shuffled his feet. He'd never been to a brothel in his life before, but he'd presumed it would be like any other business and he would be invited in, no questions asked. In hindsight, he realized what a ridiculous assumption that had been. Prostitution was still illegal, as far as he knew, so of course they wouldn't let any old Tom, Dick, or Harry walk in off the street. But he'd come this far, so he wasn't about to give up now.

'I was, um, told I could get a good time here,' he said, trying not to stare at the tattoo of a thick snake that rose up from the woman's wrinkled cleavage and wrapped itself around her turkey neck.

'By?' she demanded.

'Er . . . *Dave*?' He blurted out the most common name he could think of.

'Dave who?' The woman narrowed her eyes and shoved her sleeves up, revealing yet more tattoos on her arms.

'I don't know him all that well, so I'm not sure what his surname is,' Evan said, half-expecting her to slam the door in his face. 'He's got grey hair and a bit of a limp,' he embellished, guessing that most of her customers were getting on a bit, like the two he'd seen tonight. 'Drinks in the Dog and Duck.'

The woman looked him up and down, then jerked her chin up at him and opened the door a little wider to allow him entry. Closing and bolting the door when he stepped into the dingy hallway, she turned to face him.

'This your first time, son?'

Cringing with embarrassment, Evan nodded.

'OK, well this is how it works,' she said. 'It's eighty for an hour, fifty for half. If you want extras, you settle up when you've finished and I've seen what state you've left her in. Just so you know,' she went on, a clear warning in her voice. 'I've got security. And if you get too rough, you'll be walking out of here with a cunt where your cock used to be. Got that?'

Disgusted by her coarseness, Evan muttered, 'Got it,' and pulled out his wallet. Sliding two twenties and a ten out, he handed them over – praying, as he did so, that Marie wouldn't question why the Christmas bonus he'd received from work had gone down so fast, because this would be bloody hard to explain.

The woman snatched the notes and shoved them into her pocket, and then opened an internal door and led him down a narrow corridor. At the end, she ushered him into a shabbily furnished lounge area, where five young women wearing skimpy underwear were huddled together on a long sofa, while two others were perched on tall stools at a tiny bar in the corner.

'Take your pick,' she said.

Evan felt a fresh fire burn his cheeks as he looked at the girls. The two at the bar appeared to be a fair few years older than the others, and one was blonde, while the other was a red-head, so he dismissed them and turned his attention to the ones on the sofa. He'd hoped he might recognize the one he'd glimpsed through the van window the previous night, but they all had the same dark hair and olive complexions.

'Come on, son, don't stand there gawping all night,' the woman said impatiently. 'You're not fuckin' window shopping.'

'Sorry,' Evan muttered. 'I'll, um, take her.' He nodded at one of the girls.

'Up you get,' the woman barked, kicking the girl's foot when she didn't immediately move. 'And make sure you give him a good time for his money.'

Evan picked up the warning behind the words – and he guessed the girl did, too, because she was visibly trembling when she stood up. She raised her eyes briefly before quickly lowering them again, and he was surprised to see that they weren't brown, as he'd expected, but light blue; the pupils two tiny pinpricks in a sea of ice. His gaze instinctively slid to the crook of her elbow, and his suspicions were confirmed when he saw faint puncture marks and bruising.

'Summat wrong?' the boss woman asked, narrowing her eyes when she saw what he was looking at.

Evan remembered why he was there, and shook his head. Seeming to buy it, the woman turned back to the girl, and said, 'Room two. Half hour.'

Following the girl up a steep set of stairs and into a bedroom, Evan looked around in disgust when she closed the door behind them. The threadbare carpet showed no hint of its original colour beneath the grime of a thousand punter-footsteps, and the grubby bedding didn't look as if it had seen the inside of a washing machine in decades. A lamp with a red chiffon scarf draped over it sat on the bedside table alongside a box containing tubes of KY Jelly, condoms, and antiseptic wipes. It was depressingly clinical, and he suspected that the metal bars barricading the window were designed to keep the girls in rather than intruders out.

Expressionless, her gaze on the floor, the girl sank down on the edge of the thin mattress and started unhooking her bra. Evan's frown deepened. He enjoyed the female form as much as the next man, especially when it belonged to a girl as pretty as this one probably was when she wasn't stoned out of her mind. But this wasn't what he'd come for, so he held out his hand to stop her.

'You're all right, love; you don't need to take it off. I only want to talk.'

229

The girl looked up, her hands still behind her back.

'You no want sex?'

Evan shook his head and sat down at the other end of the bed.

'I want to ask you some questions – if that's OK?'

'I no talk,' she said, eyeing him warily as she quickly refastened her bra. 'Is not allow.'

Conscious that the old woman could be outside listening, Evan lowered his voice, and said, 'I only want to know if you're one of the lasses I saw getting dropped off in that van? From the farm?'

The girl didn't answer, and Evan guessed that she *was* one of them when he saw the fear in her eyes.

'Please don't be scared,' he said, holding out his hand to show he meant her no harm. Quickly withdrawing it when she shrank back, he said, 'What's going on here, love? Are you and your friends being forced to do this? Is it those men who brought you here, or her downstairs?'

'Please leave . . .' the girl whimpered, rising unsteadily to her feet. 'I am try to be good like they tell me, but you are cause trouble for me.'

'I promise I won't tell them you've spoken to me,' Evan reassured her, as he, too, stood up. 'But that farm where you're staying belongs to my dad, and I'm worried about him.'

'You need *leave*,' the girl repeated, the effect of whatever drugs she'd taken clearly not powerful enough to override her terror. '*Please* . . .' she implored, as tears began to trickle down her cheeks. 'If men find out, they will be angry, and . . .'

She tailed off without finishing the sentence, but Evan easily filled in the gaps.

'I know you're scared,' he said quietly. 'And I'm going to help you, I promise. But I need to know how many men are at the farm? And is my dad involved?'

The girl edged away from him without answering, and Evan cursed himself for diving straight in without thinking how she might react when she made for the door. Rushing across the room, he placed his hand on the wood to prevent her from opening it.

'Please, love, let me explai—'

Wincing when the girl let out a blood-curdling scream, he whispered, 'I'm sorry! Please stop screaming. I wasn't going to hurt you, I swear!'

It was too late. The door burst open, and the old woman barrelled in, followed by a huge man with the biggest biceps Evan had ever seen, and a neck so thick it looked like his head was sitting directly on his shoulders.

'What's going on?' the woman demanded, looking from Evan to the girl. 'What's he done to you?'

'I haven't touched her,' Evan said truthfully, keeping a wary eye on the man.

'You must have done *something*,' the woman argued. 'You've only been in here two minutes, and look at the fuckin' state of her.'

The girl had stopped screaming, but tears were still streaming down her face, and she cowered like a terrified puppy when the woman stared at her and asked what had happened.

'He – he say he not w-want sex,' she stammered. 'And he was ask about men who bring us here.'

'Is that right?' The woman narrowed her eyes and glared at Evan.

Guessing that he was about to be ejected, he held up his hands, and said, 'It's OK, I'm leaving.'

Before he could move, the bruiser lunged at him and hurled him across the room, and stars exploded behind his eyes when his head smashed into the wall. The last thing he heard before blacking out was a scream, followed by the whip-crack of a slap.

Big Shirl gazed down at the man on the floor and prodded him with the toe of her boot. Getting no response, she jerked her head at the bouncer, saying: 'Put him away.'

The bouncer nodded and, scooping Evan up off the floor as if he weighed nothing, slung him over his shoulder and carried him out onto the landing. When he'd gone, Big Shirl turned back to the now-sobbing but no-longer-screaming girl, and demanded to know exactly what had happened.

When the girl had told her everything, Big Shirl locked her in the room and made her way downstairs, tapping a number into her mobile phone as she went.

'It's me,' she said when her call was answered. 'We've got a problem. You'd best get your arse back here ASAP!'

30

On a dark backstreet on the outskirts of the city centre, Nick shoved his phone into his pocket and looked around for Gaz. They had driven over here to collect money from the street girls after dropping the foreign ones off at the brothel, and he'd been about to punish one of the junkie slags for trying to conceal a twenty in her shoe when Big Shirl's call came through. The cagey bitch had refused to tell him anything over the phone, but it sounded urgent, so he reluctantly let the tart off with a warning and summonsed Gaz with a shrill whistle before jogging back to the van.

Arriving at the house ten minutes later to find all the security gates locked, Nick hammered on the metal bars with his fist until Big Shirl opened up. Gesturing for him and Gaz to come inside, she quickly relocked the gate and then locked and bolted the door.

'What's happened?' Nick asked, wondering if one of the girls had OD'd.

'A bloke turned up and picked one of the new ones,' Big Shirl explained over her shoulder as she walked down the hallway and slotted a key from the huge bunch she was carrying into the lock of an internal door. 'Only he tells her he don't wanna fuck, he wants to *talk*.'

'Is that all?' Nick pulled a face. 'You made it sound like a fuckin' emergency.'

'He was asking questions about *you* lot.'

'What kind of questions?' Nick asked, watching his step as he followed her down a rickety flight of wooden stairs to the dimly lit cellar.

'How many of youse are at the farm, and if her and the others are being forced into this.'

'Are you fuckin' kidding me?'

'That's what she said.' Big Shirl shrugged and pushed the cellar door open.

Nick brushed past her and strode into the dank-smelling chamber. Tiny, their man-mountain Romanian security guard, was standing behind a chair, upon which an unconscious, bloody-faced man was slumped with his chin on his chest, a filthy rag in his mouth, and ropes binding his ankles to the chair legs and his wrists together behind his back.

'Is he a regular?' Nick asked Big Shirl.

'First time I've ever seen him,' she replied, pulling a pack of cigarettes from her pocket and slotting one between her teeth.

'Are you serious?' Nick glared at her. 'Why the fuck did you let him in if you didn't know him?'

''Cos he reckoned another punter sent him, and he looked all

234

right, so I give him the benefit of the doubt,' Big Shirl snapped, her eyes glittering evilly in the flame of her cigarette lighter.

'You're going fuckin' doolally, you,' Nick sneered. 'Didn't that last raid teach you nothing?'

''Ere, who d'ya think you're talking to like that?' she retorted angrily, jabbing him in the chest with her fingernail. 'You ain't bullying me like you bully them soft cunts up there, so wind your neck in before I snap it!'

Nick curled his lip at her and turned back to the man on the chair. Instantly recognizing him when Tiny grabbed his hair and yanked his head up, he muttered, 'What the fuck's *he* doing here?'

'He must have followed us,' Gaz said, also recognizing him. 'K said he looked suspicious when he left the other day, but I wonder how much he knows?'

'Soon find out,' Nick said, taking a picture of Evan on his phone before lashing him across the face with the back of his hand.

Evan's eyes flickered open, and Nick leaned down and tore the gag out of his mouth.

'Yeah, that's right, fucker, it's *me*,' he snarled, nose to nose. 'What you doing here, then, eh? *Daddy* tip you off, did he?'

Evan's heart was pounding so hard he could hardly breathe. His dad obviously *did* know what was going on, or the man wouldn't have asked if Frank had tipped him off; but the scathing way the man had referred to him told Evan that he'd been right to suspect he was in danger.

Nick's mobile phone suddenly started ringing. Straightening up, he answered it.

It was Karel.

'Are you there yet?'

'Yeah, just,' said Nick. 'It's that cunt who turned up at the farm yesterday – the old fucker's son . . . Yeah, he's still here. Tiny sparked him and tied him up. What do you want us to do with him?'

Nick nodded as he listened to Karel's instructions, and Evan felt sweat trickle down his back when the man looked down at him and grinned slyly, before saying, 'No problem, boss. I'll give you a bell when it's done.'

'Whatever you're planning to do to me, you won't get away with it,' Evan spluttered. 'My wife's expecting me home soon, and she'll ring the police if I don't turn up. And they'll go straight to my dad's place, 'cos that's where she thinks I am.'

'Know your trouble . . . ?' Nick drawled as he slotted the phone back into his pocket. 'You're too fuckin' nosy for your own good. You shoulda pissed off home like your old man told you to, but you had to go and stick your snout where it don't belong, didn't ya? And now you're gonna pay for it. Any last words for your pa before you go?'

'You can't be serious?' Evan squawked, struggling against the restraints when the man pulled a gun out of the waistband of his jeans. 'You can't fucking *shoot* me.'

'Wanna bet?' Nick drawled, grinning as he released the safety catch. 'But first . . .' He rammed the end of the barrel into Evan's mouth. 'You're gonna answer some questions.'

31

Irena looked drained and miserable when she unlocked Frank's door the following morning. The air in the room was still stifling, but he was dressed and sitting in the chair by the boarded-up window when she entered. Watching as she placed the cup she was carrying on the bedside table, he said, casually, 'Sleep well?'

Irena hesitated, and Frank saw wariness in her eyes when she glanced over at him and nodded. Guessing that she was wondering why he was being civil to her after their last bitter exchange, he gave a half smile, and said, 'That's good. And are you and Karel getting on OK?'

Frowning now, Irena said, 'Why are you ask this?'

'I thought I heard you crying last night,' he said. 'So I thought you might have fallen out?'

'No.' She shook her head. 'We are happy.'

'Sure about that?' Frank raised an eyebrow and looked pointedly at her cheek. 'Nasty bruise you've got there.'

'I fall.' She self-consciously covered the spot where Karel's backhanded slap had landed a couple of days earlier. 'Is nothing.'

Unable to keep up the pretence, Frank gave her a pitying look.

'Oh, come on, Irena, that's exactly what you said when I found you that night, battered to within an inch of your life. Only I'm assuming it was Nick's handiwork that time, seeing as Karel was in prison at the time. Am I right?'

Irena turned to the door without answering, and Frank said, 'I know you'll probably tell me it was *part of the plan*' – he made quotation marks in the air with his fingers – 'but why did Karel let Nick do that to you if he cares about you as much as you claim he does?'

Again, Irena hesitated, and her expression had hardened when she looked back at him.

'I know you are say these things to make trouble, but it will not work,' she said. 'Karel is good man, and he love me.'

'No, he doesn't,' Frank argued. 'Or he wouldn't have gone in there while you were sleeping last night, and—'

He caught himself before the rest of the words came out and released a weary sigh. He had intended to tell her about Karel and the girl, but his instincts told him that would cause more trouble for him than for Karel. Irena was bound to tell the man what he'd said, and Frank had already witnessed his violent streak first hand, so it wasn't worth it.

'What were you going to say?' Irena pressed, suspicion in her eyes.

'Nothing,' said Frank. 'You were right: I was trying to stir things up. Forget it.'

Irena continued to stare at him for several moments. Then, quietly, she said, 'I know you think I have cold heart, Frankie, but I honestly never meant for you to be hurt.'

Frank didn't reply, but his eyes betrayed the emotion her words had stirred in him. Hearing her call him by that name brought back memories of the time they had spent together before this nightmare began. It might all have been a lie on her part, but he'd felt genuine affection for her, and, despite his determination not to, he still felt an urge to protect her.

Irena glanced at the clock on the bedside table, and said, 'I need make breakfast. Drink tea while is still hot. I will bring food for you when I have finish.'

Reminded of something that had come into his mind during the long, hot, restless night, Frank said, 'Subject of food, I don't suppose you could nip over to Yvonne's and see to the animals, could you? Only it's been a few days now, and I'm worried they'll starve if they don't get something soon.'

'I will try,' she agreed.

'One more thing . . .' Frank said before she moved. 'Is there any chance I can go to the bathroom to empty that?' Embarrassed, he nodded toward the stinking vase of piss.

'I will ask one of men to take you,' she said, backing out onto the landing.

As she turned the key in the lock, raised voices drifted up from the hallway. Curious, Frank got up and went over to the door. He'd heard the girls being brought back earlier than usual last night, and a lot of shouting and door slamming had followed. Whatever had happened, it clearly hadn't been resolved yet if the foul-mouthed insults he could hear Nick firing off right now were anything to go by. He didn't recognize the other man's voice, but he was disappointed that it wasn't Karel, because if those two went head to head, the gang would implode and his ordeal would be over.

The voices faded away, and Frank, none the wiser, picked up the tea Irena had made for him and carried it to his chair.

Frankie . . .

Recalling the way she had spoken his name, Frank shook his head as he sank down on the seat. For a moment there, he had allowed himself to believe she might still have feelings for him. But who was he kidding? She loved Karel, and she would stay loyal to him to the bitter end – no matter how badly the bastard treated her.

Downstairs, Irena prepared breakfast as the men came in from the caravan and took seats at the table. Nick and Gaz were still bickering, but she was relieved they were no longer shouting, because there was always a risk it might turn physical when things got that heated – and a very real chance, when Nick was involved, that someone could end up getting stabbed or shot.

Like Frank, she, too, had sensed that something bad must have happened last night. But she couldn't ask Karel about it, because he still wasn't speaking to her. He blamed her for Frank's attempted escape, despite the fact that his men had also been here and security was their job – a job they were extremely well paid for, while she received nothing for all the cooking, cleaning, and washing she did. Theirs was a male-dominated world, and the women they allowed into it were viewed as little more than maids and on-tap pussies. But Karel had told her she was different. He'd said he loved her, and that he wanted to marry her and have children with her.

If he cared about you, he wouldn't have gone in there while you were sleeping last night . . .

She studied Karel's face out of the corner of her eye as she plated the food. Frank's bedroom sat between theirs and the one in which the girls were being held, so they were the only rooms he could have heard Karel going into. He'd insisted he had only said it to cause trouble, but instinct and past experience told Irena otherwise. Viktorya wasn't the first girl to catch Karel's eye, but Irena knew better than to confront him about it. If she forced his hand and he made the wrong choice, it could only end one way: Viktorya would take Irena's place, and Karel would make Irena take hers. And she would rather die than go back to that life, so she would keep her mouth shut – and pray that Karel's interest in Viktorya died as quickly as it had with the others.

32

You're too pretty to waste, so I'm going to keep you for myself . . . And if you're good, I'll make you my number one girl. You'd like that, wouldn't you?

The whispered words were at the forefront of Viktorya's mind as she broke through the fog, but they evaporated when her eyes flickered open, and she recoiled in disgust when she saw a filthy foot lying on the pillow in front of her mouth. The other girls had still been out the last time she'd been conscious, but they were back now, and she had to squeeze herself out from between their naked bodies.

The room was stiflingly hot, and the combined odour of sweat and stale cigarette smoke made her feel nauseous. Sitting up, she dropped her feet to the floor and gazed around. The lamp on the bedside table was switched on, and she frowned when she saw that the window had been boarded over. When had that happened? And how had she not heard the nails being hammered into the wood?

Struggling to remember, she stared at the bruises on her

thighs. The colours had intensified since the last time she'd looked at them, but – thankfully – the pain had lessened.

Apart from the ache between her legs, which felt new and raw.

A vision of the boss man's face flashed before her eyes, and she remembered the words she'd heard as she was waking. But had she dreamed them, or had the man actually spoken them? she wondered.

Twisting her head at the sound of a groan, Viktorya peered at the faces of the sleeping girls. They had all looked so young and pretty when she'd met them in the back of that van, but dark shadows now encircled their eyes, and their cheeks were sunken. The girl closest to her rolled over, and she frowned when she noticed several puncture marks in the crook of her elbow, and crusted sores on the back of her hand which looked like cigarette burns.

Curious to know if the other girls were similarly scarred, Viktorya raised the edge of the quilt and scanned their naked bodies. They all bore the same puncture marks and bruising, and she squeezed her eyes shut when an aural memory of them crying and pleading for mercy came back to her. The painkillers had clouded her mind and made her think she had dreamed those pitiful cries, but she now knew that it had been real. And she also knew that it wouldn't be long before she, too, suffered the same fate.

I'm going to keep you for myself . . .

Viktorya's dark eyebrows crept together when the words replayed in her mind. This time, they were accompanied by a sharper vision, and she knew that the boss man *had* been here. He'd climbed into bed with her, and had told her that he would treat her well if she pleased him – although she wasn't sure why he'd made it sound as if she had a choice, when they both knew she'd have been powerless to stop him from taking whatever he wanted from her. But if agreeing to go along with his proposal saved her from suffering like the other girls, she would be a fool to refuse.

Decided, she lay down with her back to the others. As sorry as she felt for them, they were strangers, and she doubted they'd give *her* a second thought if they were offered the same opportunity, so why should she worry about them?

33

Following the argument of that morning, things had quietened down in the house, and Frank counted off day after boring day of captivity as the intruders went about their daily lives as if they owned the place.

It was ten days since they had muscled their way in, and Frank pretty much knew their routine by heart. Irena, despite her insistence that Karel loved her, seemed to be little more than a housekeeper for him and his gang. Every morning she made them a full cooked breakfast, and would then clean up and wash their clothes and bedding while they went about their business. She would cater for them again at lunchtime, and then dinner. Once they'd eaten, Nick and the other man would take the girls to work, and Irena would invariably go to bed – alone – while Karel stayed downstairs, drinking, smoking, and playing cards with the rest of the men into the early hours.

Tonight, the enforced inactivity and boredom was wearing Frank out, but he was finding it difficult to sleep in the airless, stale-smelling room, even though he had stripped down to his underwear and was lying on top of the bed. It was gone midnight when he heard the familiar creak of bedsprings and the low murmur of voices through the wall. Unwilling to listen to any more of the disgusting grunting he'd been subjected to all week, he rolled over and plucked a cotton wool ball out of the bag Maureen had kept in her bedside cabinet. As he was about to plug his ears, a shrill whistle rose up from the front of the house, followed, a few seconds later, by the thunder of footsteps running up the stairs.

Sliding off the bed at the sound of someone rapping sharply on Irena's bedroom door, Frank rushed over to the door – praying that she would wake up and catch Karel red-handed as he came out of the girl's room. Disappointed when Karel emerged onto the landing before she did, he pressed his ear against the wood in time to hear Karel hiss, 'What the fuck's all the noise about?'

'Someone's coming,' a man replied quietly. 'I was out front and saw headlights coming this way. And it's definitely not Nick, 'cos they were too low down for a van.'

Irena's door suddenly opened, and Frank could hear the sleep in her voice when she asked what was going on.

'Someone's coming,' Karel told her. 'Go down and get rid of them.'

A vehicle turned onto the drive and came to a stop, and Frank heard its door slam shut and someone walk heavily across the gravel. The doorbell rang, and Irena answered it. Her voice was too low for Frank to hear what she was saying, but he had no such problem with the caller's voice, and his heart lurched when he realized it was his daughter-in-law. Marie never visited of her own accord, so he wondered if Evan had sent her to pick up the bits and pieces he'd left behind. Or maybe something had happened, and she'd come to deliver the bad news?

Dreading it being the latter, Frank jerked away from the door when the key turned in the lock. It was Karel, and he had the shotgun in his hands.

'You've got a visitor,' he hissed. 'Get dressed.'

'It's my son's wife,' Frank said, quickly pulling his pyjama bottoms and dressing gown on. 'Evan's probably sent her to pick his stuff up.'

'Get rid of her, or I'll kill her,' Karel warned, shoving him out onto the landing with the barrel of the gun digging into his spine.

Marie was demanding to speak to Evan when Frank reached the hallway. Forcing himself to act naturally, he walked up alongside Irena and gave his daughter-in-law a questioning smile.

'Hello, love. What are you doing here at this time of night?'

Switching her angry gaze from Irena to him, Marie said, 'I want to see Evan. *She* reckons she hasn't seen him, but I know he's here, so tell him to stop hiding and come out and face me.'

'He's not here, love,' Frank replied truthfully. 'Did he tell you he was coming over tonight?'

A flicker of uncertainty flashed into Marie's eyes, but she quickly blinked it away and raised her chin.

'You know damn well he hasn't been home since he came to

help you with your cars last week, so stop covering for him. He hasn't been in work since, and none of his mates have seen him, so he's *got* to be here.'

'I promise you he's not,' said Frank. 'He did call round last week, but we had words and I told him to leave. I haven't heard from him since.'

'So where *is* he?' Marie's voice had risen in pitch, and tears were glistening in her eyes.

Frank had never been overly keen on the woman, but she looked so distraught, he had to stuff his hands into his dressing gown pockets to keep himself from reaching out to her.

'I honestly have no idea, love. Knowing him, he's probably been on a bender, and now he's hiding out somewhere, trying to pluck up the courage to face you. I'm sure he'll turn up soon, so why don't you go home and get some sleep, eh? You look exhausted.'

'Of course I'm exhausted,' Marie replied spikily. 'I've been ill all week, and I've barely had the energy to get out of bed, so I didn't need to be worrying about Evan on top of it all.'

'Have you tried ringing him?' Frank asked.

'Numerous times,' said Marie. 'And I've left loads of messages, but he hasn't answered any of them. And *you* haven't answered when I've tried to ring you,' she added accusingly. 'That's why I know you're covering for him.'

'My phone's got a fault,' Frank lied. 'I haven't heard it ringing.'

'Mobile broke as well, is it?' Marie gave him a disbelieving look.

Frank gave a guilty little shrug, and said, 'I'm sorry, love, but I don't know what else to tell you.'

'I know you're lying,' Marie sniffed, taking a tissue out of her pocket and swiping at her nose. 'I've given it a week, but enough's enough. If he's not man enough to face me, you can tell him not to bother coming back this time. I've bent over backwards to put things right since he came home after stopping here the last time he walked out, and everything's been great, so I don't understand why he's doing this.'

'I am sure Even is not try to hurt you,' Irena interjected.

The sound of her voice ignited a fire in Marie's eyes.

'His name is Ev-An,' she corrected her angrily. 'And don't you *dare* talk about him like you and him are friends. He's told me all about you, waltzing in here and taking advantage of a lonely old man, and he's as disgusted by you as I am!'

'That's enough,' Frank said, desperate to get her out of there when he heard a creak on the stairs behind him. 'Just go home, Marie.'

Rounding on him, Marie yelled, 'Don't tell me what to do, 'cos you're as bad as *her*! You call yourself a father, putting that tart before your own children when their mum isn't even cold in her grave yet? And to think I forced Evan to ring you on Christmas Day, because I knew he was missing you. It's no wonder him and Jo don't want anything to do with you. You're a disgrace!'

'Do not talk to Frankie like this,' Irena jumped to Frank's defence. 'He is good man, and is not his fault his son is liar.'

'Irena, don't,' Frank said quietly.

'No, is not fair,' Irena persisted. 'She is disrespect you, and she need to know truth.'

'What truth?' Marie demanded, staring at Frank. 'What's she on about?'

'It's nothing,' Frank said, furious that Irena had been about to repeat the accusation she'd made against Evan when he now knew it to be a lie. 'It's late, and we all need some sleep, so go home.'

'I'm not going anywhere until you tell me what she meant.' Marie stood her ground.

'I've already told you I haven't seen Evan, and I don't know where he is,' Frank said with finality. 'Now go *home*, Marie.'

Narrowing her eyes when he made to close the door, Marie said, 'I know you lot have never liked me, and I bet you're made up now he's left me, aren't you? Well, you know what, you can go to hell, 'cos I'm getting a divorce and cutting the whole rotten lot of you out of my life!'

She turned on her heel at that, and marched back to her car, and Frank's heart went out to her when he saw her swiping tears off her face as she drove away.

'I am sorry if I speak out of turn,' Irena murmured, touching his arm. 'But she would not leave, so I was try to—'

'Don't touch me!' Frank snapped, slamming the door shut and glaring down at her. 'This is all *your* fault.'

'What was that?' Karel demanded, trotting down the stairs.

Frank turned to face him, his expression pure ice. Evan had

gone AWOL, and Jo was safe in Australia, so he figured now was as good a time as any to take a stand.

'You heard,' he said brusquely. 'I had to stand there and watch *her* break an innocent woman's heart, so that's another life you two have ruined.'

'Who the *fuck* do you think you're talking to?' Karel thrust his face into Frank's and stared into his eyes.

Too angry to be intimidated, Frank slammed his palms against the man's chest and pushed him away, yelling, 'I'm talking to *you*! The piece of shit who robs decent, hard-working people, and tortures defenceless women!'

Winded when Karel drove a fist into his stomach, Frank doubled over, but he looked up and let out a little laugh.

'That all you got, big man?'

The second punch connected with his nose, and his legs buckled when white-hot pain exploded behind his eyes. A vicious kick in the ribs sent him flying against the blood-splattered wall, but still he refused to give in.

'Go on, then!' he challenged, staring up at Karel from the floor. 'What are you waiting for? You're gonna kill me anyway, so fucking *do* it!'

It was the first time Irena had ever heard him use that word, and Frank almost laughed out loud when he saw the expression on her face.

'What's up, love? Haven't shocked you, have I? Well, it's not half as shocked as you're going to be when you find out what he's been doing with that girl for the last few nights.'

Infuriated, Karel released the gun's safety catch and aimed it at Frank's head.

'*No!*' Irena squawked, leaping forward and tugging on his arm. 'We need him alive or this will all be over!'

'He knows that, and that's why he's not gonna do it,' Frank said, praying that the man's ego wouldn't compel him to prove otherwise. 'He knows about us, as well – don't you, Karel? You know she was sharing my bed right up until the day you and those other thugs turned up here? That we had sex every night, and she told me she loved me.'

'Is lie!' Irena spluttered, her face draining of colour. 'Do not listen, Karel. He is try to cause trouble.'

'Come off it,' Frank snorted. 'You might have fooled me, Irena, but you're sure as hell not fooling him, 'cos he already knows you're a whore. Isn't that right, Karel?'

With a roar of fury, Karel smashed the barrel of the gun down on Frank's head before turning on Irena.

'Karel, don't!' she cried, throwing her arms up to protect her face when he raised his fist.

'Shut your mouth,' he spat, his punch glancing off the side of her head. 'You've been asking for this all fuckin' week!'

The back door suddenly opened, and two of the men ran in. Dragging Irena out of their way, Karel said, 'Took your time, didn't you?'

'Sorry, boss,' Jacko apologized, casting a hooded glance at Irena, but making no move to help her. 'We were doing a recce of the fields.'

'Put him in his room while I deal with her,' Karel ordered, nodding toward Frank who was sprawled on the floor.

'Karel, you are hurt me!' Irena cried when he dragged her along the hall.

'Hurting you?' he spat, slamming her up against the wall and holding her there with his hand around her throat. 'Think yourself lucky I haven't fuckin' *scalped* you!'

'He was lie,' she whimpered, her hands fluttering over his as she forced herself to meet his gaze. 'You are only man I love, and he know this, so he is try to punish me by lie to you.'

'You really think I'm that fuckin' stupid?' Karel laughed, his breath thick with alcohol. 'I've known all along, you thick bitch.'

'No . . .' Irena tried to shake her head, but he was holding her too tightly.

Karel's lip twisted into a sneer.

'I don't give a flying fuck what you and him did, sweetheart. The only thing that pisses me off is that cunt thinking he's got one over on me. And *you*, lying through your teeth when I gave you the chance to come clean.'

Irena swallowed nervously and forced herself to refocus. Karel had beaten her before, and he had humiliated her on numerous occasions. But the benefits of being his woman had outweighed the pain, and she refused to lose the privileges she had earned over something that had been his idea in the first place.

When Nick had come across this place after Karel's arrest, Karel had told her, during a prison visit, to do whatever it took to get her foot through the door. She had known exactly what he meant, because it hadn't been the first time he'd asked her to use her body for his gain. But, foolishly, she had forgotten how quickly he could change his mind: that what he considered acceptable one day, could become a sin worthy of retribution the next. As soon as he'd laid eyes on Frank his expression had changed, and she had known he would react violently if he heard what she'd done, so she had lied. That had been a mistake, but she could turn this around. She *had* to.

'Karel, I love you, so I will tell truth,' she began, tentatively. 'I did sleep in bed with him, but only because you tell me to secure house for you. This is all I do, and I swear I did *not* make sex with him.'

Karel tightened his grip on her hair.

'Is truth!' she repeated, tears of pain and fear swimming in her eyes. 'I *would* have done it – for *you*. But he did not ask me to, and I did not offer.'

'So why sleep in his bed?' Karel asked, his eyes still sparking with suspicion.

'To make him believe I have genuine feeling for him,' she replied earnestly. 'He was meant to think you are my brother until I have marry him and is too late for him to stop us. This is why I need to make relationship seem real. And it was work – until he see you and become suspicious.'

'Oh, so it's *my* fault you fucked up, is it?' Karel raised an eyebrow.

'I am not blame you,' Irena said, her legs shaking with relief when she saw that the flames in his eyes were beginning to die down. 'I love you, and I have suffer without you. Frank realize this, and he is jealous. This is why he lie: to push us apart.'

Karel brought his face down close to hers and stared into her eyes.

'Like I said, sweetheart, it ain't even about you fucking him, it's about you lying to me. Now fuck off. I've got stuff to do.'

Unable to stop herself, even though her instincts were screaming at her to keep her mouth shut, Irena said, 'What about girl?'

Karel's eyes narrowed, and Irena cowered when he raised his hand. She'd been sure he was going to punch her again, but instead, he grasped her chin tightly in his hand, and said, softly, 'You know better than to question me, Irena. I've given you a lot of leeway, but that can easily change – and you wouldn't want that, would you?'

In pain, her lips distorted by his grip, Irena whispered, 'No.'

'Thought not.' He grinned. 'Now, like I said – fuck off, before I change my mind and beat the shit out of you.'

Irena didn't need telling twice, and she scuttled away as soon as he released her. Jacko and the other man had come back downstairs by then, and they looked as embarrassed as she felt when she brushed past them and ran up to her room.

34

Marie cried bitter tears on the drive home. She didn't understand why Evan had bothered coming back to her if he hadn't intended to stay. *She* hadn't gone after *him*, he'd come to her, tail between his legs, begging for a second chance. He'd said he loved her, and had sworn that he'd never cheated on her, and never would. And, like a fool, she had believed him.

Since he'd come home, she had been making a massive effort to put the spark back into their marriage. Evan hated that she let the dog lick her face, so she'd put a stop to that; and she had taken to cleaning the house while he was at work, so it was nice for him to come home to. She'd even started wearing the sexy underwear he liked, despite the fact it made her feel fat and ugly. In return, Evan had been coming home straight from work instead of sloping off to the pub; and he'd started paying her little compliments instead of constantly criticizing her. And last week, the night before he'd disappeared, he had bought her flowers for the first time in years. They had been half-dead, and some of them hadn't even survived their first night in the vase, but it was a romantic gesture, and she had really thought they were turning a corner. So why had he abandoned her again?

It had to have something to do with what that woman had said before Frank had shut her up. She'd said that Evan was a liar, and that Marie deserved to know what he was really like, and the only conclusion Marie could draw from that was that Evan was cheating on her, and Frank and his bitch knew exactly where he was – *and* who he was with.

Convinced that she was right, Marie marched inside when she got home and, ignoring her beloved dog when it bounded out into the hall to greet her, dragged a suitcase out of the cupboard under the stairs and carried it up to the bedroom. Throwing it onto the bed, she unzipped it and tipped the contents of Evan's drawers into it, before chucking the contents of the laundry basket on top. If this new woman of his wanted him so badly, she was welcome to him *and* his stinking under-pants and sweaty socks!

Drawers and laundry basket empty, Marie opened the ward-robe and pulled out his shirts and trousers. Pausing when she came to the suit he had bought for their wedding six years earlier, she clutched the jacket to her breast and sank down on the bed when she picked up the faint scent of his aftershave.

Something hard was pressing against her breastbone, and she reached into the inside pocket and pulled it out. It was the passport Evan thought he'd lost after his last trip abroad, and she flipped it open and looked at the photo he had always complained made him look older than his dad. A wave of sadness washed over her as she stared into the familiar eyes, but it was quickly replaced by anger when she remembered that he was probably lying in another woman's bed right now; having sex, and telling the bitch he loved her.

Hurling the passport across the room, Marie yanked at the jacket, desperately trying to tear the material with her bare hands. When that didn't work, she snatched her nail scissors up off the bedside table and hacked at it instead.

Exhausted after a few minutes, she was stuffing the ruined jacket into the suitcase along with his other clothes when the house-phone started ringing. Dropping everything, she threw herself across the bed and snatched up the receiver.

'Evan?'

'No, it's Jo. Isn't he there? Only I've been calling his mobile for the last few days, and he hasn't answered or rung me back.'

Irritated that her sister-in-law hadn't even had the grace to say hello, Marie said, 'No, he's not here. I haven't seen him all week – but you probably already knew that, didn't you?'

'No, I didn't,' said Jo. 'Has something happened?'

Marie clenched her teeth when she thought she detected a hint of glee in her sister-in-law's tone. Jo was another one from Evan's family who'd never liked her – and the feeling was mutual. Jo had looked down her nose at Marie from the moment Evan had introduced them, and Marie couldn't stand her. The bitch thought she was a cut above everybody else, and her daughter was a pampered little princess who was going to grow up to be a snob, same as her mother.

'Hello . . . ?' Jo said. 'Are you still there?'

'Yes, I'm here,' Marie said. 'And, no, nothing's happened. Not that *I* was aware of, anyway,' she added bitterly. 'You're probably best calling your dad if you want to speak to him, 'cos that's where he's hiding.'

'Really?' Jo sounded confused. 'I thought they weren't talking?'

'They weren't,' said Marie. 'But Evan was missing him, so he went round to sort it out. Last I heard, they'd made up, and Evan was going round to help him with his cars. But your dad reckons he hasn't seen him, so I haven't got a clue what's going on. All I *do* know is, he's been lying to me for weeks: telling me that bitch is a dog, when she's not; and that she's not there any more, when she is.'

'What bitch?'

'The foreign one your dad's shacked up with.'

'Oh . . .' Jo murmured. 'She's still there, then?'

'Like you didn't know,' Marie said tartly. 'You and Evan have been thick as thieves these last few weeks, and I know you've been talking about her, so stop treating me like an idiot.'

'I don't think you're an idiot,' Jo argued. 'I know we haven't always seen eye to eye, but you're my brother's wife, so I—'

'Oh, *please*,' Marie interrupted scornfully. 'Why don't you ever say what you really think, Jo? You're so bloody patronizing, it's sickening. I know damn well none of your lot can stand me, but I never cared as long as me and Evan were all right. But we're finished now, so you can drop the act.'

'You want me to drop the act, do you?' Jo replied sharply. 'Fine, I'll tell you what I really think of you. You're one of the rudest, most miserable people I've ever met, and I wish my brother had never met you, because he can do way better. I'd even prefer him to be with Irena – and that's saying something, considering the lies she told about him after they kissed!'

Marie's mouth had fallen open, and her heart was pounding so hard she felt light-headed. It hadn't even crossed her mind that Frank's girlfriend might be the one Evan had been cheating with, but it all made sense now. He'd called the woman a dog, when in reality, as loath as Marie was to admit it, she was extremely attractive – and exactly his type, with her blond hair, big blue eyes, and slim figure. And he and Frank had fallen out when he'd stayed there that week, so his dad had probably caught them at it. *That* was why he'd come home that night. Not because he loved her and wanted to be with her, as he'd claimed, but because Frank had kicked him out and he'd had nowhere else to go.

Marie didn't realize Jo had hung up until the dial tone filtered into her thoughts. Still reeling, she replaced the receiver in its cradle and glanced at the clock on the bedside table. All she wanted to do was jump in the car and drive round to all of Evan's mates' houses until one of them told her where he was. But it was gone 2 a.m., and they all had children, so she resigned herself to the fact that she wasn't going to get any information tonight.

Unable to face sleeping alone, she undressed and climbed

into bed, calling the dog up to lie beside her. Then pouring herself a large drink from the bottle of vodka that was standing on the bedside table, she set her alarm for 6 a.m., determined to drive over to Evan's workplace and catch his mates before they went in. They had all denied seeing him, but one of them had to know where the cheating bastard was hiding. And when she got her hands on him, he was going to wonder what had hit him.

35

Viktorya couldn't sleep. She'd been restless ever since the boss man had rushed out of her room earlier, and time seemed to have come to a standstill as she waited for him to come back.

Determined to be alert when he came to her, she deliberately hadn't swallowed the painkillers she'd been given today. As a result, she had been awake when the horrible blond man had come into the room earlier that evening, and she had watched his reflection in the dressing-table mirror as he'd given each of the girls an injection before molesting them and ordering them to put on the flimsy underwear he'd brought in for them.

Surprisingly, the girls hadn't resisted, and Viktorya had realized as she'd watched them lick their lips in anticipation of the needle, that they were starting to need whatever drug he was giving them. That realization had made her all the more determined to take the boss man up on his offer, because the thought of being forced into a life of prostitution, addiction, abuse and pain, terrified her.

Still hoping that the boss man would come back to her, she rolled over to face the door when the key turned in the lock several hours later. Disappointed when the blond man herded her room-mates in and ordered them to strip, she watched as the zombie-like girls obediently shed their flimsy underwear and handed it to him before flopping down on the mattress.

Scared that she was about to miss her chance when he turned to leave the room, she quickly sat up, and said, 'I need to see boss.'

Nick stopped at the sound of her voice, and turned his head. 'Is that right? And why's that, then?'

'Is between me and him,' Viktorya replied, her heart racing. The man's aura was sinister, and she felt vulnerable in his presence.

'Ah, well, you're gonna have to wait,' Nick said quietly as he walked around the bed. ''Cos he's with his missus, and he can't be disturbed – if you get my drift?'

He made a thrusting motion with his hips inches from Viktorya's face, and she swallowed the bile that flooded her mouth when she recalled seeing him do the exact same thing to one of the girls earlier tonight – minus the jeans that were now covering his erection. As scared as she was, Viktorya raised her chin and forced herself to maintain eye-contact with him. She knew he'd mentioned the boss's woman to make her think she meant nothing to the man, but she knew better. The boss had promised that she would be his number one, and she intended to claim that position by whatever means necessary.

'I need speak to him,' she repeated. 'And if you do not bring him, I will tell him what I see you do to these girls tonight.'

'And . . . ?' Nick jeered, his sour breath settling over her face when he leaned down and placed his hands on either side of her. 'He might have the hots for you right now, darlin', but I guarantee that won't last, so don't be thinking you're something special, 'cos you ain't. He'll fuck you till he's bored, and then he'll ship you out to earn your keep with your mates.'

'He say he is want to keep me for only him,' Viktorya argued, refusing to be swayed. 'And he has promise to make me number one girl.'

'I wouldn't let our Reeny hear you saying that, if I was you,' Nick snorted. 'She ain't gonna give him up without a fight, and she'd make mincemeat of you. So how's about you and me make a little pact, eh? I won't tell Reeny you're after her man, and you can give me a bit of what you've been giving Karel. Yeah?'

Revolted by the idea of this animal putting his filthy hands on her, Viktorya drew her head back and spat in his face. Then, opening her mouth wide, she screamed out the name she hadn't known until that moment: '*KAARRREEEELLL . . . !*'

Jolted into action, Nick threw his hand over her mouth to silence her, and let out a strangled cry of pain when she sank her teeth into his flesh. Raising his fist to punch her, he hesitated when the door opened and light filtered in from the landing.

'What the fuck are you *doing*?' Gaz hissed, staring in at him.

At the sound of his voice, Viktorya released her grip on Nick's hand and scrambled off the bed.

'Help me!' she cried, running to Gaz. 'He was try to rape me!'

'Was I fuck,' Nick countered, wiping the spit off his face with his sleeve and stuffing his injured hand under his armpit. 'I was trying to shut you up, you stupid bitch.'

'Why are you even in here?' Gaz asked. 'You were only supposed to be locking them in.'

'You what?' Nick glared at him. 'I don't answer to you, you little prick.'

'No, you answer to Karel,' Gaz reminded him. 'And he specifically told you to leave this one alone, so, if I was you, I'd get out of here before he wakes up and catches you.'

'Catches him doing what?' Karel asked, walking in at that exact moment and looking from Gaz to Nick.

'Nothing,' Nick muttered, flashing a hooded look of warning at Gaz. 'I was only getting the tarts' underwear off 'em for the wash, and this crazy bitch started mouthing off.'

'I ask speak to you,' Viktorya said, rushing to Karel's side and clinging to his arm. 'He say no, and then he hit me and try to rape me.'

'No, I fucking didn't!' Nick protested, turning to Gaz. 'You saw everything. Did it look like I was trying to rape her?'

Gaz gazed coolly back at him, and his silence weighed heavily in the air for several moments. But just as Nick was beginning to think the man was going to throw him under the bus, Gaz looked at Karel and shook his head.

'He'd only been in here a minute, and she was biting him when I walked in.'

'You bit him?' Karel raised an eyebrow and peered down at Viktorya.

'Yes,' she replied, no trace of remorse in her voice. 'He put hand over my mouth when I call for you, and I could not breathe, so he deserve.'

Karel chuckled softly, and grinned at Nick and Gaz.

'I like this one. She's got balls.'

'And teeth,' Nick muttered, still rubbing his hand. 'I wouldn't mind, but I was only trying to protect you. She was yelling her head off, and I didn't think you'd want Reeny to hear her and start asking questions.'

'Do I look like I give a fuck what Irena thinks?' Karel scoffed. Then, turning to Viktorya, he said, 'Go get yourself cleaned up, darlin'. The bathroom's at the end of the landing. And wash this.' He stroked her greasy hair. 'I want it looking as nice as it did when you first got here.'

Gaz frowned when, smiling like a cat that had got the cream, Viktorya sashayed out of the room. He couldn't blame her for jumping at the chance to escape the hell her room-mates had found themselves in, but she was fooling herself if she thought she was in for a free ride with Karel, because the man respected nobody – not even Irena, who had stood by him through thick and thin and deserved to be treated a damn sight better.

Turning to leave the room, Gaz cast a quick glance at the girls who were now huddled together in the bed, and his stomach churned when he saw how ruined they looked compared to a week ago. When he'd first started working for Karel, he'd only been involved in the drugs and protection side of the business, and he'd been fine with that. But everything had changed since moving out here. Now he and Karel's rabid sidekick, Nick, were tasked with keeping the street and brothel girls in line, and he hated it. But people who tried to walk away from Karel had a habit of disappearing without trace, and Gaz wasn't stupid enough to think he'd fare any better, so he had no choice but to stick around until he found a safe way out.

Irena had been sleeping, but she woke when the overhead bedroom light suddenly came on, and she squinted in the glare. The mattress dipped behind her, and she snapped her head round when she heard a little giggle.

'Oh, good, you're awake,' Karel said, smiling at her when she gazed blearily up at him. 'We've got a guest.'

Irena blinked to clear her vision, and her blood ran cold when she saw Viktorya perched on the edge of the bed with a towel wrapped around her damp body. There had been other women in the past: some Karel had picked up in clubs and had wined and dined like normal dates; others, like Viktorya, who he'd picked out from his stable. But he had never brought one of them into their bed while Irena was in it, and that told her she'd been right to be worried about Viktorya. Not only was the girl stunningly beautiful, with her dark-lashed azure-blue eyes, her flawless complexion, and her perfect body, but she was also more than a decade younger than Irena.

'Where d'you think you're going?' Karel asked when Irena slid her legs out from beneath the quilt and stood up.

'You have made your choice, so I will sleep downstairs,' she replied.

'Like hell you will,' he snorted. 'You're my woman, and you'll go when I tell you to.'

Confused, Irena hesitated.

'I do not understand.'

'Oh, I think you do,' Karel said, his eyes never leaving hers as he pulled the towel off Viktorya and tossed it aside before turning the girl around by the shoulders. 'What d'ya reckon?'

Irena's mouth had gone dry, and she self-consciously crossed her arms over her own breasts when Karel started fondling the girl's.

'Back in bed,' Karel ordered huskily. 'You, me, and little Vicky are gonna have some fun.'

Barely able to breathe, Irena croaked, 'Please, Karel, do not do this. You say you love me.'

'And you said you didn't screw that old fucker, but we both know you did,' Karel replied smoothly as he loosened the belt of his dressing gown and let it drop to the floor, revealing his erection. 'Now get back in the fucking bed, or you'll be sleeping with Nick from now on. Is that what you want?'

Aware that he would carry through with the threat and hand her over to Nick if she argued, Irena bit down hard on her lip to keep herself from crying, and climbed back under the quilt.

36

Up and out by six fifteen the next morning, Marie drove over to Evan's workplace and parked outside the main doors. It was all locked up at the front, but she could hear music and banter coming from the side of the building, and she made her way round there when she recognized the voice of Billy Hicks – the man Evan had lied about giving lifts to the hospital.

'I've never seen owt like it in me life,' Billy was saying when she reached the open workshop doors. 'There was a horse with a dick the length of a hosepipe, and the bird was givin' it pure—'

He abruptly stopped speaking when another man spotted Marie and nudged him, and he and the others turned to face her.

'You can't come in here, love,' one of them said. 'Reception opens at eight, so you'll have to come back later.'

'I'm looking for Evan,' Marie said to Billy. 'Have you seen him? Any of you?' she added, including the others now; some of whom she recognized, some she'd never seen before.

'I told you when you rang the other day, he hasn't been in all week,' Billy reminded her.

'I'm not talking about here,' she said. 'I'm talking about *anywhere*. You're his mates; one of you must know where he is?'

'Not me.'

'Me neither.'

The men all shook their heads, and Billy shrugged.

'Sorry, love.'

Marie stared at him before sweeping a gaze over the others.

'One of you knows something,' she said accusingly. 'Did he tell you to lie to me? Are you all in on it? Laughing at me behind my back?'

'Come on, don't get upset,' Billy said, walking over and ushering her back out into the alley when tears started glittering in her eyes.

'Don't touch me!' She jerked away from him. 'I know all about the stupid *bro code*, and I can see you're all lying through your teeth. Just tell me where he is. I promise I won't let on that I got it from you.'

'For the last time, I don't know,' Billy insisted. 'And I've got to set my machine up before my boss gets here, so—'

'Billy, *please*,' she implored. 'I'm his wife; I've got a right to know.'

'For fuck's sake, leave the man alone and go home,' one of the others called out from the doorway.

'It's no fuckin' wonder he's done one, state of her,' someone else muttered from inside.

'Take no notice,' Billy said apologetically when her cheeks flared. 'None of us has seen or heard from him. And, between you and me,' he went on quietly as he walked her along the alley, 'he'll be getting his cards if he doesn't show his face ASAP. So if you *do* manage to find him, give him a heads up, yeah?'

He left her with that, and headed back to the workshop. Unsure where to go from there, Marie pulled a tissue from her pocket and blew her nose. Behind her, someone wolf-whistled, and she snapped her head round to see which one of Evan's loutish workmates was taking the piss. But the whistle hadn't been aimed at her, she realized; it was for the woman wearing stiletto heels, a short skirt and low-cut top, who was unlocking the door directly facing the entrance to the workshop.

Recognizing her, Marie's blood boiled, and she turned on her heel and marched back up the alleyway, yelling, 'Oi, *you*! Laura, or whatever your name is, I want a word!'

'Me?' Laura Weston hesitated and gave her a bemused look. 'About what?'

'My *husband*,' spat Marie. 'I should have known he'd go crawling back for more when he's got *them* under his nose day in day out!' She jabbed a finger at Laura's enormous breasts.

'You what?' Laura almost laughed in her face. 'I haven't got a clue who you're talking about, sweetheart, but I think you've got the wrong person.'

'Don't pretend you don't know him when I caught you with him in the pub,' Marie bellowed, oblivious to the men chuckling as they watched the show from the workshop doorway.

'Oh, yeah . . .' Laura drew her head back and smirked. 'I remember you now. Evan's crazy bitch wife.'

'Where is he?' Marie demanded. 'What's the address? I said what's the fucking *ADDRESS*?'

'First off, you'd best stop yelling in my face before I punch your lights out,' Laura warned. 'And, second off, I haven't got a clue where he is, so quit making a show of yourself.'

'*Liar!*' Marie hissed, her body quivering with rage. 'You *told* me you'd been screwing him, so don't bother denying it now!'

'I said I *could* have, if I'd wanted him,' Laura corrected her. 'But I was only winding you up, you dozy cow. What did you expect after chucking my drink in my face?'

'I don't believe you.'

'I don't really care *what* you believe,' Laura said dismissively. 'And if you don't mind, I've got a showroom to open.'

'JUST TELL ME WHERE HE *IS*!' Marie wailed.

'I . . . don't . . . *know*,' Laura repeated slowly, tiring of the conversation. 'But he's not with me, 'cos I'm spoken for.' She held up her left hand and flashed an engagement ring at Marie. Then, giving a tight smile, she walked inside the building and slammed the door shut.

Humiliated, Marie turned to Billy, but he shook his head and retreated into the workshop, quickly followed by the others. Cheeks on fire, she fled up the alleyway and climbed into her car. It felt like a huge conspiracy that everyone was in on except her. Wherever Evan was, he clearly didn't want her to find him, and that hurt, because she'd done nothing wrong. But he'd made his choice, so she was going to have to accept that it was over for good this time.

Swiping at the tears that were running down her face, she threw the car into gear and headed home.

37

Frank's head was banging when he woke up, and he grimaced when he looked in the dressing-table mirror and saw a lump the size of a tangerine on the side of his head, and dried blood on his face and neck. Untying his dressing gown belt when he felt a sharp pain in his side, he gingerly touched the bruised flesh, half expecting to find a rib poking through. Relieved to see that wasn't the case, he carefully moved over to the side of the bed and opened his drawer to look for painkillers.

The strip of heart tablets Irena had brought up to him several days earlier was sitting at the front of the drawer, so he popped one into his mouth and dry-swallowed it. There were only two left, and it occurred to him that his repeat prescription would already have been sent to the village pharmacy. If he didn't go to collect it, they would ring him; and if he didn't answer, their delivery woman, Anita Reynolds, would bring it round. And she was one of the biggest gossips in the village, so when she saw Irena, she'd go straight back and tell everyone.

But so what if she did? It wouldn't change anything. Gossiping or not, they would still be free to go about their lives, and he would still be imprisoned here, at the mercy of these thugs.

The door opened behind him, and he turned his head as Nick entered. In a fighting mood, despite the injuries Karel had inflicted on him, Frank glared at the man.

Unfazed, Nick grinned, and said, 'Up and at 'em, Granddad. It's time you started earning your keep.'

'No,' Frank replied, stubbornly staying put. 'If you want me to get up, you'll have to *make* me.'

He'd fully expected the man to go for him, but he hadn't expected the speed of the attack – or the strength with which the much shorter man managed to pin him down on the bed.

'Still don't get it, do you?' Nick snarled, his eyes glittering as he pressed the blade of the knife he'd pulled out of his pocket against Frank's throat. 'You ain't in control here, and you'll do as you're fuckin' told – or else.'

'Do your worst,' Frank hissed, bucking his hips to try and dislodge the man. 'My kids are out of reach, so you can't do a damn thing to them. It's just you and me, so why don't you put the knife down and take me on man to man?'

Nick gave a throaty chuckle and pressed down harder on the blade, drawing blood.

'Oops,' he drawled, wiping it off with his fingertip and smearing it on Frank's cheek. 'Now look what you've made me do.'

'Do it again,' Frank challenged. 'Cut my fucking head off and nail it to the gate post, if you want, but I'll *never* take orders from you!'

Karel strode into the room and tutted when he saw Nick sitting astride Frank on the bed.

'What the fuck are you doing?' he snapped. 'I told you to fetch him down, not shag him.'

'And I will,' said Nick, still staring at Frank. 'Soon as he realizes who's boss.'

'Well, it isn't *you*, that's for sure,' spat Frank. 'You're nothing more than his sidekick.'

The dart hit its target, and Frank laughed when he saw anger flare in Nick's eyes.

'Go on then, dickhead, *do* it!' he goaded when the man raised the knife into the air.

'Get off him,' Karel ordered, his tone bored now.

'Nah, man,' Nick argued. 'I ain't having the cunt think he can talk to me like that.'

'I said get off him,' Karel repeated. 'I've got something to show him.'

Nick hesitated for a moment. Then, grin returning, he jumped off the bed.

Sensing that something bad was about to happen, Frank eyed the men warily as he sat up.

'What's going on?'

'If I didn't need you, I'd have killed you by now,' Karel said, as casually as if they were mates having a friendly chat. 'But you know that, don't you? And that's why you've suddenly developed balls. But let's see if we can't change that, eh?'

An icy hand clutched Frank's heart when the man brought

a photograph up on the screen of his phone and showed it to him.

'No . . .' he croaked, staring in horror at the image of Evan gagged and tied to a chair in a dimly lit room, his head at an angle, his face battered almost beyond recognition.

'You've only got yourself to blame,' Karel said, putting the phone away again. 'If you'd got rid of him like I told you to that day, he'd have been OK. But you had to go and make him suspicious, so now he's paying the price.'

'But I didn't say anything,' Frank argued, his voice as weak as he physically felt. 'You were there – you heard everything.'

'I know what you *said*,' Karel agreed. 'But you obviously gave him some sort of signal, 'cos we caught him spying on us the next day. And why would he do that, unless he knew something was wrong?'

Frank's knuckles were bone white, and his fingernails were cutting into the flesh of his palms. This was why Marie hadn't seen Evan all week. He hadn't left her, he'd been kidnapped.

'Where is he?' he asked. 'Is – is he . . .' He tailed off, unable to voice his fear.

'Not yet,' Karel said, guessing what he meant. 'But he will be if you give me any more trouble.'

Tears of relief flooded Frank's eyes and he held up his hands.

'OK, you win. I'll do anything you want, but let my boy go. *Please*, I'm begging you.'

'Awww . . . he's such a good daddy, ain't he?' Nick said sarcastically.

'Sure is.' Karel grinned. Then, to Frank, he said, 'Anyway, now you know what's at stake, I think I can trust you to behave, so I'm going to give you a bit of rope.'

'What do you mean?' Frank asked, wary again.

'I'm going to let you go downstairs,' Karel explained. 'You'll be able to make yourself a brew whenever you want; take a bath, go to the loo without asking permission. I'll even let you take a walk around the garden and get a bit of air, if you want. So what d'ya say?'

A deep crevice had formed in the centre of Frank's brow. Was this some kind of trick? Was Karel toying with him? Dangling the carrot of freedom, only to snatch it away and tell him it was a joke when he said yes.

'Come on, Frankie.' Karel sighed. 'Don't take too long or I might change my mind.'

Convinced it was a trick, but desperate for it not to be, because he'd barely eaten in days and desperately needed to clean himself up and brush his teeth, Frank met the man's gaze and nodded.

'Can't hear you,' Nick said, pushing one of his ears forward.

'Yes,' Frank muttered – ashamed of himself for being so weak as he added, 'Thank you.'

'See, I knew me and you could be buddies if we made the effort,' Karel said, clapping a hand down on Frank's shoulder and giving it a squeeze. 'Wow, you're wasting away, mate. Best go and make yourself a butty, 'cos you're gonna need to stay fit now you're working for me. But get a wash first, eh? You're not looking your best, and we need you on tip-top form for the wedding.'

Stomach churning at the reminder of the man's plan to marry him and Irena off, Frank nodded and stood up.

In the bathroom a few seconds later, he closed the door and leaned heavily against the sink. Someone had smashed the mirror, and numerous weary eyes looked back at him when he stared into it, each of them surrounded by a deep, dark hollow. His skin was grey, and the peppery half-beard he was sporting made him look like his father.

Squeezing his eyes shut when the image of Evan, shackled and beaten, flashed into his mind, he shook his head slowly. He wasn't a violent man by nature, but these people were evil, and if he survived this, he would make it his life's mission to kill each and every one of them for what they had done to his son.

But who was he kidding? There was only one way this was going to end, and it didn't involve him walking away. As Karel had said, he would already be dead if they didn't need him, and it was only a matter of time before he'd served his purpose and they disposed of him.

He opened his eyes and stared at the jagged shards of mirror-glass. Maybe he should do the job for them and put an end to this, he mused. If he cut his wrist or throat deeply enough, they would never be able to stem the bleeding, and when he was dead they would be forced to abandon their plans and leave.

Really? an internal voice argued. *You really think they'd give up just because you're dead?*

He shook his head in reply. Of course they wouldn't. They were too smart for that. They had been planning this for months, and they wouldn't throw it away because of a minor inconvenience like Frank dying earlier than he was supposed to. If anything, they would probably go ahead with the wedding using one of Karel's men as a stand-in, safe in the knowledge that nobody who knew the real Frank would be present to out the man as an imposter.

That was certainly do-able, but would Karel take that risk when he'd not long been released from jail, knowing that, if it went wrong, he'd have the police crawling all over him? No, he wouldn't, Frank decided. He was going to do this exactly as he'd planned, and that was why he'd taken Evan hostage: to ensure that Frank didn't do anything to fuck it up for him.

Heartsore at the thought of his son being hurt because of him, the last spark of hope died in Frank's eyes. He had always tried to be a good father, but now, when he ought to have doubled his efforts in light of them losing their mother, he had failed his children in every possible way. Marie had been right to call him a disgrace, and if, by some miracle, he and Evan came out of this alive, Frank would do everything in his power to make it up to him – and to Jo.

Resigned to the thought that, whichever way this turned out, his children probably wouldn't want to have anything to do with him, Frank washed the blood off his face and brushed his teeth, then shampooed the grease out of his hair before heading back to his room to change into clean clothes.

BRUTAL

When he went downstairs a short time later, Irena was coming out of the kitchen with the overflowing laundry basket in her hands, and their eyes met for a brief moment before, blushing, she scuttled into the utility room. Walking on into the kitchen, Frank stopped and looked around, drinking it all in. It was the first time he'd stepped foot in there since arriving home after visiting Yvonne on Christmas Day to find Karel and Nick with their feet under the table, and his heart cried when he saw the state of the place. Irena had kept it tidy when it had been the two of them, but he guessed she was overwhelmed by the volume of people she was now catering for when he saw the dirty crockery stacked on the ledge beside the sink, and the empty whisky bottles and crumpled beer cans heaped in the corner beside the overflowing bin. The table was littered with playing cards and used glasses, some of which still contained dregs of alcohol; but he was more upset about the china saucers from a tea set Maureen had inherited from her mother being used as ashtrays – along with the tabletop, which was scarred with numerous burn marks. The lack of respect was staggering, but he didn't know why he'd expected better of these animals.

A girlish little giggle drifted out from the living room, and Frank looked round to see Karel coming out into the hall with his arm around a young, barefoot girl dressed in a long shirt. She was extremely pretty, with dark-lashed blue eyes and long black hair, and Frank instantly recognized her as the one he'd seen smile at Karel on the day the girls had first arrived.

Realizing that she must also be the one he'd heard Karel having sex with, he understood why Irena had looked so miserable. If Karel was no longer trying to hide the relationship from her, she had to be afraid that her days were numbered.

Karel had been nuzzling the girl's neck, but he stopped when he spotted Frank watching them, and looked him up and down before giving an approving nod.

'Looking good, Frankie boy. What d'you reckon, darlin'?' He nudged the girl. 'Handsome fucker, ain't he?'

Viktorya cast a disinterested glance at Frank, and shrugged. 'He is not so handsome as you, I think.'

'Smart girl,' Karel chuckled, slapping her on the backside before ushering her into the kitchen and taking a seat at the table. 'Have you had anything to eat yet, Frankie?'

Frank shook his head and eyed the girl from the corner of his eye when she perched on the man's lap and looped her arms around his neck. She had a self-satisfied smile on her lips, as if she'd won some kind of prize, but Frank had a feeling that her joy wouldn't last too long, and he pitied her almost as much as he pitied Irena.

'Hurry up and grab a butty,' Karel said, leaning forward to take a cigarette out of a packet on the table. 'It's gonna be a busy day.'

Curious to know what the man had in store for him – and still convinced that this sudden display of magnanimity was a trick Karel had dreamed up to torture him – Frank walked over to the fridge. It was mainly filled with beer cans, but he found an open packet of ham and a half-loaf of bread in the salad drawer, and carried them over to the ledge.

As hungry as he'd been all week, his stomach was now in knots, and his appetite had evaporated. But he didn't trust Karel, and he knew it could be a while before he was fed again if the man locked him back in his room, so he made the sandwich and took a seat at the end of the table.

He'd no sooner taken his first bite than Nick appeared in the doorway and jerked his chin up at Karel, and he watched from beneath his lashes as Karel pushed Viktorya off his lap and stood up. Nick was holding a rucksack, and Karel took it from him and handed it to the girl, then shooed her up the stairs, telling her to go and get dressed.

When the girl had gone, Karel and Nick went into the living room and closed the door. Alone, Frank stared at his keys, which he'd noticed on the ledge beside the kettle. Then, standing up, he looked out through the window and quickly scanned the back garden. None of the other men were out there, and the caravan curtains were closed, which made him think they must all still be sleeping. Heart pounding, he tiptoed over to the ledge and reached for the keys. If he was quick and quiet, he could sneak past the living room door and let himself out. Then he could lock Karel and Nick inside, jump into his car, and drive to the police station.

And then what?

Even if he managed to get out without being caught, the village police station worked on a skeleton crew and was rarely open whenever he drove past. And if he was lucky enough to find a copper there today, they would have to call for reinforcements once they learned there were weapons in the house, and that would give Karel and the others ample time to make their getaway. And where would that leave Evan?

In no doubt that they would kill his son, Frank put the keys down and went back to his seat to finish the sandwich.

Karel walked in as he was about to wash his plate, and said, 'Leave that. Irena can do it when you get back.'

'Get back?' Frank repeated.

'I've got some friends coming over, so I need you to take her to pick up some supplies,' Karel said. 'She knows what I want. And, here . . .' He pulled Frank's wallet out of his pocket and tossed it to him. 'Put it on your card.'

Frowning, sure that he'd misheard, Frank said, 'You want me to take Irena shopping?'

'That's right,' Karel affirmed, picking up the keys Frank had put down and tossing them to him before ushering him out into the hall. 'It's time the locals saw you out and about with your lovely fiancée. That way, it won't be so much of a surprise when they hear you're tying the knot.'

'What if I see someone I know?' Frank asked. 'They're bound to ask what's happened when they see the state of me.'

'Just act naturally,' Karel said. Then, dropping the genial tone, he looked Frank in the eye, and said, 'I'm trusting you, Frankie. Don't make me regret it, or you know what'll happen.'

'I won't,' Frank replied. Then, remembering his medication,

he said, 'Is it all right if I go to the pharmacy and pick up my prescription while we're there, only I'm almost out of tablets?'

'Of course,' Karel said, smiling again. 'See how much easier it is when you stop trying to fight me? And once we get that date booked, you'll be on your way to getting your life back.'

Considering what he knew of the man's illegal activities, Frank very much doubted he'd be allowed to walk away when this was all over. But he was more concerned about Evan than himself, so he asked, 'And what about my son? Are you going to let *him* go when I've done what you want?'

'Hey . . . whaddaya take me for?' Karel drew his head back and splayed his hands. 'Do I look like the kind of man who'd go back on his word?'

It was like a scene from *The Godfather*, and Frank was reminded of a saying his father used to roll out whenever he came up against someone dishonest. *I don't know what's worse,* he'd say; *people who lie, or people who think I'm stupid enough to believe their lies.* That was Karel to a tee – although Frank doubted the man gave a toss whether Frank believed him or not.

Karel glanced at his watch and yelled for Irena to get a move on, then bounded up the stairs. Almost immediately Nick came out of the living room and strolled over to Frank.

'Enjoy your freedom while it lasts, Granddad. But don't be getting any silly ideas while you're out there, 'cos we've got eyes and ears *everywhere*. One wrong move and your boy's a goner.'

He mimed pointing a gun between his own eyes and pulling

the trigger, before continuing: 'And when that's done, I'll take a little trip to Australia to meet your daughter and her little one. What was her name again? *Em-i-ly?*' He spaced the name out, as if savouring it, and breathed in deeply through his nostrils. 'Mmmm . . . I can almost taste her already.'

Disgusted, the sandwich churning in his gut, Frank glared at him, and spat, 'You sick fuck!'

'You better believe it, Frankie baby.' Nick grinned. 'Now you just keep that in mind while you're on your jollies, and everything'll be sweet – yeah?'

He winked, then sauntered away, and it took every ounce of self-control Frank possessed not to leap on his back and pummel him to death.

38

In the car a few minutes later, with Irena sitting as stiff as a rod in the passenger seat beside him, Frank turned the key, and, acutely conscious of Karel and Nick watching from the porch, crunched it into reverse and backed it off the drive before setting off along the lane.

When the house had faded into the distance, he glanced round at Irena. Her gaze fixed on the windscreen, her lips barely moving, she said, 'Do not speak. Karel may be listen.'

Unsure how that would be possible unless the man had bugged the car, Frank scanned the dashboard and the sun-visors for hidden microphones or cameras. Nothing appeared to have been tampered with, but he wouldn't put anything past Karel, so he drove on in silence until they reached the village.

In the car park behind the supermarket, he climbed out and walked round to open Irena's door. As he waited for her to get out, he cast a surreptitious glance around, looking for signs that they had been followed, or that somebody had been sent ahead to keep an eye on them. There were a fair few people milling about. Most he recognized, but there were a few strangers, and these he kept in his peripheral vision as he unhooked a trolley from the line and followed Irena into the store.

They had reached the end of the first aisle when somebody called Frank's name, and he froze when he glanced back and saw a woman he vaguely recognized from one of Maureen's knitting or book groups hurrying toward him. Unsure what to do, he looked to Irena for direction, and turned back to the woman when she gave a tiny nod.

'I thought it was you,' the woman said breathlessly. 'I've been meaning to pop round and see you, but you know how it is. Something always seems to come up at the last minute, and everything else flies out of your head.'

'Mmmm,' Frank murmured, struggling to remember her name. Was it Elizabeth, or Edna?

'Sorry I couldn't get to the funeral,' she went on. 'I wanted to pay my respects, but I'd just had my bunions done, so I couldn't get out. I bumped into Mrs Caldwell a few days later, though, and she said it all went well.'

'Mrs Caldwell?' Frank repeated blankly.

'Yvonne,' the woman elaborated. 'From Rose Cottage.'

'Oh, yes, of course,' Frank said, ashamed to realize that he'd as good as forgotten about his neighbour.

'Terrible business, all that,' the woman went on. 'Still, I suppose it's a blessing she doesn't know what's going on, because I'd be absolutely petrified if I found out I had a tumour eating into my brain and there was nothing they could do about it.'

'Sorry?' Frank's eyebrows crept together.

'Oh, didn't you know, love? Sorry, I assumed you'd be first to hear, what with you and her being neighbours. I only found out because our Janet's started working at Leeds General. They reckon it could have been there for years, and that bang on the head triggered it to start growing. She's not going to last much longer by the sound of it, bless her.'

Saddened to hear that Yvonne was in such a bad state, Frank shook his head. None of this was his doing, but he felt responsible, nevertheless. If he hadn't taken Irena in that night, Karel and his gang would have had to find somewhere else to set up camp, and Yvonne would have carried on living her life as normal. Instead, he'd set in motion a lethal chain of events that had affected everybody close to him.

The woman had noticed the lump on the side of his head, and she peered at it, saying, 'Ooh, that looks nasty, love. What on earth happened?'

'He have accident,' Irena said before Frank could answer. 'But is OK; I have been take care of him.'

'Oh . . .' the woman replied coolly, looking at her for the first time. 'I'm sorry, I don't think we've been introduced.' She held out her hand. 'I'm Elaine – a friend of Frank's wife.'

Still smiling, Irena shook it, saying, 'Is nice to meet you. I am Irena – Frankie's fiancée.'

'Fiancée?' Elaine's pencil-thin eyebrows shot up, and she switched her gaze back to Frank. 'That's a bit fast, isn't it? It's not even a year since . . .'

She tailed off without finishing, but Frank got the message loud and clear, and he clenched his teeth. He barely knew the woman, and Maureen had only ever mentioned her in passing, so they'd hardly been the friends she was making them out to be. But even if she'd been Maureen's best mate, and his relationship with Irena *hadn't* turned out to be an absolute sham, it would still be none of her damn business.

'Shall we go, darling?' Irena gave a little tug on his hand. 'We need finish shop.'

Elaine's face was a mask of pure disapproval, and she looked Irena up and down before giving Frank a curt nod goodbye and walking away. As he watched her go – no doubt desperate to tell everybody about his shocking betrayal of his late wife – Frank snatched his hand from Irena's and shoved the trolley round to the next aisle.

'I am sorry,' she said quietly, rushing to catch up. 'I know this is difficult for you, but is difficult for me, too.'

'Really?' he hissed, glaring at her. 'It's *your* innocent neighbour who's dying of a brain tumour because that thug whacked her on the head, is it? *Your* son who's been battered and held hostage to keep you in line? *Your* daughter and granddaughter being threatened with *rape*?'

Irena took a step back, her face bleached of colour.

'Don't act like it's got nothing to do with you, because it's your fault,' Frank snapped. 'If you hadn't lied to me and let those animals into my house, none of this would be happening.'

'You are wrong,' Irena replied quietly. 'Nick was the one who find house, and they would have done this with or without me, because Karel needed place to—'

'Oh, I know what he needed,' Frank cut her off. 'A place to hide out while he gets his filthy business up and running again. What I don't get is what's in it for *you*? You're the one who had to do all the dirty work, but he's not exactly bending over backwards with gratitude, is he?'

'You do not know him like I do,' Irena protested, trotting out the same line she always used whenever Frank criticized Karel. 'He is good man, and he—'

'Oh, give it a break, for Christ's sake,' Frank groaned. 'Are you seriously that blind? If he had any respect for you, he wouldn't be flaunting that girl under your nose. But you don't even seem to care that he's screwing her.'

Two bright spots bloomed on Irena's cheeks, and Frank sighed and shook his head.

'I don't get you at all. I know you're scared of him, because I've seen how you react when he gets angry. But you're not stupid, so why do you stay with him when he treats you so badly?'

A veil came down over Irena's eyes, and she said, 'We need finish shop and go home. Karel will be wonder why we are take so long.'

'I very much doubt he's sitting there watching the clock,' Frank sniped. 'He'll be too busy fucking your replacement.'

Irena turned and walked away without answering, and Frank followed as she snatched items off the shelves and tossed them into the trolley. She claimed that she and Karel were in love, but Frank had seen little evidence of that so far – definitely not from Karel's side. The man exuded power, and Frank imagined it was easy for him to fool women into thinking he cared about them when he turned on the charm. But Irena wasn't a love-struck teenager; she was an intelligent woman in her thirties, who ought to have the sense to walk away when a relationship turned as sour as theirs clearly had. But if she was content to be used as a doormat, there was no point trying to reason with her.

39

Three of Karel's men were outside admiring a Range Rover with a full body kit and blacked-out windows when Frank and Irena arrived back at the house after calling in at the pharmacy. It was parked behind the Transit, so Frank pulled up alongside it and turned off the engine. Irena went straight inside, leaving him to unload the shopping. As he was struggling up the path with several bulging carrier bags, one of the men walked over to him and held out his hand.

'Let me take them for you, mate.'

Surprised by the man's civility, because it was such a huge contrast to the violence and threats he'd received from Karel and Nick, Frank thanked him and passed the bags over. That tiny act of kindness had brought tears to his eyes, but he quickly blinked them away before hefting the boxes of wine inside.

The living room door opened as he entered the hallway, and Viktorya came out wearing a short, tight-fitting red dress, and a pair of high-heeled shoes. Her pretty young face was perfectly made-up, and the glossy curls in her long hair bounced around her shoulder as she tottered unsteadily into the kitchen. Frank guessed that the bag Karel had given her that morning must have been the one she'd arrived with, and that this outfit was one of the ones she had chosen for the glamorous life she'd been promised in England.

Irena was already in the kitchen, and she flashed the girl a dark look before hanging her coat behind the door and pushing up her sleeves to empty the shopping bags.

Viktorya caught it and, a mean light flaring in her eyes, she said, 'What is problem, old woman? Are you jealous because Karel want me more than you?'

'You are just doll he is play with,' Irena retorted dismissively. 'He will soon tire of you and put you back with others. But I will still be here.'

'You are the one he will tire of,' Viktorya countered, a sly smile on her glossy lips as she ran her hands over her breasts and down over her hips. 'Why would he want you when he can have this?'

Irena's brilliant-blue eyes sparked with rage, and she slammed down the plastic bottle she was holding so hard the lid popped off and milk exploded all over her. Sensing that she was about to lose it when Viktorya started laughing, Frank rushed over to her and thrust a tea towel into her hand, whispering, 'Don't rise to it; that's what she wants.'

'What's the joke?' Karel asked, appearing in the doorway.

Frank glanced round and saw that the man had changed into an expensive-looking suit. He'd also shaved, and his freshly washed hair was slicked neatly back. He looked good, and Frank could almost physically feel the confidence radiating from him. Whoever his guests were, Frank figured they had to be important for Karel to go to so much effort for them.

'I spill milk, and she think is funny,' Irena muttered, using the tea towel to wipe her top.

'She slam bottle because I tell her she is finish,' Viktorya said, linking a possessive arm through Karel's. 'She is ugly old woman, and you should make her work with other girls to punish her for disrespect me.'

'You're a smart-mouthed little bitch, aren't you?' Karel grinned, looping his arm around her waist.

'I am pussy cat,' she replied silkily, staring seductively into his eyes as she pressed her breasts against his chest. 'But I have sharp claw,' she added, casting a sly glance back at Irena. 'And I will fight for what I want.'

'Yeah, well, you can save all that for later,' Karel chuckled.

Nick walked in behind them, and smirked when he saw the murderous look on Irena's face. Glaring at him, she turned her back and unwrapped the huge slab of beef she'd bought at the supermarket.

'Leave that,' Karel said when she slapped the meat down on the chopping board. 'I've got a job for you.'

'It need to go in oven, or it will not be tender for dinner,' she replied tersely.

'I said leave it,' he repeated, dropping the arm from around Viktorya's waist.

Irena stopped what she was doing and turned round when he walked over to her. The blank expression she'd perfected was firmly in place, but Frank could tell she was nervous when he saw the vein pulsing in her throat.

'What you want me do?' she asked.

'Not me, Abdul,' he said, brushing the hair back off her face and looping it behind her ear. 'He's asked for you, so go get changed and wait for him in the bedroom.'

Irena's cheeks had been flushed, but every ounce of colour had now drained out of them, and her eyes widened.

'No . . .' she croaked, shaking her head. 'Please do not make me do this, Karel.'

'Aw, sweetheart,' he crooned, making her flinch when he raised his hand and cupped her cheek in his hand. 'You know I wouldn't if I didn't have to, but he's asked for you, so what can I do?'

'Send *her*,' Irena said, jerking her chin up at Viktorya. 'She is younger and prettier. He will prefer her.'

'He wants *you*,' Nick piped up, using his knife to slice open one of the boxes of wine Frank had carried in. 'And you're getting on a bit now, so you should be flattered he's still willing to pay for it.'

'Karel, *please*,' Irena implored, ignoring Nick. 'I will do anything you ask of me, but not this.'

To the side, Frank stared at Irena as Nick's words sank in. So *that* was why she accepted the shit Karel threw at her, he realized. The story she'd told him – about being tricked into coming to England and forced into prostitution – had been true. Karel owned her, just like he owned the other girls, and the partial freedom she'd gained from being his woman was infinitely preferable to being forced to sleep with multiple strangers.

Irena was crying now, and Karel grasped her face in his hand, and hissed, 'Pack it in before he hears you, you stupid bitch. If you fuck this up for me, I'll make you wish you'd never been fuckin' born. D'ya hear me?'

'*Please . . .*' Irena sobbed, clutching at the lapels of his jacket. 'Don't make me do this!'

Irritated, Karel slapped her hands away and pushed her up against the ledge. Then, raising his hand, he snapped his fingers at Nick, saying, 'Get something to shut her up. Oral not spike.'

Nick walked over to the fridge, and a chill skittered down Frank's spine when the man took out a bottle of Oramorph. It was one of Maureen's, and he'd meant to return it to the pharmacy after she passed away. But like so many other things he'd meant to do in those dark days, it had completely slipped his mind.

'You can't give her that,' he said when Nick shook the bottle. 'It's dangerous.'

'Not as dangerous as sticking your beak in where it ain't wanted,' Nick replied, shoulder-barging him into the table.

Wincing when his hip connected with the wood, Frank said, 'I'm serious. You can't mess with that stuff. It's lethal if you give it to someone who doesn't need it.'

'Best shut your gob, then, or you'll be having some an' all,'

Nick warned, yanking a drawer open and pulling out an oral syringe.

'Karel, I love you,' Irena sobbed. 'And you say you love me. We are meant to be marry and have children. You promise.'

'And how d'you reckon that's gonna happen when you're getting hitched to *him*?' Karel replied smoothly, nodding at Frank.

'But this was *your* idea,' she reminded him desperately. 'You say I must marry him so we can take house. I did not want any of this. All I want is *you*.'

'Shouldn't have fuckin' lied to me then, should you?' Karel said coldly, reaching for the oral syringe when Nick had finished filling it. 'Now quit whining, and open up.'

Irena clamped her lips together and shook her head, but she couldn't move, because Karel had her pinned against the ledge.

'Stop it!' Frank yelled, lurching round the table when Karel grabbed her hair and yanked her head back.

'Don't even think about it!' Nick warned, leaping in front of him and thrusting the knife under his nose. 'Unless you want me to make a call and have your fucktard son's head blown off? And, trust me, I'll be more than happy to oblige if that's the road you wanna go down. Now, what's it to be . . . *her*, or *him*?'

Every fibre of Frank's being screamed in frustration and rage as he watched Karel force the plastic tube into Irena's mouth and depress the plunger. He'd never hated anyone as much as he hated these two men right now, but he'd be putting Evan's life in jeopardy if he tried to fight them, so he had to back down.

Sinking onto a chair, he dropped his face into his hands, unable to watch as Irena spluttered and choked on the liquid. Still holding her hair, Karel held her head back until she had no choice but to swallow.

'There we go,' he said, releasing her when she gulped. 'Now you won't feel a thing, and it'll all be over before you know it.'

'I'll go and top up Abdul's glass while we wait for that to kick in,' Nick said, reaching for a bottle of wine.

'Nah, we've wasted enough time,' Karel said. 'Just give him some gear and take him up to the bedroom. The farmer's, not mine.'

Nick put the bottle down and, taking a plastic bag out of a cupboard, extracted a wrap of white powder from it before leaving the room. Frank heard him talking to someone, then, seconds later, a huge shadow passed by the crack in the door, followed by heavy footsteps on the stairs. As the thudding steps moved along the landing above, Frank looked at Irena out of the corner of his eye. The fight had drained from her eyes, and he guessed the morphine was already taking effect when her shoulders sagged and her head began to loll forward.

Karel slipped his arm around her waist to hold her up, and then turned to Frank.

'You'll have to do the cooking tonight,' he said. 'My friend's going to be hungry by the time he's finished, so make sure there's plenty. She'll help you if you need a hand.' He nodded at Viktorya.

'I am not cook with him,' she protested. 'I am stay with you.'

'Women, eh?' Karel rolled his eyes at Frank. 'Give 'em an inch, and they want the whole ten – with balls on top.'

Disgusted, his voice as cold as ice, Frank said, 'I don't need any help.'

'Suit yourself.' Karel shrugged. 'But you'll be tasting everything before any of us touch it, so think again if you were planning on adding any special ingredients.'

With that, he half-walked, half-carried Irena out of the room, and Frank released a shuddering breath and placed both hands on the tabletop when Viktorya tottered behind him. He'd never felt so powerless in his entire life, and the guilt and shame was burning like acid in his gut.

40

It was almost three hours before Abdul came back downstairs, by which time Frank had finished cooking. Karel, Nick, Viktorya, and the guests ate in the living room, and the men who were standing guard ate outside, leaving Frank alone in the kitchen.

He was still sitting at the table, his plate of food untouched, when Nick brought a stack of empty plates in and dumped them on the ledge. Watching as the man opened the cupboard and took out the bag of drugs, he said, 'Where's Irena?'

Nick walked out without answering, and Frank shoved his chair back and scraped his now-congealed food into the bin. As he was running hot water into the sink to do the washing up, the man who'd helped him with the bags came in with his and his friends' plates.

'Cheers for that,' he said, putting them down on the ledge.

Frank paused what he was doing and, twisting his head, watched as the man walked out of the room.

'Yo, Gaz . . . check this vid,' one of the men in the porch said when he opened the front door and stepped outside. 'It's one of them—'

The door closed before Frank could hear any more, and he frowned thoughtfully as he turned back to the dishes. The man, Gaz, wasn't like the others. There was intelligence in his dark eyes that made Frank wonder why he'd got himself mixed up in all this. He appeared to be around Evan's age, and he was a good-looking lad, so why was he holed up here with these criminals when he could be making something of his life?

Before Frank could think any more about it, the living room door opened, and he glanced back over his shoulder when Karel, Viktorya, and Nick came out into the hall, followed by two strangers, one of whom was quite tall and muscular, while the other was as wide as he was tall, with thick rolls of fat cascading down his neck that made it impossible to see where his bald head ended and his shoulders began.

Nick suddenly turned and walked into the kitchen, and Frank quickly averted his gaze and reached for a tea towel to dry the dishes. It was pitch-dark outside, and he could see the reflections of the people in the hall clearly in the window. Watching as Karel, Viktorya, and the strangers left the house, he switched his gaze to Nick, and saw that the man had laid a pack of syringes on the table and was now unwrapping a bag of brown powder. Guessing that he was preparing injections for the girls before he took them to work, Frank clenched his teeth. He despised drugs and the destruction they wreaked in ordinary people's lives. That was why he'd ploughed his redundancy money into the farm in the first place: to get his young son and daughter away from the heroin and cocaine that had been flooding the streets of Manchester at that time, before they reached the age where he could no longer control who they hung about with – or what they got sucked into. Yet, now, because of his own bad decision, those very same drugs were wreaking havoc right under his roof, and there wasn't a damn thing he could do about it.

The sound of a powerful engine roaring to life outside broke the silence, and a few seconds later the front door opened. Frank had expected Karel and Viktorya to walk in, but, instead, it was Gaz and the other two men who entered. They were speaking quietly, so he didn't catch everything they were saying, but he gathered from what he did manage to hear that Karel and the girl had gone off with the men to celebrate something.

Nick had finished preparing the syringes by then, and he carried them upstairs while the other men helped themselves to a glass of whisky. Unsure what he was supposed to do, Frank pottered about putting away the dishes and wiping ledges and the cooker.

Nick came back down a few minutes later, and dumped a handful of now-empty syringes in the bin.

'Yo, Granddad, it's bedtime,' he said when he noticed Frank was still there. 'But I think you might wanna change your sheets before you get your head down,' he added, grinning slyly. 'It's a bit of a mess up there.'

Frank went into the utility room. A neat stack of sheets were sitting on a shelf alongside a stack of towels, and he took one of each and carried them upstairs. As he passed the bathroom, he hesitated when he heard the sound of running water. Guessing that Irena must be taking a shower, he walked on to his bedroom and switched the light on.

The scene made him stop in his tracks, and he stared at the bed in horror. He'd expected there to be bodily fluids on the sheet, but what he hadn't expected was blood. And there wasn't only a bit, there was a *lot*. It was everywhere . . . on the sheets, the headboard, even on the wall; and there was a thin trail on the carpet leading from the bed to the door.

Heart pounding, he stepped back onto the landing and peered down over the bannister rail. He could hear the men talking in the kitchen, but nobody was in the hallway, so he tiptoed back down to the bathroom and tapped quietly on the door. The water stopped, and he whispered, 'Irena . . . it's me. Are you OK?'

No answer came, but he heard what sounded like a groan.

'I know you're probably too scared to talk, but I'm worried about you,' he whispered, his lips pressed up against the wood. 'If you can hear me, just tap once to let me know you're OK. Can you do that?'

A few seconds passed, and then a tiny tap came through the wood.

'Thank God,' he murmured, releasing a shaky breath. Then, aware that he didn't have much time, he said, 'Karel and the girl have gone out with those men, and Nick and Gaz will be taking the other girls to work soon. The rest of them are drinking in the kitchen, but they'll probably go out to the caravan when the others have gone, so if you want to talk . . . well, you know where I'll be. OK?'

Another pause, and then another tiny tap. About to speak again, Frank changed his mind and rushed back to his room when he heard footsteps in the hall.

Nick strolled into the doorway a few seconds later and shook his head as he eyed the blood.

'What a mess, eh? You'd think the fat fuck'd have a bit more consideration, considering how long he's been waiting to get another shot at our Reeny. But that's Arabs for you. No fuckin' manners.'

Sick to his stomach, Frank didn't reply; he just grabbed a corner of the sheet and started tugging it off. When Nick pulled the door shut and locked it, Frank tossed the ruined sheet into the corner. The blood had soaked through to the mattress beneath, so he covered it with the towel before putting the clean sheet over it. His pillows and quilt had been dumped on the chair, so he propped the pillows against the headboard to cover the blood, and threw the quilt over the sheet.

Glad that the heating was still on, because he was shivering from head to toe, Frank lay on top of the bed and listened as Nick corralled the sluggish girls out of their room and down the stairs. Usually the man spent a little time in there after administering the injections, and from the disgusting things he'd heard through the wall, Frank hadn't needed to guess what he was doing to them – or, rather, what he was making *them* do to *him*. The guests had obviously eaten into his fun time tonight, and Frank heard the front door opening and closing, followed by the sound of the van driving away.

Several minutes of silence passed, and then Irena's bedroom door opened and closed. Scrambling into a sitting position, Frank tapped on the wall.

'Irena . . . ? Are you there?'

'Yes, I am here,' her voice came faintly back to him. 'But I do not want to talk, so go to sleep, Frankie.'

'I just need to know you're OK,' he said. 'Did that man hurt you?' Grimacing as soon as the words left his mouth, he said, 'Sorry, that was a really stupid question. I know he's hurt you, because I've seen the blood. But how bad is it?'

'I will survive,' Irena replied.

'I'm so sorry,' Frank said guiltily. 'I should have helped you, but there was nothing I could do to stop them. They showed me a picture earlier. It was of Evan. They're holding him some- where, and he was hurt, and they said they'd kill him if I tried to help you. I'm so sorry, love.'

On the other side of the wall, Irena sighed. Then, her voice flat and drained of emotion, she said, 'Is OK, I understand. I need sleep now. Goodnight, Frankie.'

'Night,' he replied, keeping his ear pressed against the wall until he'd heard the squeak of her bedsprings.

Turning round when all was silent again, he lay back and threw his arm over his eyes. At the beginning of this nightmare, he'd thought that Irena could hold her own with Karel, but it had all been a facade. Karel had always held the power, and she had played the part of the loving, dutiful partner to perfection, probably desperately hoping that, one day, he would actually see her as something more than a slave he'd granted favours to. But now he'd switched his attentions to the younger girl and had shown Irena that she meant nothing to him, she seemed to have given up.

After everything she had done, the jeopardy she'd placed both him *and* Evan in with her lies, Frank knew he ought to be glad that she was now suffering. But she was as much a victim in this as he and Evan were, so all he felt was guilt and concern, and he mentally renewed the vow he'd made to her before he'd realized her actual involvement in the take-over. If he ever got out of this – as increasingly unlikely as that was looking – he would do everything in his power to help her to escape from Karel and this life.

41

'Oi, watch it!' Jordan King yelped, struggling to keep his balance when his friend banged into him from behind. 'I'm right on the fuckin' edge here!'

'Sorry,' Keegan Brown sniffed, shoving his glasses further up his nose and peering over the edge. Squinting when the sunlight bounced off the murky water below, he said, 'Shit, that's a long way down, Jord. You sure about this?'

'Yeah, it'll be sick,' Jordan grinned. 'Zack and Leo are planning on doing it Saturday, and they'll be gutted when we beat 'em to it.'

'It's a long drop,' Keegan said again, stepping back when he experienced a sudden sensation of falling.

'We ain't doing it from up here, knobhead,' Jordan laughed. 'We'll go round the side and climb down to that ledge.' He pointed out a slab of rock jutting out over the water on the opposite side. 'That's still high enough to look boss in a vid.'

'What if we fall?' Keegan asked.

Jordan peered at him through narrowed eyes.

'You scared?'

'*No!*'

'Yeah, you are. You're shitting it.'

'All right, so maybe I am,' Keegan admitted. 'It's dead muddy, and no one ever comes up here, so we'll never get found if we slip.'

'You can swim, can't you?'

'Yeah, but that won't save me if I smash my head on a rock, will it? Come on, man, let's sack it off and go home.'

'You can piss off if you want, but I'm doing it,' said Jordan. 'Chloe'll be well impressed when it gets millions of hits.'

'She's Decca's bird,' Keegan reminded him. 'And he'll kick the fuck out of you if he thinks you're after her.'

'Whatever,' Jordan said dismissively. 'Come on.'

Keegan bit his lip when his friend started kicking a path through the brambles to get to the other side. His instincts were telling him to forget the stupid plan and go home, but Jordan was determined to go ahead with the dive with or without him. And if it went wrong and people found out Keegan had deserted him, he'd get the blame.

'OK, wait up,' he shouted. 'I'll film you, but I ain't diving.'

'Puss-*ay!*' Jordan jeered. 'Pussy, pussy, puss-*ay!*'

'Fuck off,' Keegan muttered, following as his friend forged ahead.

A few minutes later, they emerged into a clearing where the ground was scorched and the vegetation frazzled.

'What the fuck's gone on here?' Jordan said. 'It looks like

someone's had a barbecue, or summat. You'd think they'd be more careful since they had all them fires on the moors last year, wouldn't you?'

Two evenly spaced lines in the soot had caught Keegan's eye, and he followed them until they disappeared over the side. Guessing that a vehicle had been torched and pushed over, he walked up to the edge to take a look. He hadn't really expected to see anything, so when he spotted the back end of a burned-out car some fifteen feet below, its front end wedged in a gap between two rock ledges, he murmured, '*Whoa* . . .'

'What's up?' Jordan walked up beside him and followed his gaze. Laughing when he saw it, he said, 'That's what the idiots get for following the SatNav. Someone my dad works with ended up in a lake the other week. Got to be thick as pig-shit not to see that coming.'

'That doesn't explain how it set on fire,' said Keegan, still staring at it. Then, squinting, he leaned forward with his hands on his knees. 'I think someone's in it.'

'Fuck off,' Jordan jeered. 'It'll be them bottle-bottoms making you see things.'

'I'm serious,' Keegan insisted. 'Look . . .' He pointed to the right-hand side. 'In the driver's seat.'

Rolling his eyes, sure that his friend was imagining things, Jordan followed his finger.

'Shit, yeah, you're right,' he said when he saw what his friend had seen.

'What should we do?' Keegan asked.

'Go down and take a proper look,' Jordan said, wriggling his arms out from the straps of his rucksack. 'We can take pictures and put them on Insta.'

'It's too dangerous,' Keegan argued. 'That ledge is the only thing holding it up, and the slightest movement or extra bit of weight could send the whole lot down – you with it.'

'So what do you suggest, Brainiac?' Jordan asked, already slipping his blazer off. 'Leave it, and let Zack and Leo take all the glory when they find it on Saturday? I don't think so, mate.'

Keegan thought about it for a second and slid his phone out of his pocket.

'Don't take pics from up here,' Jordan said, folding the blazer and placing it neatly on the rucksack. 'You need to get up close.'

'I'm not taking pictures, I'm calling the police,' Keegan said.

'What?' Jordan pulled a face. 'Nah, man, what's the point in that?'

'That could be someone's mum or dad, for all we know. People could be looking for them.'

'So what? It's nowt to do with us.'

'It will be if it gets on the news,' Keegan said pointedly, holding Jordan's gaze as he waited for his words to sink in.

It took a few seconds, but Jordan eventually got it, and a slow smile spread across his handsome young face. Getting a few views on Instagram and YouTube was nothing compared to being hailed a hero on national TV, and he was already imagining the attention he was going to get from Chloe at school tomorrow.

'Yeah, man.' He nodded. 'Do it.'

PART THREE

42

'Fuck!' Nick muttered, watching as the girl's eyes rolled to the back of her head.

On the bed beside her, their own eyes glued to the syringes he hadn't yet used, their track-marked arms wrapped around their skinny, naked frames, their lips flicking over their dry lips, the other girls were waiting for their fixes. But they would have to wait a bit longer, because Nick had a disaster on his hands.

Yanking the syringe out of the crook of the girl's elbow, he grabbed her by both arms and shook her roughly, then dropped her back onto the bed and slapped her face twice. Her rolled-back eyes didn't correct themselves, and her body moved as a result of the slaps, but there was no reaction to the pain.

Nick put his ear to her mouth.

Nothing.

Shoving his distaste aside, he blew air between her lips, and then pressed down hard on her chest several times before putting his ear to her lips again.

Still nothing.

Jumping up off the bed, he rushed out of the room, ignoring the other girls when they started whining that they wanted theirs.

Karel was sitting in the kitchen, with his new plaything on his lap and a rolled-up banknote inserted into his left nostril, hoovering up a thick line of coke.

'One of the tarts has OD'd,' Nick announced.

'What?' Banknote still in place, Karel looked up at him.

'I'd just given her a fix, and her eyes rolled back,' Nick explained. 'I've tried mouth to mouth, and all that shit, but she ain't responding.'

'I will go,' Irena volunteered, dropping the tea towel she'd been using to dry the dishes Frank had washed.

'You can try, but it won't do no good,' Nick said, reaching for an open bottle of whisky and taking a swig.

'How the fuck did you manage that?' Karel demanded, unceremoniously dumping Viktorya on the floor when he leapt to his feet and slapped the bottle clean out of Nick's hand.

'It ain't my fault,' Nick complained as the bottle flew across the room and shattered against the wall. 'I give her the same amount as last time, and she didn't fuckin' die then, so how was I supposed to know she'd kick it this time?'

'I told you this new batch is stronger,' Karel yelled. 'Why d'you never fuckin' listen, you brain-dead piece of shit?'

'It ain't my *fault*,' Nick repeated angrily, the coke he'd snorted before heading upstairs making him feel invincible. 'If you wanna blame anyone, blame the cunt you bought it off. I fuckin' told you to stick to our usual man, 'cos at least we can trust his shit.'

'So now you think you know better than me?' Karel shot back furiously.

'About this, *yeah*!' Nick argued. 'I ain't being funny, man, but I'm the one who handled everything while you was on lock-down, and I had run-ins with that twat when I found out he cuts his shit with rat poison. We put good stuff out to make the fuckers come back for more, not fuckin' kill 'em! But, hey . . . what do I know?' He spread his arms. 'It's your business, and you know best.'

'Yeah, I fuckin' do, and you'd better remember that in future,' spat Karel. 'It's my shit you wasted; my money you've poured down the drain.'

As the men continued to argue, Frank focused on his breathing in an effort to calm his pounding heart as he took over the drying of the dishes. Since the visit from Karel's enor-mous friend a couple of weeks earlier, there had been a shift in the dynamics of the gang. Irena barely talked any more, and Frank could tell she was in pain as she moved slowly from one task to the next. But the visit seemed to have had the opposite effect on Karel, and his celebrations hadn't stopped since he'd returned that night. His drug-taking was completely out of control now, and Frank rarely saw him without a straw up his nose. He was also drinking whisky like it was water, and his mood could switch from genial host to raging psychopath in the blink of an eye. Unfortunately, Nick was like that naturally, and the combination of volatile personalities was making the atmosphere in the house feel like a pressure cooker. The other men had felt it, too, Frank was sure, because they seemed to be on edge far more than usual, as if they were waiting for the ticking bomb to explode.

Irena had come back downstairs. Spying her in the doorway, Karel stopped arguing with Nick and jerked his chin up at her.

'Well?'

She shook her head.

'Fuckin' great!' Karel muttered, running his hands through his hair. 'So now I'm a tart down.' He turned back to Nick. 'More money down the fuckin' drain.'

'It ain't my fault,' Nick said for the third time.

'I don't wanna hear it,' Karel snapped, slumping down on his chair and snatching up the banknote he'd dropped. 'Take the others to work, then come back and clean your mess up.'

'So you want me to drive to Manchester and back, *twice*?' Nick asked.

'You got a problem with that?' Karel snarled.

Nick thought about it for a second, his eyes fixed on Karel's. Then, tutting, he said, 'Nah, I ain't got no problem.'

'Good,' Karel said coolly. 'And make sure that one's arms and legs are straight while you're up there, 'cos you don't want it stuck in some weird position that'll make it hard to get rid of when you get back.'

Nick barged past Irena without answering, and marched up the stairs. When he'd gone, Karel dumped a pile of coke on the tabletop and roughly chopped it into two lines before snorting them both. Throwing his head back as the powder burned a path from his nose to his brain and rushed through his veins, he gritted his teeth and slammed his hands down on the table.

The noise startled Frank, and he turned his head in time to see Karel pummel his chest with his fists before leaping to his feet.

'Right, go and get tooled up and start the beemer,' Karel ordered Jacko. 'We're going to pay a little visit to the cunt who sold me that shit.'

Jacko nodded, and made his way out to the caravan. Seconds later, Nick came down the stairs, shoving the girls, who had now had their injections and didn't seem to know or care where they were, ahead of him.

'Let's go,' he said, jerking his head at Gaz.

Gaz got up and reached for his jacket, and Frank noticed him give an unimpressed shake of his head before following Nick out to the van.

Only one of Karel's men remained in the room. Frank didn't know this one's name, because the others only ever seemed to address him as '*Yo!*' He raised an eyebrow when Karel said, 'You stay here and keep guard, Scotty. Anything happens, shoot the fuckin' lot of them.'

'Wait for me,' Viktorya squawked, hurrying after Karel when he strode out into the hall.

'You ain't coming,' he said, yanking his coat off a hook behind the front door.

'I am not stay with *her*,' she protested, glancing nervously back at Irena. 'She hate me.'

'Grow up,' Karel said dismissively, pushing her aside and marching out, slamming the door behind him and locking it with the mortice key.

Scotty had gone outside, and Frank saw the flare of a lighter in the darkness outside the kitchen window as the man paused to light a cigarette before heading over to the caravan, no doubt to get his gun. Alone with Irena when Viktorya scuttled up the stairs, Frank sank down onto a chair.

'She's dead, then?' he said. 'The girl upstairs?'

'Yes,' Irena said quietly. 'I try, but it was too late.'

Frank peered at her face before she turned away from him, and said, 'I'm sorry, love,' when he noticed tears glistening in her eyes.

'You should go to your room,' she replied, taking a sheet of kitchen paper off the roll and dabbing at her eyes, her back still turned. 'You do not need to see what happen when they come back.'

'I don't want to leave you on your own,' Frank argued.

'I do not need company,' she insisted. 'Please, just go.'

Aware that she was struggling to contain her emotions, Frank stood up.

'If you need me, you know where I am,' he said.

Her reply was a curt nod, so Frank left her and went upstairs. Viktorya had locked herself in the bathroom, and he could hear water running into the bath as he passed the door. In his bedroom, he sat on the chair by the boarded-up window and stared at the wall separating his and Evan's rooms. Behind those bricks a young girl was lying dead on the bed that he, in a different life, had bought for his young son. He didn't know which girl it was, because he'd barely recognized the skeletal creatures Nick had herded out through the front door a few minutes earlier. But, whichever one it was, she hadn't deserved to die like that, and Frank couldn't stop thinking about her poor parents. They must have been so happy when they'd waved her off at the airport, he imagined; so grateful to the man who had paid her fare and promised her a wonderful new life in England, where the streets were paved with gold. They had probably waited patiently for her to contact them and tell them all the amazing things she had done since arriving: the visit to Buckingham Palace, the shopping trips, the meetings with the agents who were going to propel her into stardom. And what were they thinking now? he wondered; all these weeks later, and not even a phone call to tell them that she'd landed safely. Would they be thinking she was too busy to contact them, or would they be tearing their hair out with worry; trying desperately to contact somebody in authority who could help them to trace their beautiful daughter and send her home?

That was exactly what Frank would have done if Jo hadn't contacted him as soon as she'd landed in Australia. And she wasn't young, vulnerable, and alone, like that poor girl in the next room had been; she was a married woman with a sensible head on her shoulders and a husband to protect her.

Thinking about the word 'alone', his thoughts turned, as they so often did, to Evan, but he shut the images out before they had a chance to take hold. Evan was fine, he told himself firmly. OK, maybe not fine, but at least he was safe, wherever he was, because Karel needed him to keep Frank on track, so he wasn't going to let anything happen to him. So, as long as Frank was still necessary to the plan, Evan was safe – and that was what he had to cling to in order to keep himself from doing something stupid.

Like trying to escape now there was only one man around to stop him.

One man who had been ordered to shoot not only him, but also Irena and Viktorya if anything happened.

Shaking his head, Frank dismissed the idea as quickly as it had entered his mind. He was in his bedroom with an unlocked door for the first time in weeks, yet *still* he was powerless, and he began to understand why Irena had given up.

43

'It's been declined.'

The girl pulled the bank card out of the machine and shoved it across the counter, while simultaneously pulling back the bag containing a litre bottle of vodka and four tins of dog food.

'What do you mean, declined?' Marie asked, her cheeks flaming when she heard one of her neighbours, who was behind her in the queue, whisper something to the woman standing next to her. 'Try it again.'

The girl rolled her eyes and shoved the card back into the machine. Sure that she must have hit a wrong digit the first time, Marie re-entered her pin. But the girl shook her head and pulled the card out again.

'Declined,' she repeated, her voice unnecessarily loud, Marie thought, as she added, 'Insufficient funds.'

'But that's wrong,' Marie argued. 'I've got money in my account.'

'You'll have to take it up with your bank,' the girl said unsympathetically.

'It's nearly ten o'clock,' Marie reminded her. 'They're shut.'

'So, wait till morning,' the girl snapped. 'Now, unless you've got cash, or another card you want to try, you need to move and let me serve someone else, 'cos we're shutting in a minute.'

Too embarrassed to continue arguing, Marie snatched her card off the counter and barged her way out of the shop. How could her account be empty? It didn't make sense. There had been seven thousand in there the last time she'd checked.

But when *had* she last checked?

Oh, God . . .

Realizing that it had been in the week before Evan had left, and that she'd been too wrapped up in misery to think about checking it since, Marie rushed home and logged into their online banking account. Her fears were confirmed when she saw that Evan had transferred six thousand pounds into another account the day after leaving, and the one thousand he'd left had already been swallowed up by the rent and various direct debits. The rest, she had spent on food and booze – more booze than food – leaving her with precisely seven pounds and eighty pence.

'No . . .' She stared at the screen in disbelief. 'He wouldn't do this to me . . .'

But he had, and she let out a roar of anger, causing the dog to jump off the sofa and run for cover.

'You bastard!' she screamed, slamming her fist down on the tabletop. 'You absolute fucking *bastard*!'

The fury made her want a drink, but all of the bottles lined on the hearth were empty, so she lit a cigarette and took a deep drag. Soothed by the nicotine, she closed the banking screen and brought up Facebook. She'd given up on searching for Evan after the confrontation with that bitch at the car showroom and his friends at work, but she wanted – *needed* – her share of the money they had saved, so she would have to find another way to track him down.

It took several attempts before she managed to crack the password on Evan's Facebook account. He claimed not to bother with the site, but he'd already been proved to be a liar, so she wanted to check his relationship status, to see if he'd changed it from Married to In A Relationship.

He hadn't, which dashed her hopes of finding the name of the woman he'd run off with; and he hadn't updated his status, or commented on anything in over a year. Next, she opened up his messages, to see if he'd been chatting to some bitch behind her back; maybe arranging to meet up with her.

Nothing.

He'd never bothered setting up a Twitter or Instagram account, but he and Marie shared this laptop, so she closed his Facebook page and went into the history to see if he'd logged in to any online dating accounts.

Again, nothing.

At a loss as to what to do next, Marie sighed when the dog slunk back into the doorway and whined. Remembering that he hadn't been fed, she slammed the laptop lid down and heaved herself out of the chair. Thanks to Evan, there was no dog food, but there was a chunk of stale Spam in the fridge, so she would give him that.

She was on her way into the kitchen when the doorbell rang. Telling the dog to wait a minute, she went to answer it. A man and a woman were standing on the step, and the woman said, 'Mrs Peters?' when she peered out at them.

Wary, because they looked official, and she thought they might be from the council, that maybe someone had reported the dog for barking again, Marie folded her arms.

'Yes.'

The woman flashed a police badge at her.

'I'm DS Strachan, and this is my colleague, DC Ogden. Is Evan Peters your husband?'

Marie frowned.

'Yes. But if you're hoping to find him here, you're out of luck, 'cos he walked out a month ago, and I haven't seen him since.'

'Can we come inside?' Strachan asked, her face giving nothing away.

The dog bounded into the hall and started barking. Grabbing his collar to stop him from going for the pair, Marie said, 'Just give me a sec to put him in the kitchen,' and closed the door.

Something in the woman's tone had unsettled her, so she locked the dog away before letting the officers in.

'Sorry about the mess,' she apologized, rushing into the living room ahead of them and scooping up the empty bottles on the hearth, and the chocolate wrappers littering the floor and sofa.

'Don't worry about it,' Strachan said, sitting on an armchair as Ogden took a seat at the end of the sofa.

Conscious of the stench of stale cigarette smoke and unwashed dog, Marie perched at the other end of the sofa and stuffed the rubbish out of sight down the side.

'So what's going on?' she asked, looking at them in turn.

'A car was found last week in Derbyshire,' Strachan said, resting her elbows on her knees. 'It was burned out, but we've managed to salvage the chassis number, and it came back as a Volvo estate registered to this address. Could you confirm that your husband still owns it?'

'As far as I know?' Marie shrugged. 'But I haven't seen him since he walked out, so he could have sold it, for all I know.' Then, frowning, she said, 'Here, I hope you don't think *I* set it on fire to get revenge, or something, 'cos I don't even know where he is.'

'I'm sorry to have to tell you this, but there was a body inside the vehicle,' Strachan said. 'And we're trying to establish if it's your husband.'

'What?' Sure that she'd misheard, Marie drew her head back. 'Are you serious?'

Strachan nodded, and Ogden said, 'I'll make a brew,' when Marie's face drained of colour.

He left the room, and the dog started barking again, followed by the sound of the back door being opened, and claws skittering across the floor tiles before it closed again.

'I know this is a shock,' Strachan said. 'So is there someone you'd like to call before we go on? Someone who can come over and sit with you?'

Marie stared blankly down at the floor. Frank had been ignoring her calls since their argument, and her own parents were holidaying at their caravan in Wales. She didn't want any of her nosy neighbours coming in and seeing the state of the place; and none of her so-called friends had been round to see how she was getting on since she'd told them about Evan leaving, so she wasn't about to ring them.

'No.' She shook her head. 'But I'll be OK.'

'Are you up to answering some questions?'

Marie nodded and clasped her hands together between her knees.

'You say your husband's been gone for a month?' Strachan started. 'Can I ask why you didn't report him missing?'

'Because I didn't think he *was*,' Marie replied truthfully. 'I assumed he was at his dad's, like last time.'

'Last time?'

'Yeah, we had a misunderstanding a few months back, and I kicked him out,' Marie said, blushing at the memory of the scene she'd caused in the pub. 'He stayed at his dad's for a week, but they had a falling-out and he came home. We cleared the air, and everything was fine. Or, at least, I *thought* it was.'

'So he didn't seem unhappy or depressed this time?'

'No.' Marie shook her head. 'He went on a bit of a downer at Christmas, but that was understandable, 'cos it was the first since his mum died, and him and his dad still weren't talking.

Frank – his dad – had moved some woman in, you see, and Evan and his sister weren't happy about it. That's why they'd fallen out, but I could tell Evan was missing him, so I made him talk to him on Christmas Day.'

She paused when the door opened and Ogden came in carrying a cup of tea. Thanking him when he handed it to her, she took a sip to lubricate her dry mouth. She wasn't sure why she was offloading on the woman like this, but now she'd started, she couldn't seem to stop.

'It didn't go too well on the phone, so Evan drove over there the next evening. He was there for a few hours and said it was all sorted when he got home, and I was pleased when he told me he was planning to go there after work the next day to help his dad with his cars. He said it might turn into a late one, so I wasn't concerned when he didn't come home that night. But he didn't come back the next night, either, and neither of them was answering their phones.'

'Didn't you go over to try and talk to him?'

'Not straight away, no. I wasn't very well that week, and Frank's never really liked me, so I didn't want to mug myself off by going over there, like I was desperate, or something. But when it got to a week, I couldn't take it any more – the not knowing, and that. So I drove over there to have it out with him. Only Frank said he hadn't even been there, and then his girlfriend made a dig about Evan being a liar, so we had a row and I came home. And then Evan's sister rang and told me he'd kissed Frank's girlfriend, and that's when I realized he'd only come back because Frank had kicked him out and he had nowhere else to go.'

The hurt and anger about the betrayal had returned, and her hands were shaking so badly, she spilled scalding tea on her thigh.

'Shit!' she hissed, slamming the cup down on the table and rubbing her leg. 'Sorry . . . it just makes me so mad to think about all the lies. I thought we were back on track, I really did, but he was using me.'

'He didn't seem unhappy?' Strachan asked.

'No!' Marie snapped. 'I already told you, I thought he was fine. Why do you keep asking that?'

'I'm trying to establish his frame of mind the last time you saw him,' said Strachan. Then, reaching into the bag she'd placed at her feet, she took out a sheet of paper and handed it over. 'Do you recognize this jacket?'

Marie stared at the black-and-white photograph. It was a still taken from CCTV footage, and the central image was a rear view of a man wearing a jacket with a distinctive logo emblazoned across the back of it.

'It's Evan's work jacket,' she said. 'He was wearing it when he left that morning. But what does this mean?'

'Given the condition of the victim's body, a visual identification isn't possible,' Strachan explained. 'Your husband's the registered owner of the car, but he hadn't reported it as stolen, and he himself hadn't been reported as missing, so we decided to do a few checks before approaching you. This is not the kind of news we want to deliver if we've got the wrong person, as you can probably imagine.'

'What kind of checks?' Marie asked.

'We tracked the vehicle's movements prior to it arriving at the quarry,' said Strachan. 'The quarry's located in a remote area which doesn't have CCTV coverage, but we were able to pick up images of the car passing through a village several miles away. We hadn't been able to see the driver's face, so we back-tracked from the point it went off the radar. This image was picked up at a motorway service station an hour before the car arrived in the village.'

Marie stared at the photo again, and frowned.

'What is it?' Strachan asked.

'He looks like he's lost weight,' Marie said, her tone sad. 'Evan really likes his food, so I'm guessing his new woman hasn't been feeding him very well. Either that, or he's been working it off – *physically*,' she added bitterly, breathing in deeply at the thought of Evan having rampant sex with a faceless sex goddess.

The officers exchanged a surreptitious glance, then Strachan said, 'If you look at the date and time in the corner, you'll see that this image was captured at two fifteen a.m. on the twenty-eighth of December, Mrs Peters. And you said your husband left here on the morning of the twenty-seventh – is that right?'

'Yeah.' Marie nodded. 'I remember because it was his first day back at work after the Christmas holidays.'

'That image was taken the same night, going into the next

morning,' Strachan reiterated. 'And there's no way he could have noticeably lost weight in that time.'

'I don't understand what you're saying.' Marie was confused.

'OK, forget about the jacket for a minute, and take another look at the picture,' said Strachan. 'Would you say that's your husband – from the shape of him, the length of his legs, the way he's standing, etcetera?'

Marie stared at the picture again. Strachan had told her to forget about the jacket, but her eye was continually drawn to the logo, because that was the only real detail she could see. The figure did look slimmer than she remembered Evan to be; the shoulders not as broad, the legs maybe not as long. But that could be a result of the angle the picture had been taken from, she supposed. She'd once overheard two teenage girls discussing the best angles to hold a camera for the perfect selfie, and they had reckoned that an overhead shot made them look much slimmer and shorter than a straight-on shot. That, added to the fact that she hadn't actually laid eyes on Evan in a while, made it possible that she'd exaggerated his size in her mind's eye.

'I honestly don't know?' She sighed. 'Maybe. Yeah, probably. Oh, God, I don't know.'

'Take your time,' said Strachan.

Marie looked again, then shook her head.

'No, it's not him. He's bigger than that. The jacket's definitely his, though. See that bit . . .' She pointed out an untidy section where the material joined the waistband. 'I sewed that, so you'll easily know it's his if you've found it, 'cos I made a bit of a mess of it.'

'I'm afraid we don't have the jacket, because all material items were destroyed by the fire,' Strachan said, taking the picture back and putting it away. 'I just wanted to see if you recognized it, because we didn't get a visual of this person's face, but he was tracked getting back into the car after purchasing a pack of cigarettes, which he paid for using your husband's debit card.'

'Doesn't that prove that it *was* Evan, then?' Marie asked.

'Not exactly,' said Strachan. 'He used the contactless function rather than entering a pin, so it's possible the card could have been stolen along with the jacket and the car. As I explained earlier, this isn't the kind of news we'd want to deliver to the wrong family, so we do everything in our power to ascertain the victim's identity before we approach their loved ones.'

Marie nodded her understanding. Then, chewing on her lip for a second, dreading the answer, she said, 'Was – was anyone with him at the service station? A woman, I mean?'

'As far as we can tell, he was alone,' said Strachan. Then: 'Can I ask if you have children? We managed to recover a sample of DNA from the scene, but your husband isn't on our database, so we'll need to check it against a close relative in order to see if it's a match.'

'We haven't got kids,' Marie said quietly. 'We tried, but . . .' She tailed off and shrugged. 'That's why I got the dog.'

'It's OK.' Strachan gave her an understanding smile. 'Now

we know his father's alive, we'll see if he can provide us with a sample instead. Providing he's your husband's biological father?'

'Oh, Frank's definitely his dad,' Marie said with certainty. 'Evan's the image of him, and Maureen wasn't the kind to cheat.' *Unlike that bitch Frank's with now*, she thought but didn't add.

'One last thing,' Strachan said. 'Did your husband own or have access to any guns that you know of?'

'No.' Marie shook her head. 'Frank used to own a shotgun when he was still farming, but I think he got rid of it when he had his heart attack. Why do you ask?'

'We recovered a gun at the scene, along with the corpse,' said Ogden.

Flashing him a disapproving look when Marie visibly blanched at the word corpse, Strachan said, 'There was significant damage to the skull and facial bones which indicate he'd been shot at close range.'

'Oh, my God!' Marie gasped. 'You think Evan shot himself? Is that why you kept asking if he was depressed? No way . . .' She shook her head. 'Evan would *never* have done that. One of his mates hanged himself a few years ago, and he went mad; said it was the most selfish thing anyone could ever do.'

'OK, we'll leave it at that for now,' said Strachan. 'If you could give us your father-in-law's address?'

'Yeah, course, I'll write it down for you,' Marie said, fishing a pen out of her handbag and looking around for paper.

Ogden took a notepad out of his pocket and passed it to her.

Thanking him, Marie scribbled Frank's address and handed it back.

'What do I do now?' she asked, a sudden flutter of panic churning in her stomach. 'About Evan, I mean. If he's . . . won't I need to contact an undertaker, or something?'

'Not just yet,' Strachan said kindly. 'There's still a chance it might not have been him in the car, so let's wait until we know for sure.'

Hoping against hope that the woman was right, Marie nodded, and pushed herself up to her feet to show them out. She'd been cursing Evan for weeks, wishing disease, catastrophe, and even death on him. But now there was a possibility that he actually *was* dead, the guilt was tearing her apart.

As soon as the pair had gone, Marie let the dog back in and lit a cigarette. Then, rooting her mobile phone out of her handbag, she dialled Frank's number. As usual, his phone went straight to voicemail, but, this time, instead of hanging up, she decided to leave a message.

'Frank, it's Marie,' she said, her chin wobbling as the reality of what she'd heard washed over her. 'I know you're not talking to me, but I really need to speak to you, so please pick up – it's important.'

She waited a few seconds, to give him time to pick up if he was listening. He didn't, so she said, 'Look, something's happened. I can't tell you what it is over the phone, but the police are on their way to yours. Please call me back as soon as you can. And I'm sorry for what I said,' she added, sniffing back a tear. 'I was angry, but I didn't mean it. You've been a great dad to Evan and Jo, and . . . Please just ring me back. *Please.*'

She cut the call at that and, dropping the cigarette into the ashtray, sobbed into the bewildered dog's fur.

44

Frank was still in his room when the Transit pulled up outside, and he heard two sets of feet crunch across the gravel, followed by a key being slotted into the front door. It didn't open, and Nick's complaining voice rose up to him, saying, 'Why the fuck's he put the mortice on?'

'Why d'ya think?' Gaz replied gruffly.

The crunching started up again as the men walked round to the back of the house. A few seconds later, Nick bounded up the stairs and threw Frank's door open.

'Get your arse downstairs, Granddad. I've got a job for you.'

'What kind of job?' Frank eyed him warily from the chair.

'Just fuckin' move it, and quit asking stupid questions,' Nick snapped, already moving to the next room. 'Gaz . . . get up here!' he yelled as he unlocked the door. 'I ain't doing this by myself!'

Unsure what the man had in mind for him, but all too aware that, whatever it was, it wouldn't be good, Frank reluctantly got up and made his way out of the room. Viktorya popped her head out of the bedroom she was now sharing with Karel and Irena, but immediately withdrew it when she saw him and slammed the door shut.

Gaz was coming up the stairs as Frank walked down, and Frank saw the anger in his eyes as they passed and guessed that he and Nick had been arguing again.

Irena was in the kitchen pouring whisky into three glasses when Frank walked in. His mouth was parched, and he instinctively reached for one, but Irena threw out her arm to stop him.

'No!' she said sharply without looking at him. 'These are for the others.'

Holding up his hands, Frank went over to the sink and poured a glass of water from the tap. He'd just taken a sip when Nick and Gaz came downstairs carrying a rolled-up quilt between them. It was filthy, but Frank instantly recognized it as being Evan's, and his heart lurched painfully in his chest when he picked up on the all-too-familiar odour of death coming from it.

'What are you going to do?' he asked, staring in horror at the wispy hair sticking out of the top of the rolled quilt.

'Shut it!' Nick hissed, dropping his end of the bundle and shoving him forcefully down onto a chair. Then, turning to Gaz, who was carefully setting down his end, he said, 'Quit fucking about, and go fetch the chainsaw. The pigs are waiting to be fed.'

Frank's face drained of blood when he realized what was

about to happen, and his heart was pounding so hard he thought he might faint.

'Have drink first,' Irena said, shoving the glasses into both men's hands, before handing the third to Scotty, who had just come inside.

'We'll have it later,' Nick said, eager to get on with things.

'No!' Irena said firmly. 'You need be calm, or you will make mistake.'

It was the first time she'd sounded like her old self in weeks, and Gaz nodded.

'She's right,' he said to Nick. 'You've been acting like a fucking maniac all night, so drink it and calm down, or we could really mess this up.'

Nick tutted, and then downed the liquid in one.

'There,' he said, slamming the glass down on the ledge. 'Happy now?'

Gaz nodded and sank his own drink, quickly followed by Scotty.

'Right, get back outside and keep watch,' Nick ordered Scotty. 'Make sure there's no sneaky farmers hanging about on the back field, 'cos I want this over with as quick as.'

'Please don't do this,' Frank croaked. 'It's barbaric. Think about her parents—'

'I thought I told you to shut it,' Nick roared, kicking him and the chair over.

'Pack it in!' Gaz snapped. 'We haven't got time for this. If you're gonna do it, just fuckin' do it!'

Flashing him a dirty look, Nick pushed past him and made his way outside.

'Please don't let him do it,' Frank begged Gaz as he hauled himself up off the floor. 'You're not like him, and I know you don't agree with any of this. But it's not too late to start over. I've got money; I can help you. You just need to—'

'Oi, dickhead, don't be telling him what he needs to do,' Nick sneered, walking back in at that exact moment and kicking the door shut behind him. 'He'll do as he's told – same as you. Now, quit snivelling like a little bitch, and start this fucker up.'

He shoved the rusted chainsaw he was carrying into Frank's hands.

'You'll be doing the honours,' he said, grinning nastily. 'And no funny business, or the grunts'll be getting double rations tonight.'

'No!' Frank spluttered, throwing the ancient piece of machinery onto the table. 'I can't!'

'Oh, I think you can,' Nick drawled. 'Or your dickhead son is gonna—'

His voice petered out, and a look of confusion came into his eyes as he stumbled against the table.

'What the *fuck*?' he said, his voice sounding suddenly slurred.

At the exact same time, Gaz's legs gave way, and Frank watched in confusion as the man sank slowly to the floor. A bang outside the back door brought Frank's head around, and he gaped at Irena.

'What's going on?'

'I have drug them,' she replied coolly, her gaze fixed on Nick, who was still holding himself up on the edge of the table, desperately trying to fight the effects of whatever she'd given him.

'You backstabbing fuckin' whore,' he wheezed, his head wobbling as he tried to focus on her face. 'I'm gonna . . . fuckin' . . . kill ya.'

'I do not think so,' she replied, her voice as icy as the glare in her eyes. 'You are monster, and is *your* time to die, not mine.'

'Irena, what the hell are you doing?' Frank gasped, frozen to the spot as he watched her shove Nick onto the floor with her foot before skirting round him and reaching up to the top of the fridge for the key to the gun cabinet.

'Is over,' she said, her hands shaking wildly as she unlocked the cabinet and took out the shotgun. 'I need make this stop before they hurt anyone else.'

'But they've got Evan,' Frank reminded her. 'And they're the only ones who know where he is. If you want out, go, I won't try to stop you. But I need to stay. I'll sign everything over to them, then they can do whatever they like with me. But I need to know Evan's safe.'

'Do not be a fool,' Irena said, struggling to cock the gun so she could check if it was loaded. 'They will never let him go. And they will never let you go, *or* me,' she added. 'As soon as we are marry, they will kill us both.'

Viktorya appeared in the doorway, and let out a little cry of fear when she saw the men on the floor.

'What is happen?' she asked, her voice tiny. 'Where is Karel?'

'Not here,' said Irena, snapping the gun shut. 'Do not worry, I am not blame you,' she went on, her voice softening a little. 'You are little girl, and you made choice to protect yourself. But you need go . . .' She gestured toward the door. '*Now*, before they wake and is too late.'

'No, you will shoot me,' Viktorya cried, staggering backwards and running up the stairs.

A key turned in the lock of the front door, and Karel came into the hallway. Shedding his jacket as he walked, he didn't notice what was happening until he reached the kitchen doorway. When he did, he stopped and looked at Irena before glancing down at Nick on the floor, then over to Gaz, before coming back to Irena.

'What the fuck are you doing?' he growled. 'Give me that, you stupid bitch!'

'Stay there or I will shoot you,' she warned, her teeth bared, her eyes filled with hatred as she aimed the gun at his chest. 'I have suffer enough because of you, but this is finish. You took everything from me, and you made promises you were never going to keep. And after everything I did for you, you sell me to that monster and laugh at my pain. Now *I* have power, and you will let us go. But, first, you will tell Frankie where his son is.'

'Is that right?' Karel smirked, his narrowed eyes glittering brightly.

BRUTAL

Before Irena could reply, the back door flew open and Jacko charged in, knocking her to the ground. The gun went off, and Frank fell to his knees and covered his head with his arms.

45

'What was that?' Strachan slammed her foot down on the brake pedal and gaped at Ogden.

'Sounded like a shotgun going off inside,' he said. 'Put it in reverse, and back out slowly,' he went on, his voice calm, his gaze fixed on the front door of the house they had just pulled onto the drive of.

Strachan did as he'd said and reversed back out onto the lane – and carried on going until she had put a couple of hundred feet between them and the house.

Ogden spoke into his radio as she killed the lights and climbed out, informing the dispatcher of the situation and giving the address.

Strachan was some way ahead when he finished the call, and he ran stealthily after her, sticking close to the hedgerow.

Touching her arm to stop her before she reached the driveway, he pointed to a gap in the hedge that would allow them to go down the side of the house without anyone seeing them. He had no idea what was going on in there, but the daughter-in-law had mentioned that the owner of the house used to own a shotgun before he'd retired from farming. She'd also said that she *thought* the man had got rid of it, but that meant there was a chance that he hadn't, and he wasn't taking the risk.

The two detectives made their way down the side of the hedge until they reached a gap through which they could see the back of the farmhouse. The kitchen light was on, and Strachan nudged her colleague and nodded toward the prone body of a man she'd spotted lying some feet away from the back door. Ogden saw it and gestured with a finger that they should go back to the car and wait for the ARU to arrive.

Before they could move, the back door opened, and a woman was shoved roughly outside. She fell and cried out in pain when she sprawled face down on the gravel. A man walked outside holding a shotgun.

'Think you're so fuckin' clever, don't you?' he spat, aiming the gun at her back. 'Well, let's see how clever you are when your brains are splattered all over the fuckin' countryside, eh?'

Strachan heard a click, and a rush of adrenaline coursed through her veins. She had a split second to act, but that was all it took for her to pull the Taser off her belt and throw herself through the hedge to get a clear shot at the man's thick neck.

He started convulsing as soon as the wire attached itself, and Strachan, still half crouching, ran over and kicked the gun he'd dropped out of his reach.

Another man lurched out through the door, and Ogden yelled, 'Stay where you are, or you're gonna get the same!'

The man glanced at him, saw the Taser in his hand, and ran hell for leather across the garden, leaping over the fence into the field beyond.

'Leave him!' Strachan yelled when Odgen made to give chase.

Rushing over to the woman instead, Ogden dragged her out of the light spilling from the door as the beam of a helicopter's spotlight cut through the clouds.

'How many more of them are in there?' he asked. 'Are they armed?'

'Two inside, but they are not conscious,' Irena said. 'I gave them drug, but they may wake soon. And him.' She nodded toward Scotty, who was still lying motionless.

'Are you sure?' Ogden asked her. 'There's definitely no one else?'

'Just Frankie and Viktorya,' Irena said. 'But they are innocent.'

Ogden nodded and crouch-ran over to Strachan. She'd cuffed Karel's wrists by then, and had secured his ankles with cable ties, so she left him where he was and crept behind Ogden as he made his way to the kitchen door.

Still cowering in the corner, Frank held up his hands when he saw the Taser Ogden was aiming at him.

'Any more in here?' Ogden asked.

'Only him,' Frank nodded toward Gaz. 'And the other one's on the other side of the table. There's a young girl upstairs,' he added. 'But she's not part of this.'

Ogden nodded and waved for Strachan to enter.

BRUTAL

She gazed down at Gaz and signalled for Ogden to tie him up before edging round the table to deal with the other one.

'Holy fuck!' she gasped, her eyes widening when she saw the blood and the hole in the man's back. 'This one's had it, mate.'

Epilogue

Evan's mates from work, the pub, and school, all stopped to shake Frank's hand as they filed out of the crematorium.

'So sorry, mate.'

'He was a good lad, we're gonna miss him.'

'I can't believe this, Mr Peters; I just can't get my head around it . . . Why him? He never hurt a fly.'

'If there's anything you need, give us a shout, yeah?'

Thanking them all, one by one, Frank put his arm around Jo's shoulders when she started sobbing.

'Come on, love, it'll be over soon,' he said, kissing her head. 'Give it a few more minutes, then we can go home.'

Sniffing back the tears, Jo raised her chin and shook her head.

'I'm going to take Marie back to theirs,' she said, glancing over at her sister-in-law, who was staring down at the mountain of flowers with a bereft look on her face. 'I should never have told her about Evan and Irena. Now that's the last memory she's got of him, and he wouldn't have wanted that. He was really happy that they'd sorted their differences out after all that nonsense, and he told me she'd been making a massive effort, so she didn't deserve me telling her that. I've been such a horrible bitch to her.'

'We all say things in anger,' Frank consoled her. 'But, yeah, go on . . . take her home. I'll see you back at mine later. Unless you'd rather go to your place?'

'I can't, can I?' Jo said, pulling a tissue out of her pocket. 'The new tenants are moving in first thing.'

'Well, your room's there if you want it,' Frank said, a wave of sadness washing over him when he remembered all the crying Irena had done in that room. 'I'll get Carmel to move her stuff into Evan's room, 'cos I'm sure you won't want to sleep where . . . you know.'

'I thought you said she was leaving today?' Jo sniffed.

'She was going to, but I told her she could stay a bit longer,' Frank said. Then, shrugging when Jo gazed up at him, he said, 'Yvonne's not got long, love, and Carmel hasn't seen her for years, so what was I supposed to do? The cottage still stinks of dead cat and pig, and it needs fumigating, so she can't stay there. And I'd hate to send her packing when her aunt could go anytime.'

'Poor Yvonne,' Jo sighed. 'I wish I'd been here to—'

'Don't, love.' Frank pulled her closer. 'There was nothing you could have done to stop it. Evan tried, and look what happened to him.'

'Oh, God. I can't believe he's gone, Dad.'

'Me, neither,' Frank said guiltily. 'I'll never forgive myself.'

'Don't you dare blame yourself,' Jo chided, peering tearfully up into his eyes. 'This was all Irena's doing, not yours.'

'No, it wasn't,' Frank said wearily. 'She only did what they forced her to do. She had no choice in the matter, love.'

Nodding her acceptance, Jo sighed, and said, 'Well, at least she managed to take one of them out before the others got arrested. Shame she didn't get them all, though, eh?'

'Nick was the one who killed Evan and then drove him to that quarry in the boot of his own car,' Frank said bitterly. 'And the sick bastard even wore his jacket, and got himself spotted on CCTV to make everyone think Evan had driven himself there to commit suicide. So, yeah, I'm not sorry Irena shot him. But, like I told the police, it wasn't deliberate, because she didn't actually pull the trigger; the gun went off when the other man charged in and knocked her over.'

'I told you that gun was dangerous,' Jo said. 'That's why I went mad when you told me you still had it.'

'I know.' Frank sighed. 'But it's gone now, so you won't have to worry about it again.'

'Good.' Jo gave him a sad smile. 'But you still need to sell up and get out of there. Sam's friend looked into it, and he reckons a place like yours, with all that land, would sell for over a million now, so why don't you get rid and find a nice place near me and Sam?'

'In Australia?' Frank raised an eyebrow. 'I don't think so, love. I couldn't leave your mum . . . or Evan.'

As he spoke, he gazed through the crematorium doors, taking

one last look at the curtains behind which his son's coffin lay before turning Jo away and walking her over to Marie.

'Come on, let's get you home,' Jo said, linking her arm through Marie's.

Marie lifted her tear-stained face and shook her head.

'I can't leave Evan on his own.'

'He's being looked after,' Jo said, pushing her own grief aside to help the broken woman. 'And he'd want you to be looked after, too,' she said, as she led her gently away from the flowers. 'He loved you so much.'

'Did he?'

'More than you know, love. More than you know.'

Watching as the women climbed into a car, Frank stuffed his hands into his pockets and stared down at the flowers, the words on the cards blurring as fresh tears filled his eyes.

'Excuse me . . . you're his dad, aren't you?'

Looking round, Frank smiled at the two teenaged boys in suits who were standing behind him; one of them a tall, good-looking, mixed-race lad; the other white, shorter and chubbier, wearing a pair of thick-lensed glasses.

'I'm Jordan.' The taller boy introduced himself, holding out his hand. 'And this is my best mate, Keegan.' He nodded at the other. 'I really hope you don't mind us coming, but we're the ones who found your son, so we wanted to pay our respects.'

'I don't mind at all,' Frank said, shaking his hand before reaching for Keegan's. 'If it hadn't been for you two, we might never have found him, so you're more than welcome.'

A pretty young girl had appeared at Jordan's side, and she smiled nervously at Frank as she grasped the boy's hand.

'This is my girlfriend, Chloe,' Jordan said proudly, his eyes lighting up. 'She thought you might be annoyed about us turning up uninvited.'

'Not at all,' Frank said, leaning forward to give the girl a little kiss on the cheek. 'I imagine you've had a long journey to get here, so you're all welcome to come back to the house for something to eat before you go back, if you like?'

'Thanks, but my mum's waiting for us in the car,' said Jordan.

'Sorry about your son,' Keegan added, shoving his glasses up his nose.

Nodding his thanks, Frank watched as the three scuttled away.

'That was nice,' DS Strachan said, coming over when Frank was alone.

'It was,' Frank agreed. 'Gives you hope for the future, doesn't it? You can start thinking that this generation are all trouble-makers, and then you meet nice kids like that.'

'Couldn't agree more,' said Strachan. Then, waving to Ogden when he gestured that they needed to get going, she said, 'I'm sorry, but I've got to go. Thanks for inviting us to the service; it was very moving. Evan was clearly very popular and much loved.'

'He was that,' said Frank. 'And thank *you*,' he added, gazing down at her. 'For everything. You put your life at risk to save mine, and made sure that those bastards didn't get away.'

'It's my job,' Strachan said modestly. 'But, I've got to admit there are some shouts that give me more pleasure than others. This one started off sad, but the results made it . . .' Tailing off, she winced, and said, 'Sorry. I didn't mean that the way it sounded. I know nothing will ever . . .'

'It's OK, love,' Frank said. 'I know what you meant, and I agree. The day those animals get sentenced, is the day we can all start over.'

Nodding, Strachan gave him a hug and then walked quickly over to Ogden.

'Coming to the pub, Mr Peters?' one of Evan's mates called out. 'The lads want to toast your Evan and give him a proper send off.'

Smiling, Frank nodded.

'Yeah, I'd like that.'

Arriving back at the house in a taxi a few hours and a few too many drinks later, Frank was fumbling the key into the lock when the door opened.

'Thanks, love.' He smiled at Yvonne's niece and hauled himself over the step.

'I hope you don't mind, but someone came to see you, and I let her in,' Carmel whispered, pointing toward the living room door. 'She's in there. I'll be upstairs.'

Bemused when she tiptoed up the stairs, Frank slid his jacket off and looped it over a hook before walking unsteadily down the hall. Pausing at the door when it occurred to him that it might be the old busy-body he and Irena had bumped into at the super-market that day, he took a deep breath before entering the room.

He stopped in his tracks when he saw who it was, and sobered up in a flash.

'I hope you do not mind me come?' Irena said, gazing nervously up at him from the sofa. 'I am to be sent home once I have given video evidence for court, but I could not bear to go without see you.'

'I'm glad you came,' Frank said, holding out his arms. 'Come here . . .'

In tears as soon as they touched, Irena clutched at his shirt and rested her cheek against his chest.

'I am so sorry for what happen to Evan. I never meant for him to get hurt.'

'I know,' Frank said, stroking her back. 'But stop blaming yourself, because none of this is your fault. You did the right thing in the end, and that's all that matters.'

Irena nodded, and sniffed. Then, shyly, she whispered, 'I need tell you something else before I go. I lied when I say I had no feeling for you. Before Karel came, I was start to feel happy. You are such a good man, and I know I could have had wonderful life with you. I will never know this feeling again, but this will be my punishment, so I accept.'

Frank raised her chin and gazed sadly down into her eyes.

'Don't say that, love. Too much has happened for *us* to ever work, but you deserve every bit of happiness that I'm sure you're going to find once you get home.'

A car turned onto the drive before Irena could answer, and she straightened up and pulled herself out of the embrace.

'Thank you, Frankie,' she said. 'I will never forget you.'

'Nor me you,' he replied.

Jo arrived just as the taxi that had come to collect Irena pulled away. Catching sight of the woman through the window as she waved goodbye to Frank, she raised an eyebrow as she turned onto the drive.

'Was that who I think it was?' she asked, joining Frank in the porch.

'Irena? Yes, it was. She came to say goodbye.'

'She's stunning.'

'Yep, she is.' Frank nodded. Then, slipping his arm around her waist, he pointed up at the sky. 'But see her up there . . .'

'The moon?' Jo frowned.

'Your mother,' said Frank. 'The one who's been watching over me this whole time. She's the only woman I've ever truly loved – or ever will.'

'Don't say that,' Jo murmured, resting her head on his shoulder. 'You're still young enough to start ag—'

Frank placed a finger on her lips.

'It's not going to happen, so forget it. I made your mother a promise just before you got here: that no one's ever going to come between me and you again. And I meant it.'

Nodding, Jo hugged him, and they stood together in silence

for a while, both lost in their thoughts. Then, sighing, Jo said, 'It looks like it's going to be another cold one.'

'It does, that,' Frank agreed, pushing the door open.

'You go and sit by the fire,' Jo said, kissing him on the cheek. 'I'll put the kettle on.'

OUT NOW

RUN

Mandasue Heller

When there's nothing left, and no escape . . .

After being cheated on by her ex, Leanne Riley is trying her hardest to get her life back on track, which isn't easy without a job and living in a bedsit surrounded by a junkie and a mad woman.

On a night out with her best friend she meets Jake, a face from her past who has changed beyond all recognition. Jake is charming, handsome and loaded, a far cry from the gawky teenager he used to be. Weary of men, Leanne isn't easy to please, but Jake tries his best to break through the wall she's built around herself.

But good looks and money can hide a multitude of sins. Is that good-looking face just a mask? And what's more, what will it take to make it slip, and who will die in the process . . . ?

PRAISE FOR MANDASUE HELLER

'Mandasue has played a real blinder with this fantastic novel'
Martina Cole on *Forget Me Not*

'Captivating from first page to last'
Jeffery Deaver on *Lost Angel*

When Ellie Fisher misses her train home one night, she has no idea that being in the right place at the wrong time will change her life forever.

That night she comes across Gareth, a young man about to take his own life because as far as he's concerned there is nothing left to live for. Putting her own life in danger, Ellie convinces Gareth that there is always something left. Her own life is no bed of roses, she explains, but she always pushes on.

However, good deeds aren't always repaid the way we want. Has Ellie unwittingly put her life in danger, or is the real danger a lot closer to home?